To the girls with deep hearts and
multiple backup plans . . .
And especially to Emma, who is
my guide for both.

SABÉ KEPT HER EYES CLOSED and tried not to flinch every time the brush made contact with her nose. The finishing powder had to be applied lightly, which tickled, and now was not the time for laughter. Rabé's hands were steady as she applied the last of the queen's makeup, and Sabé kept her breathing steady, too. She knew from personal experience that inhaling the powder led to a bout of sneezing, and now was not the time for that, either.

Around her, she could feel the other handmaidens going about their tasks. No one ran or let their emotions break through their professional façade, but Sabé knew that everyone was on edge. Saché finished with her hair, and Sabé braced her neck for the weight of the headpiece as Yané slid it on. Rabé pulled away the cloth at Sabé's neck, the one that kept the makeup from getting on the elabourate black dress she wore, and Sabé opened her eyes.

She looked into the queen's face. It wasn't the first time she had done so, of course, but this time felt like it was the most desperate. The measured calm of the queen's dressing room was not expended much beyond the door. Sabé could hear ships landing in the palace courtyards and the unmistakable clank of droid feet on stone. Anger rose in her. The Trade Federation could at least have used the proper docking areas. It wasn't like the Naboo defended them any more rigorously than they did the palace.

Movement in the mirror caught her eye, and Sabé saw Padmé and Eirtaé

1

return to the main chamber. *Padmé's face was scrubbed clean, all traces of her own makeup gone, and she had pulled up the hood of her flame-coloured robe to further disguise her identity. Sabé didn't need to see her face to know her thoughts.*

"The team made it to the royal ship," *Eirtaé said.* "But they were captured. Captain Panaka is waiting for us in the corridor. Where would you like to be when they get here?"

Sabé knew that Padmé wasn't going to give the answer. Once they began the decoy manoeuvre, it was all up to the queen, and right now, that was Sabé.

"Can we make it to the throne room?" *Sabé asked. Her voice was pitched low, and her sonorous tones — a much practised inflection — filled the room.*

"No, my lady," *Eirtaé said.*

"If they catch us here, in the queen's dressing room, they may underestimate us, think us unprepared," *Yané pointed out. She stood very close to Saché as they waited for Sabé to decide.*

"We will go out onto the terrace," *Queen Amidala declared.* "Have Captain Panaka join us with whatever guards he deems fit."

Rabé slipped away to see it done, and the rest of them made their way outside. Sabé put her hands on the railing, looking out over Theed. Usually the view brought her peace, but there was none of that now. Too many Trade Federation ships marred the cityscape. She heard the mechanised sound of the invading army coming up the wide marble stairs and — mercifully closer — the heavy step of Captain Panaka's boots.

Padmé crouched beside her, fixing some wrinkle in the hem of the voluminous black dress.

"We will do this," *she said, so softly that Sabé barely heard her. Sabé* reached down, and Padmé took her hand and squeezed it. "This dress has enough Karlini silk woven into it to protect you and anyone standing behind you in a firefight, and you know that's only the beginning. Naboo resists in its own way. Your people are with you, Your Highness. We are ready."

They were comforting words, and Sabé could easily imagine saying them herself, except she would never let her queen face such a dangerous situation, no matter what protections were woven into her robes. Panaka coughed, and the door to the terrace was pushed open by uncaring metal hands. It was time for Sabé of Naboo, bodyguard and handmaiden, to do her job. And she would, because that was what she had always chosen to do.

Sabé turned to face her enemies as the Queen of Naboo, and Padmé all but disappeared into her shadow.

PART I

CHAPTER 1

Padmé Amidala was completely still. The brown halo of her hair spread out around her, softened here and there by white blossoms that had blown through the air to find their rest among her curls. Her skin was pale and perfect. Her face was peaceful. Her eyes were closed and her hands were clasped across her stomach as she floated. Naboo carried on without her.

Even now, at the end, she was watched.

It was no more than was to be expected. Ever since she'd entered the arena of planetary politics, her audience had been unceasing. First they had commented on her interests and ideals, then later on her election to queen. Many had doubted her strength in the face of an invasion, when the lives and well-being of her people would be held ransom against her – hers to save if only she would give up her signature – and she had proven them all wrong. She had ruled well. She had grown in wisdom and experience, and had done both rapidly. She had faced the trials of her position unflinching and unafraid. And now, her time was ended.

A small disturbance, the barest movement through the

otherwise peaceful water, was Padmé's only warning before her attacker struck.

An arm wrapped around her waist, pulling her down into the clear shallows, holding her there just long enough to let her know that she had been bested.

The Queen of Naboo surfaced, sputtering water in the sunlight as her handmaidens – her friends – laughed around her. Yané and Saché, who had suffered for their planet during the Occupation. Eirtaé and Rabé, who had helped make sure their suffering meant something. Sabé, who took the most frequent risks and was the most beloved. Together – young and seemingly carefree – they were a force that was often underestimated. No matter how many times they were proven able, people who looked at them were blinded by their youth and by their clothing, and dismissed them yet again. That was exactly how they preferred it.

The lake country was renowned for its privacy. Here, even the queen could go unnoticed, or at least be easily overlooked. Naboo's natural heritage was to be protected and treasured, even before new treaties with the Gungans had been signed, and this had reinforced the isolation of the lakes in the region. The bustle of the capital was far away, and Padmé could have, for however small a moment, some time to herself. Well, to herself, her handmaidens, the guards Captain Panaka deemed appropriate, and all the household staff. Solitude, it turned out, was somewhat relative.

From the beach, Quarsh Panaka watched his charges frolic in the sun with an all-too-familiar expression on his face. He had argued to bring ten of his people down to the water's edge with him, and Padmé had conceded. Eventually. This give-and-take had once been his custom when it came to dealings with the queen – even if their relationship had grown colder and more formal of late. He was a professional, so he stood there and glowered, knowing that today of all days, his interference would not be welcomed.

"You let me do that," Saché said. The youngest hand-maiden wore a swimming suit cut in the same style as the rest of them, but where the others bared skin to the sun, she bared a large collection of mottled scars that wrapped around her arms, legs, and neck. Yané paddled next to her and ran her fingers through Saché's hair.

"I couldn't have stopped you," Padmé said. She shook her head, shedding drops of water – and the last few blossoms. Waist-deep in the shining lake and speaking in her own voice, she might have been mistaken for a normal girl, but even now there was something about her bearing that hinted at more. "Though I could have cried out and got a mouthful of lake water for my trouble."

"And Captain Panaka would have felt honour bound to rescue you." Sabé said it in Amidala's voice, and Saché and Yané both straightened out of reflex before Yané sent a wave of water towards the older girl as repayment. Sabé merely swept a flower from her cheek as it landed on her, and continued to float, unbothered by the ruckus. "So really, you were preserving the dignity of many, not to mention a fine pair of boots."

Unbothered, but not unaware, Sabé spoke loudly enough to be heard by all those who were swimming, as well as several of the guards, who did little to conceal their amusement.

"You have aged me prematurely, my ladies," Panaka said. There was a hint of warmth in his tone, but the uncrossable distance remained. "My wife will hardly recognise me when I go home."

"Your wife has no such problem," said Mariek Panaka from her position three paces away from him. She was not in uniform, because she had been in swimming with the queen. She was wrapped in a bright orange sarong that made her brown skin glow in the late morning sun, and her dark hair dripped down her back while the rest of her dried.

"Well," said Padmé, wading towards the shore with Sabé, as always, in her wake. "Soon we will all be able to rest."

And there it was: the veermok in the room addressed at last. Because the end was coming, and neither the beauty of Naboo's lake country nor the best of company could stop it. When the election was over and the new ruler of Naboo was announced, Padmé Amidala would be in search of a new task or calling or profession, and so would most of those in her service. Some, like Panaka, looked forward to retirement, as much as anyone on Naboo ever retired. Padmé guessed

Panaka had received several job offers, but they were past the stage where they discussed such personal matters, now. The younger ones, like Eirtaé and Saché, sought the future on their own terms. Musicians, doctors, parents, farmers, and all combinations thereof – it was a time for dreams. Change was coming, and it was coming fast. No one, not even Sabé, had dared to ask the queen about her plans.

Rabé stood up and followed the queen. Eirtaé dove down one more time – a sort of farewell – and then joined the others as they gathered themselves and left the water, too. They didn't have to, not with so many guards and Sabé besides, but they would always choose the queen when they could, and soon, they would no longer be able to.

Away from the lake house, Naboo was voting. The gears of democracy were well oiled, and centuries of tradition made the biennial event run smoothly, even with the inclusion of Gungan voters for only the second time in the planet's history. Though few of them chose to vote, Padmé knew her efforts to include them were appreciated because Boss Nass had told her as much. Loudly. Naboo was not quite as united as she might have liked it to be at the end of her four years of service to it, but the people were happy with what she had done.

Almost too happy, it turned out. A faction had tried to amend the constitution so that Padmé could run again. This had been tried only once before, during a time of great upheaval in Naboo's past, and Padmé could see no reason to fight for something she neither wanted nor believed was right. She had given four years to Naboo, and now it was time for someone else's vision, someone else's hands, to select the course. That was the soul of Naboo's democratic body, that change and service in short stretches were better than stagnant rulership, and Padmé was happy to play all the parts her role included.

"You weren't even tempted?" Sabé had asked when the messenger had come with the amendment for Padmé to read and she had returned it unsigned after the barest of glances. It was the closest they had yet come to discussion of the future.

"Of course I was tempted," Padmé had replied. She settled back in her seat, and Sabé resumed brushing her hair. "I thought of at least ten more things I could do with another term while I was reading the proposal. But that's not how our legacies work. Not here. We serve and we allow others to serve."

Sabé had said nothing more.

Now, wrapped in vivid sarongs on the beach, they retrieved their sandals and followed the guards up towards the house. When they reached the grassy hill at the base of the wide stone stairs, Padmé stopped to brush off her feet. They all halted with her.

"Sand," she said, by way of explanation.

"I'm sure the housekeeping droids appreciate your efforts, Your Highness," Eirtaé said. Her face was handmaiden-straight, so only a few people got the joke.

The steps weren't very steep on this side of the house. The port – for water vessels in this case; there wasn't really a place to land an airship – was on the other side of the estate, and those steps were cut straight into the spur on which the house was set. This way had been purposely constructed as a path to the water, and therefore it was both more beautiful and more leisurely an ascent. Padmé and Mariek led the way up, with Panaka behind them and the rest of the handmaidens and guards strung along like so many ducklings.

Sabé had paused at the bottom to fasten her sandals. Padmé saw her grimace slightly when she realised that there was, in fact, still sand between her toes. Sabé shook her shoes as clear as she could and then began to climb at an almost leisurely pace. Sabé didn't often allow her mind to wander when she was with the queen, but here and now, with so little at stake and peaceful change rapidly approaching, Padmé was happy to see her relax as Sergeant Tonra fell into step beside her. He was somewhat taller than Panaka, with white skin that was usually pale, though two weeks in the sun had reddened his face significantly. He had come down the steps just as Padmé had decided to return to the house but was not the least bit winded by his exertions.

"There are several messages for Her Highness." He spoke quietly to Sabé, but Padmé still overheard him. "None of them are urgent, but one is official and will require the queen to open it herself."

"Thank you, Sergeant," Sabé replied, ever competent. "We'll get to them presently."

Tonra nodded but did not fall back. Padmé expected Sabé to bristle, as she usually did if she thought someone meant to guard her person, even though she granted more leniency to those who had fought in the Battle of Naboo, as Tonra had. Sabé was as protective of her own privacy as Padmé was of hers – albeit for different reasons. Perhaps, Padmé decided, Sabé was finally allowing herself to appreciate the view.

The lake spread out as they climbed, its water reflecting the sky with such perfection that, but for a few waves, it was possible to convince oneself that sky and water had been somehow reversed. The green hills that rose up from the shore also descended down into the depths, and what few puffy clouds skirted the blue above were mirrored exactly in the blue below. It was as though two bowls were pressed against each other, their rims forming the treed horizon. There was no sign of human habitation jutting out from between the trees, except for the house they were climbing towards, and the sky above them was never dotted with ships or flying recorder droids or anything else that might puncture the quiet with unwanted noise.

The house itself was made of yellow rock, and roofed in red, with copper-green domes. There were several sections, each with its own purpose ranging from habitation to cooking, all linked by a series of elabourate gardens. The property belonged to the government, and Padmé had used it as a retreat for much of her career, beginning back when she was first in the junior legislative programme as a child. She didn't own any part of it, but she had influenced the layout and décor in subtle ways so that there was no doubting that it was a place she dearly loved. It was an oasis, a haven. Padmé had always come here to relax, and even though this was, in theory, the most relaxing visit she had ever taken here, it was obvious to all who saw her that she could not quite quiet her mind.

The queen had arrived two weeks earlier for the customary seclusion during the final campaign, and today was the election at last. Padmé was officially neutral with regard to her successor, though she had of course done her civic duty and cast a vote. A droid had departed with all of their ballots early in the day, but they hadn't spoken of politics more than absolutely necessary since their arrival, and not at all since that morning. Padmé had run unopposed in her second term, though there had been a few write-in candidates, as there always were. This was the first time she had been this uninvolved in her planet's politics since she began her studies. She liked it – and also found it deeply unsettling in a way she couldn't quite explain.

Padmé had hoped the exertion of swimming would help. The distance to the island was something she hadn't attempted in several months, though her handmaidens were always game to try. She'd thought the swim would at least tire her out too much to think. Instead, her thoughts had only reordered themselves. Even Saché's dunking hadn't helped.

She had a great deal to think about. Who was she, after all, when she was not Queen of Naboo? She had entered politics so early and with such zeal that she had no other identity. She had taken five handmaidens with her, and each of them had been shaped by their roles, as well, to the point where they had all taken names in her honour after she was elected. Who were they, when they were allowed to be themselves? Everyone knew that Rabé dreamed of music, while Yané dreamed of a house full of children that Saché would also call home, and so on and so on with each of the others, but it was more challenging for Padmé to see herself in any of their futures. Would they have room in their lives for Padmé when Amidala no longer held them as queen? And who would she be, even if they did?

"You're going to trip if you don't stop daydreaming," Mariek said beside the queen on the steps. "And won't that be just the way for you to end your reign, falling up the stairs because you were thinking too hard about things that are no longer yours to think about."

"I can't help it," Padmé admitted. She never could. "But you're right. I'll wait until I'm alone before I let myself drift that far."

"You'll never be alone, my lady," Mariek said. "And I don't mean all of this production, either." She gestured vaguely at the queen's retinue and smiled widely. "It will be different, but you will be different, too, and you're smart enough to figure it out."

"Thank you," Padmé said. "It's strange to want two things that are entirely different from one another. I am ready to stop, but I also feel like I could have done more."

"I know," Mariek said. "That's why I wrote you in, anyway."

"That's a spoiled ballot!" Padmé protested, stopping dead in her tracks. Everyone below them on the steps halted, too, and looked up to see what had caused the queen to stop walking. "And you're not supposed to tell me who you voted for."

Mariek began to laugh, and Quarsh stepped up to take his wife's arm.

"Don't tease the queen, love. I know from personal experience that she has her ways of making you pay for it, and even if she's pressed for time, I have absolute faith in her abilities." For just a moment, he was her captain again, the one who had trained them all so well before preparedness had turned to paranoia. Padmé missed him dreadfully.

Mariek laughed harder.

"My lady?" Panaka offered his other arm. "I know you don't need it, but I am happiest when I know you have my support."

"Of course, Captain," Padmé said rather formally. She took his arm and began to climb again. "Since I am so near the end of my term as queen, it behooves me to show measured judgement in all things."

"You have always done so, my lady, even when we disagreed," Panaka said. It was almost a peace offering. "That's why I wrote you in, too."

The Queen of Naboo laughed in the sunlight as she reached the house with her companions and her guards. The watergate stood thrown open, for this was a place of peace and reflection, and had never needed defending from a hostile force. Before them was the quiet courtyard and sun-drenched gardens where they would wait to hear the news, and behind them was the world that voted on the shape that news would take. Queen Amidala entered the house as the ruler of a planet, one last time.

CHAPTER 2

The holomessage requiring the queen's security code specifically was from none other than Chancellor Palpatine, and
though it was brief, it stated that he would soon be arriving
at the lake house to pay a formal visit. He apologised for the
short notice. The holo caused a minor stir – mostly because
half of them were still in their swimming clothes – but Padmé
had always been surrounded by consummate professionals,
and they were incredibly adaptable.

Rabé ran the brush through the queen's hair and considered the challenge before her. When packing, she and Yané
had agreed on a simplified wardrobe for everyone, Padmé
included, and accordingly had brought with them no outfits
that were entirely appropriate for such a high-level political meeting. There weren't supposed to *be* any high-level
political meetings, not at this time in the election cycle. But
Chancellor Palpatine's mere presence necessitated a certain
level of formality, and now Rabé found herself faced with a
bit of a scrabble.

It was difficult to explain, sometimes, what her position as
a queen's handmaiden entailed. Part of her task was defensive

– advisory – but part of it was also aesthetic. And part of it was giving all of the parts equal weight. It was easy for an outsider, even someone from Naboo, to roll their eyes when the queen's baggage train went by. The reams of fabric and elabourate headpieces could be dismissed as either wasteful or quaint, depending on the sentiment of the being doing the dismissing, but each piece served a particular function, as did its placement. At the very least, most of the fabrics were treated with resin that made them resistant to blaster fire. The jeweled brooches could conceal recording devices or a personal shield. The heaviest dresses maintained a physical barrier around the queen and had, essentially, an escape hatch so that Padmé could shed the entire getup – save for the utilitarian undersuit – if she needed to move quickly. The headpieces distracted from the queen's face, making it easier for a decoy to step in, if required. Rabé viewed the queen's wardrobe and accessories the same way she viewed the royal pistol: necessary components to be deployed with full awareness and cunning.

"Yané, get to work on Saché and Eirtaé's braids, please," Rabé directed. A young guardswoman appeared in the doorway, her hands folded together low across her stomach, and Rabé knew without asking that Palpatine had just landed. "The simple tripartite and the jade pins. Can you do that on yourself when you're done?"

"Of course," Yané said. "Well, I might need help with the pins at the back."

"I can do that," said Saché. "I've been practicing."

"Excellent," Rabé said. "You'll wear the dark red robes with the hoods down. Whoever's not being braided first can lay them out."

Saché was already seated, so Eirtaé got up and went into the closet. They could all hear the whirring as the droid who kept everything organised called up the garments she requested.

"Sabé, we'll have to use the lakeside gown," Rabé declared. "It's the fanciest thing we packed, and we are not expecting danger. See if you can find a jacket to cover her back, and then get us the green robes. We'll wear our hoods, even though it's too warm for it."

Sabé slid off the foot of the bed, where she'd been brushing out her own hair, and disappeared after Eirtaé into the closet.

"And what about me?" Padmé asked with an impish tone. "I don't want to get in your way."

"Oh, be quiet," Rabé said. "But how typical of the Chancellor to show up with so little warning when we are not at all prepared to receive him!"

"He's home to vote in the election," Padmé said. "But he can't stay for the inauguration afterwards. Perhaps we ought to have expected it, but it's hardly your fault for failing to read his mind when he wasn't even on the planet yet."

Rabé made an undignified sound and resumed brushing Padmé's hair. She did not enjoy being caught off guard, and to her credit, it happened very rarely. Moving with the efficiency of long practise, she wove half a dozen braids into Padmé's hair, each of them twisted with gold and silver ribbons. The braids were then pinned up in six wide loops, starting in front of Padmé's ears and circling her head on the back to give the illusion of size that was typically granted by the absent headpiece. Rabé added more ribbons so that they cascaded down Padmé's back.

"Here," said Sabé, holding up an ivory shawl. "Will it suit?"

"Yes, I think so," Rabé replied. "Can the two of you manage while I see to myself?"

Sabé nodded, and Padmé stood up. She was already wearing a shift, but the lakeside gown was backless, so she stripped to the waist while Sabé laid the dress on the floor for her to step into. Once Sabé drew the gown up to her shoulders and fastened the clasp around Padmé's neck, she arranged the shawl and all of the ribbons. She had to climb up on a stool to paint the queen's face, because Padmé didn't trust herself to sit again now that she was fully attired, but by the end of ten minutes, Queen Amidala was fully realised.

Padmé watched as Yané finished Eirtaé's braids and sat for a moment so that Saché could finish her own hair. Then they all got into the red robes while Sabé and Rabé pulled the deep green hoods over their heads, casting their faces into shadow. It really was too warm for it, but there was no helping the matter. At least Sabé had to be fully hooded at all appearances, even this late in the game when Padmé doubted they would ever have to switch places again.

"We didn't get this far by being incautious, Your Highness," Sabé said. By her own decree, Padmé was only ever addressed thus by her handmaidens when they were in company or she was in full makeup. The ceremonial tone gave Sabé's words an additional weight, making her seem too old for her young face. It was another part of their living, moving disguise.

"I know," Padmé said. "Still, for your sakes, I will try to make this as quick as possible."

The other three went on ahead. They would stand in the gallery while Sabé and Rabé stood behind the queen. The rear wall of the receiving room was almost the same deep green as their robes. If the Chancellor requested a private audience, their presence could be ignored, especially if three handmaidens clearly left the room when it emptied. There was a knock at the door, and Panaka came in when the queen admitted him.

"Chancellor Palpatine has been cooling his heels for just less than twenty minutes, Your Highness," he reported. "Mariek and Tonra are with him. He seems anxious to be underway, but is understanding of the wait."

"Thank you, Captain." Queen Amidala spoke in her oddly inflectionless tone. It was a voice Padmé and Sabé had developed together so that either of them could execute it flawlessly, though the others were all more or less proficient with it. "Please escort us to the receiving room, and we will put the Chancellor's mind at ease."

Panaka let Amidala precede him out of the room but then fell into step beside her as they walked through the wide marble hallways. Two guards walked in front, and two more brought up the rear, their boots rapping out a sharp staccato that made up for the silence with which Sabé and Rabé walked. They took a slightly circuitous route to avoid going outside – Rabé did good work, as always, but wasn't sure how those ribbons would fare in anything more than a gentle breeze – and by the time they arrived at the receiving room, the rest of the household was already assembled. Amidala took her place on the throne, with Panaka at her right hand. Her green-clad handmaidens stepped to the back of the raised platform, their hoods pulled low, and faded into the decorations on the wall.

"Your Highness." Mariek's clear voice called attention. "I am pleased to present Chancellor Palpatine."

In Theed, there would have been a great deal more ceremony. Music would have accompanied the Chancellor's introduction – something from his home province, perhaps, or whatever was fashionable at the moment – and there would have been significantly more of an audience present. The lack of pomp and circumstance did not bother Amidala, and it didn't seem to bother Palpatine, either. He strode into the room at an easy pace, with Sergeant Tonra behind him, and made his way towards the raised platform on which the queen was installed.

"Your Highness," he said, bowing from the waist. "Thank you so much for agreeing to see me. I know it was an unusual request for this time, but I cannot stay on Naboo long enough for a more customary visit."

"We are honoured by your presence as always, Chancellor," Amidala said. "Your position in the Galactic Senate gives great prestige to Naboo, and we are pleased to recognise that however we are able to."

Palpatine smiled winningly. Padmé felt Panaka relax beside her. Surely the Chancellor's good mood meant that nothing dire was happening and he really did merely wish to pay his respects before heading back to Coruscant.

"Might I trouble Your Highness for a private audience?" Palpatine asked, as expected. "I would not inconvenience the good captain by requesting a stroll in the magnificent gardens, but could we converse here, perhaps?"

Padmé made a show of leaning over to Panaka, who leaned over, as well.

"So far this has gone exactly as we hoped," he said, one gloved hand in front of his mouth. They didn't need to confer, not truly, but they were both so practised at *looking* like they were conferring that they fell into old habits without realising it.

"Indeed," Padmé said. "We will be all right here, however long he wants to talk."

"Whatever works," he replied. "I won't let him monopolise you for more than twenty minutes."

"That would be appreciated, Captain," Padmé said.

When she straightened, it was Queen Amidala who spoke.

"Friends, if you will excuse us? I would grant the Chancellor his audience."

The assembled members of the household made their bows and took their leave. Panaka was last, stopping to clasp hands with the Chancellor as he stepped off the platform. Soon enough, the room was emptied of all save four, and two of those were unobtrusive to the point of invisibility.

Palpatine stepped up onto the platform but didn't come within arm's reach of the queen.

"I know visits from me cause you something of a flutter, but I am pleased to see you," he said. He was close enough to speak at normal levels, and Padmé slid into her own voice, speaking to him as a friend.

"It's all right," she said. "To be completely honest, a distraction was both needed and appreciated today."

"I can imagine," he said. "Well, actually, I can't. Senatorial appointments are quite different, and I will never run for office again. But I can pretend I can imagine."

"I'm glad you were able to come home and vote," Padmé said. "I thought you would have to cast your ballot remotely."

"Grand gestures are one of the great joys of having power, Your Highness," Palpatine said. "And it never hurts to set a good example for public order."

He hesitated for a moment, long enough for her to see, so she didn't say anything, and waited for him to continue.

"Have you given any thought to what you'll do?" he asked.

Padmé was too well trained to slump, but to the practised eye, she did deflate a bit at the question. She had, of course, given the matter a great deal of thought, but no one had asked her this so directly yet, and now there was no getting around it. She had intended to talk it over with at least Sabé before telling anyone else, but that was no longer an option. She hoped Sabé would understand. It was, after all, hardly the only time Padmé had been forced to say something as Amidala she might have wanted to say as Padmé first.

"My greatest abilities have always been determination and negotiation." Padmé still spoke in her own voice, but Amidala lingered close by. "I know that if I applied myself, I could learn any manner of skill, but it wouldn't be something close to my heart."

"Naboo's unique culture provides all sorts of methods of expression," Palpatine said. "But there are some, like myself for example, who enter government service and never get around to leaving it."

"I have term limits to consider," Amidala said. "And I know that it is time for the mantle of queen to be passed along. However, I did think of something I could do. I am nearly done putting the initial plan together."

"If I can be of any aid, Your Highness," Palpatine said. He smiled at her, mouth curving in a way that might have been disconcerting if she hadn't known him so well. He always had so many plans underway. "I am happy to help."

"As Queen of Naboo, I had to focus my efforts on this planet, putting its needs above all else," Amidala said. She wished she could see Sabé's face. "But I have never been at ease about the situation on Tatooine, not since leaving it almost four years ago. Slavery is a blight, Chancellor, on everything the Republic stands for. I can't bring official political change, given the state of most Outer Rim planets, but I can use the assets I have to free what people I can, and to find them new homes, if they wish it."

She felt a weight lift from her chest having finally said the words and a brief whisper in her heart when she allowed herself to think of a little boy who had been cold in space and a mother brave enough to let him go where she could not.

"You mean to buy them?" Palpatine asked.

"I do not like that word, but yes," Padmé said. She did not visibly wince.

"An admirable goal, Your Highness," Palpatine said. "Though a challenging one, given jurisdictional limitations."

"I have, as you say, the rest of my life," Padmé reminded him.

"Your Highness," Palpatine said, "it may interest you to

know that I have currently sponsored a bill before the Senate to deal with this very issue. It will focus on the transportation of such unpleasant cargo through Republic space, and I am hopeful it will have a real impact on the problem. There is no need for you to embroil yourself in it."

"I know how the Senate works, Chancellor." This was said in Amidala's coldest tone, despite herself. Palpatine straightened, almost imperceptibly. "I have stood before it and pled with desperation for the lives of my people, Republic citizens, and they did nothing. It might be only a little effort, but it is mine to make."

"Of course, Your Highness." Palpatine bowed. He looked up and hesitated again. "I am sorry, but I do have some ill news to bring you after all."

"The trial?" she said. There could be only one thing that would bring him all the way home on the pretence of voting, and that was the current status of the charges against the Neimoidians who had invaded her planet four years ago and tried to have her murdered.

"Yes, Your Highness," Palpatine said. "Nute Gunray's third trial has ended in a hung jury. Not the best outcome, obviously, but not the worst, either, given the strength of the Trade Federation's legal team. The Republic lawyers must regroup, but they are already planning their next moves."

Amidala couldn't seethe in public, and so Padmé set her face in stone.

"Thank you, Chancellor Palpatine," she said, her flat voice harder than a rock. "We appreciate your continued efforts on our behalf."

"Would that I had better tidings on this of all days," Palpatine said. He drew himself up. "Your Highness, you have done great things for Naboo, and as one of your subjects, I am sad to see you go. I wish you all the best in your future endeavours, whatever path they take."

Amidala nodded, an acknowledgement and a dismissal, and Palpatine stepped down from the platform to make his exit from the room. As soon as the door shut behind him, Rabé materialised at Padmé's elbow. She had been standing out of earshot for the tones Palpatine had used, but for some reason no one had ever gotten around to mentioning that Rabé didn't need to be in earshot to understand a conversation. Lip-reading was inexact, but when paired with Rabé's Lorrdian-trained ability to read body language, people often betrayed themselves to her in ways they couldn't imagine.

"He is troubled by something," she said. "Something isn't moving as quickly as he'd like it to."

"That could be any number of things," Padmé said. She leaned back against the throne and felt the gentle touch of ribbons falling against her neck. "We will leave the Chancellor to his plans and continue to make our own."

"I'll go back and set out a garden dress for you," Rabé said.

"Thank you," Padmé told her. "Could you ask them to

serve lunch on the terrace? I know it's late and the others might have eaten, but I'm starving and the weather's too nice to eat inside."

"Of course," Rabé said, and floated off on her silent feet.

"Do you think it's a foolish idea?" Padmé asked.

"I think it's wildly impractical," Sabé said, appearing at her side and helping her to stand. "But most of your ideas are. So far you've done all right."

They were in no hurry, since even Rabé would need time to arrange for lunch. Furthermore, it gave them an opportunity to have the conversation Padmé wished they'd had before Palpatine arrived.

"Where did Rabé even find this much ribbon on short notice?" Sabé asked, stooping to retrieve those that had fallen.

"I've stopped asking that sort of question," Padmé said. "It's much easier to accept that she can get things done than figure out how she does it."

"That's true enough," Sabé said.

Padmé stopped, and turned to look directly at her.

"I don't have enough capital to free them all," Padmé said, still avoiding the word *buy*.

"Then we'll find out what they want on Tatooine and sell it to them in trade," Sabé said.

"'We'?" Padmé said, her heart in her mouth.

"Of course *we*," Sabé said. "You haven't tied your own

shoelaces in four years. You're going to need all the help you can get."

"That is not fair or true," Padmé said, laughing as she descended from the platform on Sabé's arm. She could feel more of the ribbons and one of the braids come unpinned, and the shawl was tangled up in the train of her gown now that she was moving. "Most of my shoes don't even have laces."

"That's as may be," Sabé said. "But my hands are yours for as long as you need them. I was only waiting for you to ask."

"Thank you, my friend," Padmé said, and meant it with every atom of her being.

"Come on," Sabé said. "Your hair is a disaster and I'm starving, too, and apparently we have a lot to talk about."

By the end of an hour's time, they were seated on the terrace in the sunshine, with good food and plenty of conversation to be had. Rabé had just revealed that her application to Theed's most prestigious music academy had been accepted when Sergeant Tonra arrived. Sabé hailed him immediately but stopped short of inviting him to sit by her. It was clear that he had eyes only for the queen, and he had a datapad in his hands.

CHAPTER 3

Eirtaé watched with a keen eye while everyone sat around her and ate a very late lunch. She could, if she had to, take in any number of details and analyse threat levels accordingly, but for now, Eirtaé surveyed the scene as an artist. She loved the light here in the lake country. While she knew academically that it was the same sun that shone down on Theed, her heart noticed minute differences to the quality of it. Everything seemed greener, more vivid and more saturated. The lake itself was almost too bright to look at. The marble gleamed. The Panakas seemed softer in the light here, though they never let their guards down. Saché blushed freely every time Yané looked at her. Padmé's eyes sparkled to see her friends so happy.

Except there was a bit of Theed-light in Padmé's eyes, Eirtaé saw. Padmé was with them – not Amidala – talking and laughing as they coerced their guards into telling what they planned to do after their service to the queen was up, but there was something just a little bit dimmer to her countenance. Eirtaé looked at Sabé out of habit, certain the other girl would know, but Sabé only shook her head in the particular way that meant *Later, when there are fewer eyes.*

Eirtaé would have stood to go and look out over the vista, to try again to think about how she might paint it, except Sabé's attention shifted. Eirtaé followed her gaze.

"Sergeant Tonra," Sabé called, but then didn't say anything else.

It was immediately clear why. Tonra clasped a datapad in his hands, and it was late enough in the day that the voting would be done. Theed was the last region of the planet to vote, and once time zones were taken into account, they were always finished by noon. The Naboo had more than mastered efficient democracy.

It was hardly the place for an official declaration. Padmé could stand, and then they all would, but then they would be a crowd of people standing on the terrace, and no one would be able to see. Eirtaé knew the thoughts that were cycling through Padmé's head as well as she knew her own and was therefore unsurprised when Padmé spoke.

"Please, Sergeant," she said. "If you would read the results, I know we are anxious to hear them."

Yané was holding one of Saché's hands, and Rabé had the other one. It was unclear which of them was more nervous.

"As you wish, Your Highness." Tonra bowed and turned to where Saché was sitting, and addressed his first pronouncement to her directly. "I am pleased to announce that your bid was successful, your ladyship. You are now a member of the planetary legislative assembly."

Yané let out a loud whoop and threw her arms around Saché's neck, kissing the top of her head. Rabé got out of the way just in time to clear a path for Mariek Panaka, who, in an uncharacteristic display of emotion, actually picked Saché up off the ground and swung her around in victory. She set her down just as Padmé got to her feet and crossed to where Saché now stood.

The queen held out her hands to the youngest of her handmaidens, and Saché all but threw herself into her embrace. Eirtaé could see that Padmé was whispering something in Saché's ear – advice or congratulations or both – but she wasn't bothered by not knowing what was said. Saché still wore the red she had worn when Palpatine had made his hurried visit, and Padmé had changed into a deep blue gown that was more suitable for outdoor picnicking; Eirtaé liked the colours together.

Tonra waited patiently while everyone congratulated Saché on her new position. It took quite some time. After what she had gone through during the occupation, Saché was special to every member of the Royal Security Forces. She had, after all, saved most of their lives by refusing to name them during the Trade Federation interrogation that had resulted in her scars. They had repaid her bravery with loyalty second only to the queen's, and when Saché had announced her intention to run for a seat, it was with their full support.

At last the commotion died down, and everyone's attention returned to the waiting sergeant.

"The full list of representatives is available if you would like to check it," Tonra said. "But it is my honour to tell the queen that Naboo will next be served by Queen Réillata."

The terrace was full of professional politicians, but Eirtaé was also a professional artist, so she didn't miss the tiny shifts in everyone's facial expressions. Yané's eyebrows rose a fraction of a centimetre. Rabé became very interested in the rolled fruit that had been set out for dessert. Saché was still too pleased by her own news to react at all. Sabé's face became, if possible, even smoother. And the Amidala-mask slid over Padmé's features a bit more quickly than it usually did.

"You have our thanks, Sergeant," the queen said formally, and inclined her head. "Any of you who wish to go and check local results are welcome to do so."

Panaka sucked air through his teeth.

"With your captain's permission, of course," Padmé added.

Eirtaé knew that none of them had voted for Réillata, though of course there had been no discussion as to how any of them would vote. Padmé believed that the reins of government were best passed on, and Réillata had served as queen before. She hadn't been a bad queen; she had only run once, until she declared for this current election. She had ruled for a single term when they were girls and had gone on to be a moderately successful opera singer after leaving office.

Running now as an older candidate than tradition dictated, Réillata had campaigned on the experience and stability her years afforded her. She and Padmé agreed on matters of planetary defence, specifically going forward with the projects that had not been completed in Padmé's tenure, but so did the other candidates. Jamillia, the candidate Padmé had liked the most, would be able to run again in two years, at least, and next time, Padmé would be able to support her openly rather than hold to the queen's neutrality in public.

"At least she waited until this election," Sabé said. She spoke quietly enough that the guards, even the off-duty ones who were sitting down with them to eat, knew to tune her out. "It would have been an unnecessary mess if she'd run against you directly."

"I know," said Padmé. "And maybe a balance of younger and older rulers ought to be considered. Any path can be a poor one if it goes blindly in one direction."

No one answered, though Eirtaé suspected none of them precisely agreed with Padmé. It was difficult to change course with a single election. The moment drew out long enough to be awkward before Padmé straightened and smiled.

"But we have to celebrate Saché!" she declared. "A hero of Naboo will take her seat in the government."

The guards, both sitting and standing, took the cue and immediately began telling stories of Saché's bravery during the Occupation. It was not precisely a custom, telling a story that everyone knew as a means of celebration, but it was familiar – and an excellent way to change the subject, of course. Even now, Padmé was in control of the situation.

"The Trade Federation types never guessed she was carrying messages for our resistance," Mariek said. "She was so little then."

"She's little enough now," Panaka said. "And she knows how to use it."

Saché bowed regally, though her motion was somewhat restricted by Yané's head in her lap.

"And then those damn droids caught her," Mariek continued. "Some statistical analysis of her movements or something. They took her away, and it was horrible. We could hear her screaming for hours, and we figured it was only a matter of time before they came for us. Only they never did, because she never gave us up."

"I wouldn't let them turn themselves in," Yané said. "They tried, and I ordered them not to, with what authority Queen Amidala had left with us. I knew that Saché had made her choice, and we weren't going to unmake it for her."

They'd all heard the story a hundred times, but there was no mistaking the affection in Yané's voice as she told it. The handmaidens who had accompanied Padmé offworld during the Occupation hadn't heard this tale until well after the Battle of Naboo. Perhaps that was why they never minded when it was retold. They hadn't been able to help Saché when she was captured, but they all helped her deal with the trauma afterward.

"They had to let her go, in the end." Tonra took up the story. "She stayed right in plain sight. She walked through that blasted camp three times a day, in view of all the droids and Trade Federation guards. And they'd stop her and search her, but she never had anything on her, and because she distracted them, the new messengers got through."

"My brave decoys," Padmé said, uttering the word that was almost never spoken, even now. "You have all given your best to Naboo, and to me, and I thank you for it."

Eirtaé had enough of an ego to admit she liked being thanked in public like that, but she kept her face professionally blank as she bowed to the queen. Then she got up and went over to the edge of the terrace to look at the lake, to see if this time she would be able to determine how best to capture it.

Padmé joined her after a moment, hovering outside her personal space if Eirtaé wished to be left alone, but clearly with something on her mind.

"I'm going to Otoh Gunga," Eirtaé said when it became apparent that Padmé was not going to speak first. "Their technology is so different from ours, and I want to see how it affects their art."

It hadn't been particularly easy to arrange, but Eirtaé was charming when she wished to be, and her paintings of

Naboo forestscapes were of great interest to the Gungans. They gave her a place to start, at least.

"That's wonderful," Padmé said. "Will you still paint?"

It had been Eirtaé's primary medium since she had discovered her affinity for capturing images. Understandably, no one was quite sure how it would fare underwater.

"No," she said, then amended herself. "Well, kind of, I suppose. The Gungans have a way of growing vacuum. It's how they push all the water out of their habitations before they fill them with breathable atmosphere. I would like to see what happens if instead of oxygen, the vacuum is full of pigment. It would make interesting patterns in the water, for starters, but I think it might also impact how we expand our aquaculture."

"You're going to put paint in bubbles and use the pattern analysis to improve growth of our blue-algae?" Padmé asked. Blue-algae was an excellent fertiliser. Using it on a limited number of fields had nearly doubled their output during Naboo's growing season. It was no secret that if more algae could be grown, the whole planet would prosper.

"Well, when you say it like that, it sounds all practical and not at all artistic," Eirtaé said. She laughed. "But yes, that is what I am going to do."

"It's perfect," Padmé said. "Skill and art and practicality. The very fabric of Naboo."

"Plus it smells better than the shaak scat most of the farmers use now," Eirtaé pointed out.

"Also that," Padmé allowed. There was the barest hint of a smile on her face, but it was a genuine one. Eirtaé knew that once the mantle of queen was fully passed along, Padmé might smile more freely when she was in company.

They went back to the picnic, where Mariek had procured some of Saché's favourite five-blossom bread for a true celebration of her election. They listened while Saché outlined all the places in her platform she felt she was the weakest, and offered what advice they could. Now that the results were announced, Padmé was free to speak her mind, though she limited herself to Saché's questions. Yané confessed that she had already selected – though not yet purchased – a house, and when they insisted, she called up a hologram of it.

"It's enormous," Saché said. "I'll get lost in there."

"Well," Yané said, "if you're at the legislative assembly, I'm going to have to do something. I know we had originally talked about waiting until your term was up before we decided, but I found this place, and I couldn't help thinking about it."

"I think that's wonderful," Saché said.

Naboo culture held children as precious, and therefore there were not a high number of orphans as other Mid Rim planets might have. Still, after the stresses and suffering of the Occupation, a few young people did manage to fall into the crack between extended family and government oversight. Yané had always been a frequent volunteer with those children when she was able to do so, and had spoken often of someday taking in a few of them permanently. Now that she was in a position to offer more personal aid, it was not surprising that she chose to do so.

"I have cousins there," Mariek said. "They can help you get it furnished before you move in."

"That would be wonderful," Yané said. "Thank you."

It was, Eirtaé realised very suddenly, the *last* time. It made her feel a little cold, made the sun seem a little dim, made the lake shine a little less brightly. It was the last time that all of them would ever sit like this and think about the future together. This feeling was what had made Padmé so restless all day and was probably what had made Sabé so overwhelmingly placid about everything. They were already preparing, or at least Padmé was, and she didn't want to impinge on any of their dreams by making requests.

She was a stunningly good queen, Eirtaé realised, to give them this freedom. Had she asked for their continued aid, no matter what she was going to do next, of course they would have given it. Instead, she had given them their space and held her tongue while they decided. It was a sacrifice on her part, one that Eirtaé imagined she held equal to the sacrifice the handmaidens had made when they joined her service, and it was just as happily given.

They would go their separate ways with Padmé's blessing. It would always be a little sad, but there would be new tasks to conquer and new work to do. In the last communication

Eirtaé had received from her parents, they had asked what name they ought to put on her travel papers. As a private citizen, she had needed to update some of her datawork for the journey to Otoh Gunga and for her residency there. She hadn't replied yet, uncertain as to what she would do, but now she knew it as much as she had ever known anything else.

She had taken the name Eirtaé four years ago, a bit for privacy and a bit for prestige, when Padmé had been elected, and she had sworn her loyalty and her life to Queen Amidala. She would keep that name forever. As a sign of her own status, surely, but also as a sign of respect for the queen she had served and the girl who had risked her own life for the well-being of Naboo on more than one occasion. And not just for Padmé, either, but for all of them who had served. They had chosen their names as children, newly come to power and slightly intimidated by it. They had chosen their names to bind themselves to one another, a constant reminder of the greater good they now served.

And Eirtaé would keep it. She would keep the name and the service and the friendship – though *friendship* hardly seemed deep enough a word – and while she lived, she would endeavour to serve Naboo as Amidala had done, whatever form her service might take.

She looked up, and found that Padmé was staring straight at her. As always, the handmaidens didn't need words to communicate with each other. Eirtaé didn't stand – there was no point in calling attention to herself – but she did lock eyes with the queen she loved, put her hands over her heart, and bow her head.

Padmé returned the gesture, and Eirtaé returned to her silent contemplation of the lake.

CHAPTER 4

They stood on the steps of Theed's great palace, as they had once done to meet Boss Nass in the early months of Amidala's reign. The square in front of them was even more crammed than it had been on that day, because today's celebration had no procession. The people of Naboo had come out in droves to see their new queen, and they had dressed for the occasion. The square was a riot of colour and music, and the air was full of ribbons and the flower blossoms that the children were hurling into the air.

Saché was used to being at the end of the line. Her primary task as a handmaiden had been distraction, but not in the martial sense. While she was a capable fighter and the second best shot – after Sabé – she knew her own physical limitations. Additionally, she'd joined the queen's service when she was twelve and was therefore hardly much in the way of a threat.

But people did talk to her. Apparently, she had one of those faces. And if she was last in the line of handmaidens, they viewed her as accessible. She heard a great many things by accident, too, because no one ever thought to guard their tongue in her presence. Unlike Rabé, she spied directly out in the open, and because everyone was always looking at her, the others got away with a great deal.

Now she stood next to Padmé in front of the assembled crowd and tried to remember that she had chosen public life, despite what the butterflies in her stomach were up to at the moment.

All eyes were on the queen anyway. She wore an enormous white gown that billowed around her. Her face was unpainted and her hair was simply done, wrapped up in a single coil held in place by strings of freshwater pearls. Padmé's dress shimmered, but unlike the dress she wore to celebrate peace with the Gungans, this dress had none of the ostentatious superstructure or ruffles. The dress attracted attention, but it would also be easily overshadowed the moment protocol demanded it.

At last, the great doors of Theed palace were thrown open, and an expectant hush fell over the assembled crowd. Two lines of guards came out first – Royal Security Forces volunteers. They marched down the steps, stopping when the first of them reached the bottom so that they lined the staircase. Then the sitting council came out and walked down to where Amidala and her handmaidens were waiting. Finally, after a long beat that Saché recognised as dramatic necessity, Queen Réillata appeared at the top of the stairs.

The new queen was taller than Padmé, and Saché knew from the campaign holos that she had very short hair. Of course, all of that was covered up by the royal headpiece that now crowned Réillata's head. Her face was stark white, the red of her lips and cheeks standing out as it was meant to, and she wore the red dress of Naboo sovereignty as well as Padmé ever had. She lacked, Saché thought somewhat treasonously, Amidala's inherent kindness, but every ruler of Naboo had her own style. That was, as Padmé would argue, the point.

Queen Réillata descended the steps with measured speed. This was partially to ensure everyone got a good look at her and also because the dress was something of a challenge to walk in. Réillata managed to make her poise and steady pace look deliberate, and Saché was forced to muster up some grudging respect. This was, after all, Réillata's second term, and Saché was going to be a part of her government.

Behind the new queen came the new handmaidens. Most of them were of an age with their monarch, but there was one young girl Saché knew to be Réillata's niece. She was even younger than Saché had been when she'd joined Amidala's service, and Saché wished her the best of it. Court could be a strange place, even for the most prepared.

Réillata reached the wide dais where Amidala was waiting for her. Governor Sio Bibble carried the royal sceptre, which was only ever used on this occasion, and stood between the two queens. For a moment, thanks to a quirk of the Naboo democratic process, they were both of equal rank. Then Amidala took the sceptre from the governor, bowed her head, and presented the trappings of rulership to the new Queen of Naboo.

As was expected, the cheering went on for quite some time.

Eventually, Queen Réillata passed the sceptre back to Sio Bibble and held her arm out to Amidala. Padmé took it, and the two queens walked up the stairs back into the palace. Power was now handed over symbolically, but there was still a great deal of work to be done. Governor Bibble fell into step beside Saché as they walked behind the queens.

"Congratulations on your election, my lady," Bibble said. "I'm not from your district, but it made me glad to know that you were on a ballot somewhere."

"Thank you, Governor," Saché said. "I hope my service is worthy of your enthusiasm."

"Well, you had an excellent teacher," he said. Both of them looked forward, and then Bibble smiled. "I speak of myself of course."

Saché laughed. "Of course," she said. "I have had a wide variety of politicians around me throughout my formative years."

"It is easy to make light of it now that the troubles have passed," Bibble said, uncharacteristically serious. "But I think we both know where you learned much of what you know. The people will respect you for that, and I trust you will not take undue advantage of their loyalty."

"Of course not, Governor," Saché said. She had never

mastered Amidala's voice the way the others had – her vocal range just wasn't suited to it – but she did have a formal voice to fall back on, and she deployed it now for the first time. "As I said, I hope my service is worthy of enthusiasm."

Saché wished she were walking with the others. She knew that Sabé was probably right behind her, and the rest were spaced out accordingly in the crowd that now moved inside. She was used to the view at the rear of the procession, not the head of it, and it was throwing off her groove. She wasn't even dressed as a handmaiden today. They were in soft violet hoods over dark grey gowns – the colours one wore to fade into a brightly dressed Naboo throng – and she was decked out in yellows and greens, with her face fully visible. She looked up the stairs and saw Mariek in the line of guards on the steps. The older woman winked at her, and Saché smiled.

For her last act as queen, Padmé had promoted Mariek and Tonra to captain, accepted Panaka's resignation, and selected a new sergeant named Gregor Typho, who had fought – and lost an eye – in the Battle of Naboo. All of them would have the option of staying in the Royal Security Forces or going somewhere else – they were all volunteers – but it seemed likely that Panaka would be the only one who went looking for another way to fill his days. In Saché's opinion, it was time for him to move on.

They arrived in the throne room, and Saché watched as Réillata took the throne of Naboo for the second time. Two of her handmaidens flanked her in chairs behind the long table while the other three, including her niece, stayed near the door. The governor took his seat, Panaka standing behind him in an unofficial capacity, and Padmé took a third chair by the queen. Saché moved to stand behind her but stopped when she heard Yané cough quietly. Saché froze, embarrassed, and didn't move until Sabé and Eirtaé had taken their places behind Padmé's new seat. Then she took the fourth chair, the one reserved for visiting members of the assembly. She didn't have to look behind her to know that Yané and Rabé stood there.

"We thank you for your good service to Naboo, Amidala." Queen Réillata's words were mostly formula at the beginning of her speech, but there appeared to be genuine enough gratitude behind them. "We know that you have laboured long and hard for our beloved planet, and we are grateful for your efforts."

"Thank you, Your Highness." If it cost Padmé anything to say the words, she didn't let her feelings show on her face. "I wish you a smooth and productive term as our queen."

Sio Bibble shifted in his seat. He was still holding the sceptre and couldn't seem to find anywhere to put his arms. One of the palace chamberlains appeared out of nowhere to take the sceptre from him, and he visibly relaxed when it was no longer in his care.

"Amidala." Queen Réillata dropped out of her formal

speaking voice and addressed Padmé as though they were acquaintances. "I know that we have specific parts to play in the coming days of government transition, and specific words we must say, but I would speak with you candidly, if you permit it."

"Of course," Padmé said. It was a shade more formal than her regular speaking voice, but only her handmaidens would know that.

"You have left me in an excellent position to begin," Réillata said. "We are at peace with the galaxy and the Gungans. Our food surpluses have recovered from the invasion, and the construction of the ion pulse is, I am told, entirely on schedule."

The temperature in the room dropped slightly as Panaka's face hardened. He had opposed the ion pulse quite publicly, wanting more robust defences, and his relationship with the queen and the politicians who supported it had never fully recovered. They were calling his decision to leave the service retirement, but the truth was that Padmé no longer trusted him as she once had, and neither did the incoming administration.

"As you know, Chancellor Palpatine's elevation to that position left us in something of a scramble for a Republic senator," Queen Réillata continued as though nothing had happened. "It is difficult to find politicians at that level who are willing to go to Coruscant. Senator Oshadam has been more than adequate, but she was adamant that her time of service has ended, and her timing means that it falls to me to fill her position."

"I can offer you several suggestions, if you would like," Padmé said.

Saché's unaccustomed viewpoint meant that she could see Sabé's face. Sabé was still hooded, of course, and the average observer would have been able to read nothing in her obscured expression, but Saché was hardly an average observer. She saw the briefest of flickers in Sabé's eyes and knew what Queen Réillata's words would be before they were spoken.

"Amidala," the queen said, "I was hoping to ask you to take the position, and to represent Naboo and the surrounding worlds of the Chommel sector in the Senate."

Padmé was not often at a loss for words. Even when she was, she excelled at saying something perfect and inane to cover her silence. But this time, she said nothing. Her guard was down – or at least it was as down as it ever was – and it was as though she didn't know where to look.

Sio Bibble shifted in his seat again, obviously blindsided by Réillata's request but just as obviously in favour of it, even though he was reluctant to say as much. Panaka's face was carefully blank, but there was an odd sadness to his eyes. Saché thought it looked almost like resignation. For a moment, she didn't understand, but then Padmé's gaze met hers. Because of where she was seated, Saché was the only person in the room that Padmé could look at without revealing that she was seeking an outside opinion, and so Saché let her look. It was immediately apparent that the idea of being senator had never crossed Padmé's mind, but now that it had been proposed, it was all but set in stone.

Saché remembered the last time they had stood at this precipice. She had been behind Padmé then, and hadn't been able to see her face. The long-haired Jedi had said they must go to Coruscant but had addressed his plea to Sabé, thinking she was the queen. They had practised for situations like that, the words that Padmé was to say to communicate with them without giving away their charade, but this was the most dire situation under which they had ever used them. Without hesitation, Padmé had said the words that signalled she would go, and by necessity, Saché had stayed behind.

When she had imagined sitting in the assembly, Saché had thought about spirited debates and getting good work done. She knew she would have to do most of that work alone, but she liked the idea of being able to turn to Padmé if she truly needed help, calling on her experience as Amidala for thorny problems that Saché couldn't solve. And yet here they stood again: a plea to go to Coruscant and a path that Saché couldn't take. She understood Panaka's expression with every part of her soul. Sabé thought it was a good idea, and Padmé couldn't see her, so it was up to Saché to convey the message of support from behind the lines.

She couldn't say the words back to Padmé. They would make no sense in this context, but she was still locked in Padmé's gaze, and she knew she would only have to move her mouth a little bit to get her message across.

We are brave, Your Highness.

Padmé took a measured breath, and then Amidala turned to face the queen.

"Your Highness," she said, bowing her head, "I thank you for the trust you have placed in me by asking me to do this task. I promise you, I will give the matter my fullest consideration, but I request that you wait to hear my answer until after our work transferring power to your term is completed."

"That is a suitable request," Réillata said. "We will continue on with the transition as tradition dictates."

Padmé leaned back in her chair, and only the most practised of spies would have seen Sabé's fist close in the fabric of her dress, just below Padmé's shoulder, showing unflagging support as she always did.

"Governor," said Réillata, turning to where Bibble sat. "What is next on our schedule?"

As the governor outlined their appointments for the next few days, Saché couldn't help thinking that she had done well at her first official appearance. It would be more challenging once she was truly on her own. Members of the legislative assembly had small staffs, but nothing like the close-knit cadre Padmé had built around herself. She would always have Yané, of course, but Yané wasn't part of the elected body and would have her own tasks to accomplish. Saché would learn quickly, as she had always done, and she would pay attention during important meetings rather than let her mind wander as she was doing right this very moment.

Saché managed to get to her feet at the same time as everyone else only by virtue of long practise. Padmé was smiling when she came to take her arm, and together they followed Mariek out of the throne room. Mariek led them to the guest apartments, where Saché was slightly mortified to discover she had a suite of her own.

"There's a connecting door in this one," Eirtaé announced when Saché stood awkwardly in the hallway. "We'll leave it open."

Saché was all but certain that Padmé would do as the queen requested. They had known that things would change after the election, but she didn't think any of them had imagined they would change this much, this quickly. Saché caught Padmé's eye again and saw a quiet request there: to leave thoughts of the future until after their ceremonies here were done. Saché nodded to show that she would do her best to obey, but she couldn't help the way her thoughts travelled as Yané helped her dress for the evening meal. At least tonight they were in a familiar place, if not familiar rooms, and they had an open door.

CHAPTER 5

They sat as they had done when they had met for the first time, when Padmé was interviewing them upon her election to queen. Soon after that Panaka had begun, quietly, to train them in measures far beyond those expected for their years, but for that meeting, they had been girls getting to know each other. Now there was no one in the galaxy who knew them better. With the transferral of government complete, this was to be their last night in Theed before they went their separate directions. Mariek sat unobtrusively by the unlit fireplace, and Tonra was just outside the door. There were half a dozen more guards in the vestibule down the hallway, but tonight, unless the guards were called for, Padmé and her handmaidens would be left alone.

"To Saché," Padmé said, raising her glass. "May your term be as challenging as you need it to be."

Saché raised her own glass in return, and the rest of them followed suit. Yané drank deeply. The alcohol content of the fruit juice was slight, and also: this was their only night of freedom before responsibilities set in.

"To Yané," Padmé continued. "May your house be full of joy and the happiest of clattering."

"To Rabé, may your music touch the hearts and minds of all those who hear it."

"To Eirtaé, may your art show us new pathways in places we had never thought to look for them."

They drank, and drank again.

"I would be dead without each of you," Padmé said. "And Naboo would be under the heel of those who would abuse it. I owe you my thanks and more, and so does the planet you have served."

"We know," Sabé said. Her face was Amidala-blank, even though the rest of them had put on their relaxed attitudes when they'd changed into their blue-and-ivory nightclothes.

"To Sabé," said Padmé, and raised her glass a final time. She didn't say anything else, because there was nothing else that needed to be said.

Yané stood to collect the glasses and placed them on a side table, out of the way. The circle shifted, drew closer together as they sat on cushions on the floor, and Padmé took a brush to Sabé's hair. Traditionally, none of them showed much in the way of personal affection in public. It was an identifying feature, and the strongest part of the handmaidens' defence was their anonymity. These private moments were to be treasured, and Yané hoped there would be an infinite number of them in the days to come. She leaned on Saché's shoulder.

"What will you do, Padmé?" she asked. It was a relief to say the name.

"The queen's request is reasonable," Padmé said. "Though I hadn't considered it an option until she brought it up."

"But then you'd have to leave Naboo," Saché pointed out. "Chancellor Palpatine was almost never at home when he was a senator."

"I know," Padmé said. "But things are different now, and it's possible that I could spend more time here, even if I was a senator."

"What about the answer you gave Palpatine when he asked you about your plans?" Rabé asked.

"He asked you that?" Eirtaé said, mildly scandalised. It had been a breach of protocol to ask so personal a question, even if Palpatine was a friend.

"He surprised me with the question," Padmé said. "I didn't mean to tell him before I told any of you, and then everything happened at once."

Eirtaé flopped dramatically across several pillows and looked at Padmé expectantly.

"I had thought I would go back to Tatooine," Padmé admitted, "and see what steps I could take towards freeing people there."

There was a long moment of silence, broken only by the steady brush of Sabé's hair.

"Well, you certainly never do anything by half," Mariek said. They all jumped, and Padmé waved her over. Mariek dragged a chair with her. "In case my husband has a sudden vision of me sitting on the floor while I'm on duty and a coronary as a result."

"He's retired," Yané pointed out. "I think you're actually in charge now."

"It's pending," Mariek said. "I'd hate to get ahead of myself."

"What do you think, Mariek?" Padmé asked, her eyes still firmly on the back of Sabé's head. "Do you think it's foolish?"

"Yes," said Mariek. She had been in favour of the ion pulse, which they all knew – but never discussed – had put a strain on her marriage. "But most of your ideas are, and they've turned out all right so far."

"You weren't going to go by yourself, were you?" Saché asked delicately. No one looked at Sabé.

"Of course she wasn't," Rabé said.

"Chancellor Palpatine told us he's overseeing a bill to address slavery in the Senate," Padmé told them. "He suggested I wait and see how his efforts fare."

There was another long pause.

"You could have more of an impact if you were in the

Senate," Eirtaé said. "You could help more planets than just Tatooine."

"The Senate takes years to get anything done," Yané argued back. "And we all know from direct experience how well they pay attention to events that aren't personally lighting them on fire! You would get more done with a good ship and connections on Tatooine itself."

They would have squabbled then, which was something that almost never happened in Padmé's presence, had Sabé not leaned forwards.

"If only," she said, "you knew of a way to be in two places at once."

The brush stilled.

"There's a difference between asking you to come with me and sending you alone," Padmé said. In either case, Tatooine was hardly an easy destination.

"I know," Sabé said calmly.

This was a line Yané had watched them skirt for all the years they had been friends. Padmé knew in her heart that Sabé would do whatever she asked, even if it meant Sabé's life, and therefore she was always careful never to ask too much.

"It could be dangerous," Padmé said. "You might not be able to do what we want to do."

"I know," Sabé said. "But I want to try. For you, for them, and also for me. I've done things as you that were worthy of heroism. It might be nice to do them with your backing and my own face for a change."

Padmé pulled her around so she could see Sabé's face. They were used to communicating without eye contact, but Yané understood the need for it now, when something truly important was being discussed.

"So you become the senator for Naboo and the Chommel sector," Mariek said, breaking the moment and bringing them all back into focus. "I'm coming with you, and I imagine my nephew Typho will come, as well."

"I can't take you away from home now," Padmé said. It was the closest they'd ever come to a direct discussion, such was Padmé's respect of boundaries and personal politics.

"Quarsh had his chance to travel the galaxy with you," Mariek said. "He'll understand that now it's mine."

It hung there for a moment, and then Padmé acquiesced. "All right," she said. She turned her gaze towards Rabé and Eirtaé, who were whispering in the corner.

"You are not changing your plans," she said in tones that brooked no argument.

"Padmé – " Rabé began, but Padmé held up a hand.

"No, I need you here," she said. "I need to know that Naboo is still my home, a place where art and peace are honoured the most. I want you to have that, even if I am going to have to wait for it."

"Thank you, my lady," Eirtaé said. Rabé could only nod.

"Saché, you will write to me if you need advice," Padmé continued. "Yané, if you need more funds or to exploit a connection I have, you will write, as well."

"Of course," Yané said.

"I suppose that leaves Captain Tonra for you," Padmé said, and Sabé nodded.

"This is for the best," Mariek said. "Réillata will want to fill the ranks with her own people anyway."

"We should call them in here, if we're volunteering them for extended offworld missions," Padmé said.

Yané rose to her feet and went to the door. Captain Tonra departed down the hallway to where Typho was stationed while Yané came back in and began to arrange chairs. Pillows on the floor were well enough for a private meeting, but this required something a bit firmer. The captain and sergeant could not have looked more different in appearance. Tonra was tall, with dark hair and a wide forehead. Sergeant Typho was solidly built, with brown skin and broad shoulders. He was Mariek Panaka's nephew, but he hadn't needed any help from his family connections to achieve his position. His eye patch gave him a slightly roguish appearance – which he was not above using to his advantage – and he was much more jovial than the other guards. The two held in common an unswerving loyalty to Naboo, and to Padmé herself.

"Thank you for joining us," Padmé said. She spoke in

her own formal voice, not Amidala's. Yané felt her pulse speed up. They were really doing this.

"Of course, my lady," Tonra said, though he sounded bemused.

"I have decided to accept the queen's request, and serve as Naboo's senator in the Galactic Republic," she announced. "Captain Mariek has volunteered to accompany me there as a guard. Sergeant Typho, we – I – am hoping that you will join us, as well."

Typho stood up and straightened his shoulders.

"It would be my honour, Your Highness," he said.

"I don't ask as your queen any more, Sergeant," she reminded him gently. "You would be volunteering to leave the planet for extended periods of time."

"I understand, my lady," Typho said. "I still wish to serve."

"Thank you," Padmé said. She turned to Tonra, who was waiting for her. "Captain, Sabé will be going on a separate mission that she will outline to you later in private. It is my dearest wish that you would accompany her."

Tonra and Sabé exchanged a look, and Sabé nodded.

"I will go with Sabé wherever she needs me to go," he said. "And I imagine that she will guard my back as well as I will guard hers."

"She had better," Padmé said. "I need you both."

"You're going to need new handmaidens," Yané said.

"Senators don't have them," Padmé pointed out.

"Senators have aides," Saché said. "Yours should be handmaidens."

"They're correct," Sabé said. "If you're going to make sure the rest of us are safe and protected, then you should be, too."

"It took Panaka months and months to train all of you," Padmé pointed out. "We don't have that kind of time."

"You don't need the same type of protection that you did as queen," Yané said. "The most important requirement for us was a double for your face before the rest of our skills were considered. Your new aides don't need to be limited to your appearance, as long as they can double for your brain. You need confidants you trust completely. You need people to listen at parties. You need people who fade into the background and pick up on what your opponents are trying to hide from you. If you are in dire straits, you can call in Sabé, but for everyday operations, two or three loyal handmaidens should be able to cover you."

"My niece – on the other side from Typho – Versaat is the right age," Mariek said. "I will send her a holo tonight. She isn't a physical match for you, my lady, but I know she is loyal, and she has other talents."

"There was a girl – Cordyn? I think?" Rabé said. "She was with us in Panaka's training, but she didn't make the final cut. She wasn't very good at combat, but she matched your appearance very closely, and you'll still need one double, I think, though Yané's point is a good one."

"My lady, if I may?" Typho said.

"Please, Sergeant," Padmé said. "Speak your mind."

"One of my classmates from the security forces training might suit you," he said. "She was in the top echelon of each of our courses."

"Why didn't she graduate with you?" Sabé asked.

"She stayed on to take the extra courses," Typho said.

Panaka's privately run programme for the queen's handmaidens had gone semipublic after the Battle of Naboo, and the academy began offering modified versions of his training as official coursework to be taken after graduation.

"What is her name, Sergeant?" Padmé asked.

"Dorra, my lady," he replied. "I can send her a message as soon as my shift is over."

"Do it now, Sergeant," Padmé said. "Don't worry about us. You can use the console in Saché's rooms and leave the door open to maintain your line of sight."

"Come on," Yané said to Eirtaé. "Let's go separate Padmé's gowns from the royal ones. If she's still working for the government, she can pack more than we had originally laid out for her."

"You don't have to do that," Padmé said.

"We don't," said Eirtaé. "But we will."

"I'll write messages to the applicants," Rabé said. "Or

whatever we're calling them. I suppose they hardly know they have applied. Typho, if you'll wait for a moment, we can send them all at once."

"I'll help," Saché said. "I can use my new access to track down Cordyn."

The guards returned to their positions, and Sabé and Padmé found themselves alone in the middle of a mass of pillows and chairs.

"Look at how fast the world turns when you ask it to," Sabé said.

"You should know," Padmé said. "You're the one turning it."

"I won't let you fall off," Sabé told her. She reached out, and Padmé took her hands.

"I know," Padmé said.

There was a moment of quiet between them, and then Sabé asked the last question that pulled at her.

"What are you going to tell your parents?"

"I should have already told them," Padmé admitted. "I had a free hour this afternoon, and I knew as soon as the queen said it. I knew I would serve. Am I selfish?"

"Are you doing this for your own glory?" Sabé asked. Padmé shook her head. "Then no. Generous to a fault, perhaps, and maybe someone who didn't know you would think you were selfish, but I know you, and I'd kick them."

She handed Padmé a datapad and looked up to catch

Mariek's eye. Once she had the guard's attention, she indicated that she was going to accompany Padmé out onto the balcony to make the call. Mariek nodded, and Sabé pulled Padmé to her feet.

On the balcony, she gave Padmé as much space as she could. Her position as Padmé's chief double put her closer to the official guards than the others, which was why Mariek let the pair of them out of her sight. At the core of it, though, Padmé was her friend, and she couldn't help eavesdropping.

"Hi, Mum," Padmé said. It was her most exposed voice, the one that Sabé never even tried to duplicate. "Is Dad around?"

A few moments passed, and then both of Padmé's parents glinted blue in the dim light. Her father was brushing sawdust from his hands.

"Queen Réilatta has asked me to serve as Naboo's new senator," Padmé said after a brief exchange of greetings. "I've said yes."

No one heard Padmé Amidala sound this vulnerable and desperate for approval. It would have been a political nightmare. But this was Padmé Naberrie, talking with three people she trusted absolutely.

Ruwee and Jobal shared a look, communicating as easily as Padmé could have done with any of her handmaidens, though they had a different reason to be so practised at it.

"I can't say I'm happy you'll be leaving," Jobal said. "But your father and I are so proud of you."

"Just don't forget where you came from when you get out there again," Ruwee added. "Galactic politics can make you feel small and, well, I'm sure you've already started to figure that out."

"I won't," Padmé said. "And I promise I'll be careful."

It was such an odd thing to say, like Padmé was asking permission to go on a school trip, that Sabé almost laughed.

"Give my love to Sola," Padmé said. "I'll write when I have settled in."

Sabé gave her even more distance to finish her goodbyes and didn't move for several moments after the blue light had disappeared. She watched as Padmé straightened, her professional walls and masks sliding back into place. Without a word, Sabé opened the balcony door and led her back inside.

Yané was bustling towards them with several of Padmé's plainest dresses in her arms.

"Sabé, try these on," she demanded. "They're from before the last time you grew, and if we have to alter them, I'd rather know it now."

Sabé stood still as Padmé pulled the first dress over her head and helped Yané pin the parts where adjustments needed to be made. They had grown up on Naboo, and it

had been good to them. Now it was time to grow someplace else.

PART II

FASHION-PLATE QUEEN
RETURNS TO SENATE

Longtime political followers will recall young Queen Amidala of Naboo. Four years ago she came to Coruscant and deposed the Chancellor to questionably hasten along aid for her home planet. Though no hard evidence of the Trade Federation's misdeeds was ever produced, Amidala swayed the opinion of the Senate. Her speech, which was most likely written for her, given her age at the time, was stirring . . . and we can't help wondering what she'll stir up this time.

Now a senator for the Galactic Republic, Amidala has returned. A puppet queen no longer, surely, but the question remains: who is pulling her strings now?

– TriNebulon News

CHAPTER 6

The first six weeks of any senator's term were highly controlled by Republic protocol, and at five and three-quarter weeks in, Senator Amidala had had about enough. There was a great deal to learn, but she had always been a fast learner, and being hemmed in on every side by tradition and expectation was starting to wear on her. Fortunately, her ire could find a specific target in an uncaring droid designated NON-3.

"Senator," the droid began. There was something odd about the droid's vocal processor that shifted the way it said its vowels. It always took a moment for Padmé to figure out what it was saying, but every time she had requested a repair, she had been informed there was nothing wrong. "I remind you that you are scheduled for your final tour of the lower levels of the Senate building today. On this tour, you will observe and come to understand the inner workings of the building itself, beyond its cosmetic appearance, so that you might take advantage of its many amenities while you are in the assembly."

Padmé did her best not to tear her hair out. Dormé, formerly Dorra, had done an excellent job with it today. A small mercy of the senatorial training period had been that Padmé had gotten to know her new trio of handmaidens at the same time. Each of them had done her the courtesy of taking a new name. Though the public reason given was still anonymity, Padmé did not mistake the honour they showed her.

Cordé, formerly Cordyn, who had failed Panaka's initial training because she wasn't good with a blaster, had stepped into Sabé's shoes without hesitation. She had already mastered Padmé's physical mannerisms, and she was a near perfect voice match. Dormé, who had come out of the same security training that produced Typho and Tonra, proved a more-than-capable wardrobe mistress, and Padmé knew she was already planning updates and modifications to the senatorial dresses. Versé, formerly Versaat, was a top-notch slicer, though both she and her aunt Mariek remained close-lipped on how she'd acquired those skills. In addition to fortifying Padmé's digital security measures, she was gradually reprogramming the apartment to be more functional and comfortable for the group. Mariek and Typho rounded out the rest of Padmé's closest companions, along with a few other handpicked guards.

She missed Sabé like she would miss the sun.

Perhaps that was the real reason all of the tours and orientations were starting to get on her nerves. And there seemed to be no end. She had toured every corner of the Senate building, except the private offices of the other senators, of course, and she had witnessed how the complex operated. It was almost the exact same as when she had been in the junior legislative programme, which made her feel like she was mired in busywork. She disliked the feeling tremendously and constantly battled not to take it out on those around her. She had seen very little of Coruscant in the meantime and almost no governmental procedure, except a few carefully moderated sessions with the other new senators. The outgoing Senator Oshadam was polite and helpful but clearly ready to leave as soon as she could.

"Maybe that's the point," Dormé had said. "Maybe you're supposed to meet new senators and form alliances with them."

"Wouldn't it make more sense for you to meet established senators?" Versé asked. "I mean, you can't learn very much from someone who knows more or less the same as you, and presumably all the new senators taken together can't possibly outweigh the opinions of the experienced ones."

"It will be over soon," Cordé had said. Her tone was mollifying, not patronising, which brought Padmé up short. They were all frustrated. "And then you can sit in the gallery and shout at people to your heart's content."

"When I was new to being a queen, I was already holding off a planetwide invasion," Padmé pointed out. "Now, if pressed, I could give directions to the sewage recycling facility in sublevel nine, and that's about it."

"That's not true, and you know it," Mariek had said briskly. "You could also tell people where to find the commissary."

Typho had done his best not to crack a smile while Padmé

gave an indelicate snort. Perhaps this was actually some sort of winnowing process for incoming senators and their staffs, as well. Padmé knew far more about the skills, pet peeves, and general preferences of her handmaidens now than she had when they'd all arrived on Coruscant, and at least that was something.

She would never forget standing in the senatorial residence for the first time. It had been completely stripped for her redecoration and felt like a tomb in the sky, high above the Coruscant bustle. She had stood in the vestibule for half a second too long, with her three new companions behind her, waiting. Then, before she could think of anything to say, Versé had stepped in and begun issuing directions on how to unpack, coordinating with her aunt for security. For the first time, her handmaidens had moved as one, and they had continued to do so ever since, with Padmé slowly integrating into their patterns.

NON-3 made the polite chiming noise it made when it thought Padmé had taken too long to give an answer.

"I heard you, Nonnie," she said. "Where are we supposed to meet the orientation group?"

"There is no orientation group, Senator," NON-3 said. "This is a private tour."

Mariek took three steps closer and frowned. It was difficult even now to think of her as "Captain Panaka" – though that was her name and title – except in moments like this, when the lackadaisical woman disappeared and the professional stepped in. Everyone wore a mask when it came to Amidala.

"I don't like this, Senator," Mariek said. "Why is this tour different from the others?"

"I don't know," Padmé said. She turned to the droid, which was programmed to respond only to senators and certain other officials. "Nonnie, why is this tour different?"

"I am not programmed to give you that answer," NON-3 said.

"And what is the tour's exact destination?" Padmé asked.

"The lower levels of the Senate building," NON-3 replied.

"That's unhelpful," Versé said. "Those levels are vast."

"And you've already seen most of them," Cordé added. "Unless they want you to actually go inside the ventilation ducts."

"You know what we haven't tried yet?" Dormé said, with a long look sideways at the protocol droid.

Padmé was tempted. Not to skip the tour entirely, because she would still go in handmaiden robes if it came to it, but to see if they could fool Coruscant the way they'd fooled Naboo. The first time Padmé had come here, she had been Amidala from the time they'd reached the apartment until the time they'd left. It would be interesting to see her new place of residence from a nonsenatorial point of view. She looked at Mariek, who nodded.

"All right," Padmé said. "We'll have to make the change quickly. Cordé, it will be you first."

Cordé was the closest physical match to Amidala in terms of face shape and bone structure. Padmé's skin was only a shade paler, and once Dormé worked her magic with the makeup brush, strangers had difficulty telling them apart. Cordé could stand the way that Padmé did, though she was a bit taller and had a narrower build, and her voice match could fool the security locks on their Naboo starship. Whether she could fool NON-3 was yet to be tested – they'd had no trouble with battle droids or astromechs – but there was plenty of time for that.

Versé helped Padmé into her spare set of dark blue robes and put her hair into a simple coil so that it would fit under the hood. Then she went to help with Cordé. Dormé had put her in one of Padmé's favourite gowns, a navy blue undergown with a sea green ruffled tunic over top of it and a wide navy belt to tie all the pieces together. It looked elabourate, but like most of Padmé's senatorial dresses, it was easy to move in. Padmé laced up her knee-high boots, smiling to think of Sabé as she did it, and Cordé stepped into a pair of flat shoes that looked decorative but were microfitted to her feet so that she could run or even roundhouse kick someone if she had to. Last, Dormé had Padmé sit next to Cordé as a reference for the makeup.

"Two or three more times, and I'll have it," she promised. "But I want to make sure it's perfect first."

"I understand," Padmé said, and let the artist do her work.

Padmé had only ever seen Sabé in the queen's face, and it was slightly unnerving to watch someone re-create her appearance using only normal cosmetics, but that was exactly what Dormé did. Cordé's face shape even seemed to change as lines of contouring drew attention to the parts of her that looked the most like Padmé did. It wouldn't fool a scan of cranial features, of course, but to the naked eye, they were now interchangeable.

"And a bit for you," Dormé said, coming at Padmé with a brush. "In case anyone thinks you look too much like Senator Amidala."

It took much less time to do Padmé's face, and then they stood so that Dormé could conduct her final check of their appearance.

"It's uncanny," Mariek said to her niece, and Versé nodded.

"Thank you," Dormé replied with an impish grin.

They went back into the main room of the suite, where NON-3 and Sergeant Typho were glaring at each other.

"Senator," said NON-3 in that odd, overpatient tone. It looked right at Cordé when it spoke. "I remind you that you are scheduled for a tour of the lower levels of the Senate building today. On this tour – "

"Yes, I know," Cordé interrupted. Even her impression of Padmé's irritation was perfect. "I am ready to go now."

NON-3 looked at her with unblinking photoreceptors instead of eyes and then turned without a word to lead Senator Amidala and her handmaiden to the waiting transport.

"We'll see you when you get back," Mariek said. "By which I mean Typho will tail you to the Senate, and you should call him in if you need backup."

The Senate prided itself on having its own guard, which Padmé could call on if she needed, but she knew that a trustworthy friend was worth even more than that. She looked at Typho, who gave her a small wave of encouragement.

"Good luck, Senator Amidala," Dormé said.

Versé was already sitting at a console, her fingers typing as fast as they could. Padmé knew that she would be setting up the identity of the fourth handmaiden Amidala had brought with her. They had left the entry empty for weeks, not knowing how best to employ the blank ID, but now Padmé would have to have clearance to enter the Senate, so it was time to fill in the gaps. She knew that by the time they arrived, Versé would have built her a rock-solid profile. It would, after all, mostly contain the truth.

Senator Amidala boarded the open-air transport, and Padmé followed her. NON-3 climbed in and pressed a notification board that signalled the droid driver it was time to go. Neither Mariek nor Typho liked the fact that Amidala's drivers were provided by the Senate. They would have much preferred to do it themselves, or at least to supply their own driver. Senate protocol was a fortress that Padmé was still learning to lay siege to, but she knew enough already to know that she had to pick her battles. The Senate drivers would do for now, and Padmé would win something else later as a result of her patience – though what, exactly, she could not say.

The transport joined the flow of Coruscant traffic. The wind and the hum of a thousand engines precluded any further conversation, so Padmé looked out over the city's vista instead. It couldn't be more different from Naboo. Padmé missed trees and water and birdsong. She hadn't been down to the lower levels of the city yet, but she'd heard that they were mostly dark, dangerous places. It seemed unfair that a planetwide city meant to serve as a symbol for the rest of the Galactic Republic should have that sort of underbelly, but Padmé didn't know enough about how Coruscant worked yet to fully puzzle it out.

Padmé turned to look at the Jedi Temple, her hand drifting to her necklace without her mind's direction. It was a large building that was visible from her apartment. Many of the new senators she'd met had gone to see it as soon as they could after they arrived on the planet. There were parts that were private, of course, but there were also parts of the temple that the Jedi permitted visitors to see. Padmé hadn't gone. Unlike most of her colleagues, she had met several Jedi already, and she found their manner unsettling. Perhaps if Master Qui-Gon had lived, she would feel differently. She would certainly be pleased to call him a friend, and would have been hopeful to treat with him as an ally. Theirs had been an odd relationship: she hadn't fooled him for a moment, but he had allowed her to continue fooling everyone else, which she had appreciated, as it helped preserve her own life. She knew she was not the only person on Naboo who lit a stick of incense for him at the yearly memorial for those who had fallen in defence of the planet.

She turned away from the temple and focused on their goal: the Senate building. Cordé was gripping the armrests on her chair a bit harder than was really necessary, a sure sign that she was nervous, but her face remained still and calm. The Amidala-mask was in place. Padmé had only to make sure she didn't put hers on by accident.

The transport docked at an unfamiliar door, but NON-3 didn't hesitate before leading them towards it. The droid pressed a button, and the door slid open. Amidala and Padmé scanned their IDs on the way through and passed into the building without an issue.

The issues began as soon as they entered.

"This is not right," Padmé said.

The hallway was dark, not even lighting up when Amidala's credentials were recognised. Both senator and handmaiden stayed close to the wall while NON-3 strolled down the middle of the corridor as though nothing were wrong.

"Nonnie," Cordé said as quietly as she could in her Amidala voice. "Nonnie, come back."

"Senator, we will be late." The droid was definitely slurring now. Its speech patterns were almost unrecognisable.

"I don't like this," Padmé said. She wished for the royal pistol, but arms were restricted in the Senate building, and so both of them had left their blasters at home.

"There's someone coming," Cordé said. She took several deep breaths, and Padmé knew she was preparing for several different outcomes. Padmé slid the beacon that would alert Typho to their whereabouts into her palm.

"What are you doing down here?" The challenge was issued just before the figure who spoke stepped out of the shadows, and it took Padmé a moment to place the voice.

"Senator Organa," Cordé said, her Amidala-mask still firmly in place. They – rather he and Padmé – had met briefly at one of the welcome dinners. Cordé reacted without missing a beat. "My apologies. I was told by my protocol droid that I was expected here."

Senator Organa was almost two metres tall with elegantly styled hair. He looked stern now that he had joined them in the dim light of the corridor, but the most dramatic thing about him was the heavy swoop of the cape that hung down from his shoulders.

"Senator Amidala, correct?" Organa asked, and then continued at Cordé's nod. "The only thing expected here is a team of demolition droids. This section is to be redone. It was in the day's briefing."

Cordé was momentarily flustered, though none of it showed enough for Organa to see. Padmé had read the day's briefing, and no mention of demolition had been made. The droid broke the awkward silence.

"Senator," said NON-3. "I remind you that you are scheduled for a tour of the lower levels of the Senate building today. On – "

"Enough, Nonnie," Cordé barked. The droid ceased speaking immediately.

"That droid is malfunctioning," Organa said.

"I am aware," Cordé informed him. "I have sent in several requisitions for repair, and they have all been returned to me assuring me the droid is fine."

"Let me send one." Organa pulled a datapad from a pocket under his cape and typed something quickly.

"Senator," NON-3 said, "I have been reported to maintenance. I must check in with them immediately. Can you find your way home from here?"

"I will take the senator out," Organa said.

Padmé was glad that Cordé was standing in for her. Cordé excelled at staying in character, and with her face covered, Padmé let herself seethe for a moment in the face of Senator Organa's dismissive manner.

"Thank you, Senator," Cordé said.

"I'm glad I found you before the implosions started," Organa said curtly. "You would never have made it out of there alive."

Cordé said nothing, which Padmé assumed Organa interpreted as grateful acknowledgement. Padmé had several dozen questions but couldn't ask them in her current position. Instead, she had to content herself with following the two of them back out through the door. Organa watched as Cordé boarded the transport, and then turned away as Padmé settled in beside her. They rode back to the senatorial residence in complete silence, and the droid driver didn't linger after she dropped them off.

"That didn't take very long," Mariek said when she met them on the platform. "Where's that blasted droid?"

"Inside," Padmé said. "Now."

As quickly as she could, Padmé relayed the events to the others. Typho's face got darker and darker as she talked, but no one else reacted until she was done.

"Why would there be an attempt on your life now?" Versé said. "Please don't take this the wrong way, but you haven't done anything in the Senate yet, and at this stage, Gunray's prosecution would move forwards without you."

"The death of a senator because of her own perceived foolishness could be used any number of ways," Padmé said. "To discredit Naboo, perhaps even to discredit the Chancellor, because he was in favour of my appointment."

"It doesn't make any sense," Versé said. "Even if the Trade Federation is that petty. Your death would call more attention, and you'd think they'd want less."

"I don't think anyone really knows what Nute Gunray wants," Mariek said.

"There's one upside," Cordé said. She was in the act of pulling the copper-wire headpiece off.

"Oh?" Dormé said peevishly. She retrieved the headpiece and put it back in its place on the dressing table.

"The droid driver didn't even look at you," Cordé said to Padmé. "Organa might as well have been talking to one person."

"One person he now thinks is a senator incapable of reading her own schedule or controlling her own droid!" Dormé fumed.

"It certainly didn't win Amidala any points with him," Padmé said. "And he's a powerful voice in the Senate."

"You can try again," Typho said. "I know you can win him over if you have to."

"Thank you, Sergeant," Padmé said. She furrowed her brow. "There's one thing I would very much like to know."

"Who reprogrammed our protocol droid so that it would try to arrange your death?" Versé said. She began to take the pins out of Cordé's hair, smoothing it down where the headpiece had made it stick out in tufts. If there had been any doubts about their loyalty, Padmé dismissed them all now.

Each of her new handmaidens was furious, in her own way, and ready for a fight.

"Well, yes, that," Padmé said. She had a faraway look in her eyes that she knew they all recognised. Amidala was deep into the politics now. "But more importantly: what was Organa doing there, too?"

CHAPTER 7

The fallout of NON-3's bizarre malfunction struck immediately. By the next morning, there were several holonews
articles about how the young, new-to-Coruscant Senator
Amidala had almost gotten herself killed due to a failure to
read directions. The first report, written up from a respected
news source, did mention the faulty droid in the final para-
graph of the story, but none of the more sensational holos
did. So it was that when Senator Amidala entered the Senate
for her first official session, she did so under a cloud of
curiosity.

"And apparent incompetence." Padmé slammed the
offending datapad down on her new desk.

"No one is saying that," Cordé pointed out.

"No one is *quite* saying that," Dormé amended. "They're
all getting pretty close."

Versé had remained at the residence to read all the
articles as they were published. She was running a text
analysis on them to see if she could identify a single author –
among other things – but she hadn't come up with anything
yet.

"At least Senator Organa wasn't interviewed," Cordé said. "He's not even mentioned."

"And your mysterious handmaiden is listed only as an aide," Mariek added. She was dressed in a modified version of the Naboo uniform today, since the hat, which provided protection from both the sun and potential debris, was unnecessary for the Senate floor.

"That doesn't clear up who the source is," Dormé said.

"There's nothing we can do about it, I suppose," Padmé said. "I'll just have to go out there and try not to look the fool. Maybe they'll all remember me as the young queen who unseated Chancellor Valourum instead."

"That's the spirit," said Mariek. "Now come and sit over here so that Dormé can fix your hair."

Padmé had done a bit of angry pacing after arriving at her office and had shaken down some of Dormé's pins. They had elected to dress Amidala as formally as they could for her first official appearance. They wanted to present nothing of the young girl the holos seemed fixated on. Padmé wore a stiff overdress of purple brocade, with hand-embroidered violets along the hem and cuffs. The tunic she wore underneath was violet, as well, with a collar that made it almost impossible for her to turn her head. Dormé had braided her hair in four sections, two to hang down her back, wrapped in purple ribbon, and two to be pinned up on the sides of her head, supporting the beaten copper headband.

"I feel like my skull is exposed," Padmé said as Dormé straightened the copper piece and affixed more pins in her errant hair.

"It'll catch the light, I think," Dormé said. "Anyone who glances at your pod will see you."

"And there are at least four representatives who will actually have their skulls exposed," Cordé pointed out.

"Thanks," Padmé said dryly. Cordé grinned back at her with no trace of apology. Padmé straightened, the Amidalamask falling over her features. Though she had deployed it at various points during the orientation, this was the first time Padmé had brought the full force of it to bear. All of her attendants straightened, suddenly reaffirmed of their directives. "All right, then," she said. "Let's go."

NON-3 had not yet been returned to them, so Padmé made her own way from her office to where the Naboo pod was docked. She had memorised the layout – from the technical specifications of the building, not the inane tours – and took no wrong turns, even though all the hallways looked the same. Cordé and Dormé walked behind her, clad in sober grey with their hoods pulled over their faces, and Mariek came last. She was not visibly armed, but Padmé knew her better than that.

Padmé suppressed a surge of vertigo as she stepped to the front of her pod and took her seat. The Senate room was almost incomprehensibly large, and it was filled with what felt like an uncountable number of species, all serving members of the Galactic Republic. It made her feel small in a way she did not like. It would be very, very difficult for a single voice to be heard, even if everyone followed the rules of protocol. Yet she had done it before. She could do it again.

A chime sounded, and Padmé looked down to where Chancellor Palpatine stood, flanked by his two aides.

"I declare this session open," the Chancellor said. "The floor recognises the representative from Ithor."

Ithorians did not speak Basic, so Padmé turned on her translator. As the other senator's pod detached from the side of the chamber and floated out to circle the Chancellor's podium, Padmé watched the text scroll past, reading as quickly as she could. Just when she felt she was getting a handle on the argument – something about hyperspace lane mapping and the dissemination thereof – two new speakers began to interrupt, both in Basic. One was the Trade Federation delegate, to Padmé's disgust, and the other was a human male from the Urce sector. Both were against sharing the maps, because they each felt they, separately, owned the rights to them. The combination of shouting and reading the translation was challenging to follow, and at the end of five minutes of what Padmé could only describe as squabbling, Chancellor Palpatine called for a vote.

Senator Amidala had only a few moments to decide. She knew she was prejudiced against the Trade Federation, but she tried to think on their terms for a brief moment while she made her consideration. The route through the Lesser Plooriod Cluster had been partially mapped by the Trade Federation, but for the most part, the work had been done by the Ithorians. The humans in the Urce sector had a claim only to the portion of the route in their own space, but taken together with the Trade Federation claim, they could potentially block the Ithorians into a corner, and Padmé remembered all too well how that could end up. Ultimately, she came down on the side of the Ithorians. It was their system, after all, and they had been using the lanes before the Trade Federation claimed to have mapped them. Naboo had made the mistake of displacing their planet's native population, to their eternal shame, and Padmé was determined not to be part of such actions again. She voted in favour of the motion.

"Motion fails," Palpatine announced a moment after she had pressed her selection. "The chair recognises the member from Chandrila."

A slim, red-haired human woman began to speak, and Padmé didn't have time to dwell on the failed vote. She had to move on to the new one.

It felt like it went on for hours. Motions were raised and passed to various committees, or they were voted on. Even though she had done the background reading, Padmé felt like decisions – all of them stalls – were made before they dug into the heart of any particular issue. Several bills that Padmé thought were sound failed, and even more were bounced back to the bargaining table, only she didn't know when or where that bargaining took place. At last, the chime sounded again, and Chancellor Palpatine called an end to deliberations.

Padmé slumped back in her seat, as much as her dress would allow, and tried not to feel defeated. No wonder the previous senator had resigned. Cordé coughed three times behind her, and Padmé straightened at the signal just before one of the camera droids flew up over the lip of her pod and focused its photoreceptor on her face. The Amidala-mask in place, Padmé rose gracefully from her seat and led her attendants out of the assembly. She hoped the camera had gotten whatever it wanted.

"Well, that was something," said someone beside her. Another young senator stood there. She cast about for his name.

"Indeed, Senator Clovis," she said.

He brightened. "You remember me!" he said.

Padmé didn't tell him that of course she remembered him. There had only been eight of them in the orientation group. Amidala said nothing, and Clovis's face dimmed considerably.

"There's a reception for the new senators and some guests. Chancellor Palpatine is hosting it," he said. "We all got notifications at the conclusion of the session through our NONs, but yours is still out, so I thought I should mention it to you."

"Thank you, Senator," Amidala said. Mariek blew out a breath, indicating that she had completed her verification of

Clovis's identity and words. Amidala relaxed her mask the slightest bit. "Will you walk with me?"

Clovis seemed only too happy to do so.

He talked unceasingly as they went, mostly about his own planet, Scipio, and how overwhelming everything about Coruscant was. Padmé agreed with him privately but would never be foolish enough to say the words out loud, so she kept her face neutral.

"But I suppose you know all about that by now," Clovis finished. Padmé regarded him steadily, and, as she hoped, he floundered. "I mean, because of the holos. Not that I think you're unqualified of course. Just new. Like me. We'll learn. Perhaps we could learn together?"

Padmé wished Sabé was with her. She wouldn't need eye contact to see the sardonic look on her face. Padmé had to content herself with imagining it instead.

"I imagine we will all learn soon enough," Amidala said. That seemed to please Clovis for some reason.

They reached the door. It was guarded by two red-robed and masked figures, indicating that the Chancellor was indeed within. The new guards were intimidating, a far cry from the senatorial guards she'd met on her previous trip to Coruscant. She vaguely remembered hearing that Palpatine had created his own security force, but she had not imagined they would be so extreme. Clovis walked blithely through, without a retinue, and Padmé led her own people into the room behind him. She took a breath, held it for three deliberate heartbeats, and then let it out. She could do this.

"See if you can find us something to eat," she said to Cordé. "And remind me to eat more before the next session."

Cordé melted into the crowd. Mariek followed at a respectful distance, but Dormé stuck to Padmé's side like glue. Clovis, mercifully, had disappeared.

"Ah, Senator Amidala, welcome." Chancellor Palpatine's booming voice drew the attention of everyone in earshot.

"Chancellor," she said pleasantly.

"I was so pleased you agreed to Queen Réillata's appointment," Palpatine continued. Padmé focused on him, knowing that Dormé would be silently cataloguing everyone in his orbit.

"It is my great honour to serve Naboo and to serve the Republic," Amidala said.

"Indeed," Palpatine said. "Come, let me introduce you."

It was going to be a bit like being shown at the annual midsummer livestock fair in Theed, Amidala thought. But she would rather have Palpatine's approval than be left at the mercy of whoever had read the newsnets, so she braced herself and made to follow him. One of his aides materialised beside them after only three steps and whispered in his ear.

"I'm so sorry, my dear," Palpatine said. "I must go and attend to this. You know how it is. But I leave you in the capable hands of Senator Mina Bonteri."

And he was gone, leaving Padmé in the middle of the room with a woman she had only barely been properly introduced to, and all eyes on her.

"Senator Bonteri," she said. "I'm pleased to meet you."

"The pleasure is mine, Senator," said the woman. "Will you walk with me?"

Amidala took the proffered arm, which forced Dormé to fall back half a pace – still well within earshot – and walked. It was much less stressful than walking with Palpatine would have been.

"You did well today," Bonteri said after a moment.

"How can you possibly tell?" Padmé asked, letting her mask slip down a little bit. If Bonteri was going to try to be helpful, Padmé was going to encourage her to do it.

"You're still standing," Bonteri said. "You're not attacking the buffet tables. You haven't started drinking. And you can still navigate a conversation with the Chancellor."

"I suppose if that's all it takes, then I am quite suited to senatorial life," Padmé said.

"Ah, there are her teeth," Bonteri said. "You do such a good job of playing a part, I was starting to wonder what kind of person was inside that dress."

"On Naboo, the part and the politics are the same thing," Padmé told her. "It goes a long way to preserving faith in government. I suppose I should be open to different methodologies."

"Well," said Bonteri. "No one has any faith in the Republic, so that's a good place for you to start."

"I have faith in the Republic," Padmé said automatically. And it was true. Even after that awful session, she did.

Bonteri looked at her, searching for something Padmé wasn't sure of. Whatever it was, Bonteri didn't look too disappointed when she didn't find it.

"Senator Amidala, I think you'll do all right here," she said. She sounded sincere. "But I will tell you a secret: you can do all the reading you want, believe in all the truths you think the galaxy has to offer, but the real work of the Senate is done at parties like these. A conscience vote is a wonderful thing, but allies are far better."

"Who would ally themselves with me?" Padmé asked. "I'm so foolish I follow my own malfunctioning droid into certain death."

"That's nothing to worry about," Bonteri said. "I mean, you should definitely figure out who tried to kill you, but the newsnets are immaterial."

Padmé said nothing but could not quite suppress a disbelieving sniff.

"I know it smarts your pride," Bonteri said. "But everyone would be staring at you anyway. We all remember your speech and how your words were enough to unseat a chancellor. We've all heard the Trade Federation claim you are a liar in the face of, frankly, staggering evidence that you are not. We all know that Palpatine likes you. We're just not sure if you're someone we want to work with."

"Do you have a we in mind?" Padmé said, "Or are you speaking of the entire Senate?"

"I like how you get right to the point of things," Bonteri said. "We all have our little factions. Sometimes there is overlap, and sometimes there is not. You'll have to figure that part out on your own."

"I'm working on it," Padmé said.

Bonteri paused midstep and looked over her shoulder directly into Dormé's face. Dormé's expression was politely blank, and Bonteri laughed.

"I'll bet you are," she said. She took Padmé's other hand so that they were facing each other. Padmé wondered how Mariek had managed to restrain herself from interfering. This was much more handsy than anyone usually got.

"The newsnets went after you because you were an easy story," Bonteri said. "Which is not the same as an easy target, so don't get all worked up. People already know you. You already have a good reputation. You've done half the work, and they're more than happy to make up the second half, even if it has no basis at all in fact."

"How do I combat that?" Padmé asked.

"You don't," Bonteri said. "Not directly, at least. You come to work and you do your job, and you try not to give them anything to sensationalise. They'll sensationalise you anyway, of course, but then you just ignore them."

"Thank you," Padmé said. "I didn't expect to get such usable advice from anyone, to be honest."

"The orientation brings out the very worst in all of us, I think. We're not so bad once you get to know us," Bonteri said. She looked ahead in the crowd and spotted someone she was searching for. She changed direction, pulling Padmé along with her. "Ah, Senator Organa, allow me to introduce Senator Amidala."

"A pleasure," Organa said, making no indication they had ever crossed paths before, even briefly at that dinner. "Welcome to Coruscant."

Welcome to Coruscant, indeed.

The gathering dragged on for another hour. Bonteri introduced her to even more senators, until they became a blur of faces and names. Padmé hoped Dormé and Cordé would be able to help her fill in the gaps in her memory. Most of the senators were as politely dispassionate as Senator Organa had been. A few were openly curious about her, for novelty's sake. All of that was preferable to what happened when Padmé met the senator from Targappia, a humanoid woman nearly eight feet tall, with webbed fingers and iridescent hair.

"Ah, Senator Amidala," she said. Her voice was lilting and

musical, but there was an atonal note beneath her words that more than carried her disdain for Padmé's presence. "It's so wonderful to finally meet you in person after reading so much about you in the newsnets."

Padmé nodded politely, of course, already composing lists of senators to avoid, based on those who chuckled at the Targappian's remarks.

At last, she followed Mariek into their transport, and before long they were all delivered back to the blessed quiet of the senatorial residence, where Versé was waiting for them.

"So," she said. "That bad, eh?"

"Later," Mariek said. "Give the senator some time to rest."

"No," Padmé said. "Not later. The four of us need to discuss a few things."

"We can talk while we're putting away the dress," Cordé said. "Come on."

While Dormé pulled pins and ribbons from her hair and began to brush it out and Cordé returned the purple dress to its spot in the wardrobe, the three of them recounted the day's events to Versé, who dutifully recorded every word.

"I didn't make any progress on my end," Versé said. "Though I would request that you promise me you'll never read the editorials from TriNebulon News. Or anywhere, actually."

"I don't imagine I'll have time for it," Padmé said. "But I promise."

"What are we going to do?" Cordé asked. She sat down on the foot of Padmé's bed, and Versé put her portable desk away.

Padmé turned and looked at all three of them.

"We knew that senatorial politics were going to be different," she said. "But I don't think any of us truly appreciated how much difference there would be until today."

"I could barely follow along, and I did all the preparatory reading," Cordé said. "Though the party was a bit easier to keep track of."

"That's what Senator Bonteri told me," Padmé said. "That the real work gets done at functions, not on the floor."

Dormé made a face, realising what Padmé intended to do. A soft chime sounded, and Versé looked up.

"It's your schedule for tomorrow," she reported.

"I shudder to think of it," Padmé said. She paused, and then continued. "The strengths I cultivated to be queen of a planet are going to trip me up as a senator."

"Not all of them," Cordé said loyally.

"But some of them." Dormé's loyalty was characteristically blunt.

"I can't be so distant," Padmé said. "I can't rely on people's faith in tradition. I have to be more approachable to my colleagues."

"You didn't exactly have colleagues as queen." Versé called up a new personnel profile, projecting the image so they could all see it. "So I suppose that would be the easiest place to start. It's an addition, not a replacement."

"We can rework the Amidala persona from there," Padmé agreed. "How she interacts with her fellow senators, and how the handmaidens operate, as well."

"I was thinking about new protocols while I was wandering at the party," Cordé admitted.

"And I can tell you what to avoid," Versé added.

"I suppose we can't just burn down the whole Senate and start over again with a system that makes sense?" Dormé asked.

"I'm fairly certain that would be treason," Padmé said. "We're going to have to work with what we've already got."

CHAPTER 8

Sabé had never wished for the deep calm of a Naboo lake as much as she did at this particular moment. For six weeks, she had been Tsabin, a new resident of Mos Espa, one of the spaceports that dotted the surface of Tatooine, with her partner, Tonra, whose own name was un-Naboo enough to pass. After the unrelenting suns and the unrelenting wind and the unrelenting grit of the desert planet, she longed for home. Everything she had planned to do on Tatooine had gone sideways almost as soon as she'd landed, and she'd been scrambling to right her course ever since with little success.

The local criminals didn't trust her because she was too new. By the time she'd realised – too late – that Tatooine had a nascent liberation movement, they no longer trusted her because she'd been trying to get in with the criminals. Only the sellers would talk to her, and Sabé found them almost too odious to bear. The upside of the whole debacle was that Captain Tonra had turned out to be a decent living companion. She suspected this was because he wanted her to like him, and for the most part, it was working.

They had a small house on one of Mos Espa's innumerable

side streets. It was cramped and uncomfortable and not entirely sound. In her darker moments, Sabé soothed her wounded pride by reminding herself that she wouldn't be stuck on Tatooine forever. This mostly served only to prick her conscience even more: there were plenty who had no such choice.

It was those people she had come to help, and it was those people she had, for the most part, failed.

The door slid open, and Tonra ducked inside. He was dressed nondescriptly, as was she, but he carried a pack.

"It's time," he said.

Sabé took a deep breath, calling up the Tsabin personality, and followed him out into the blistering sunlight. She wished she'd had more time to recover from the auction Tonra had been able to swindle their way into, but that was a selfish thought, too: She felt only fury and frustration. There was so much more at stake.

It was a quick walk to the spaceport, where their secondary freighter was parked. Waiting for them next to the ramp was their purchased cargo.

They were still chained.

Sabé thought she might supernova with anger, giving Tatooine another sun. Rage coursed through her – at herself, at this abhorrent system, at everything.

"Do the preflight," Tonra said, his hands on her shoulders. He let her see his own fury, smouldering no less intensely than hers but channelled in a different direction. "I'll take care of them."

The overseer pressed the control ring into her hands and was smart enough not to say anything. She all but fled up the ramp into the cockpit, unable to face the people who stood silently on the platform.

The checks done, Sabé ground her teeth as she watched out the viewport while Tonra marshalled the last few passengers up the ramp and onto the transport. Most of them were scared – and she couldn't blame them – but she was in no mood to be gentle at the moment. Tonra was good at that sort of thing, so she left him to it while she triple-checked their stores and the map of their route.

Twenty-five souls. That was all she'd managed to save. It was better than nothing, but it was still so far from *enough*, and it gnawed at her. They would only be replaced with twenty-five more.

Tatooine's was a strange economy, running on water and crime, the latter being much more lucrative. The Hutts' iron control of smuggling and trafficking was impossible for two people, both new to the planet, to overcome.

"Everyone is squared away," Tonra said, settling into the copilot's chair. "Are we ready to go?"

"Nearly," Sabé said. It would have been easier if they'd had another pilot to make this run instead of doing it themselves, but the freighter they were using was unremarkable enough and there was no one else they could trust – or who trusted them.

The freighter lifted off and headed out of Tatooine's atmosphere. Once they were in the clear void of space, Sabé set the coordinates for a planet in the Chommell sector. Karlinus was nearly as affluent as Naboo itself, and it was always looking to hire agricultural workers. One or two seasons at a fair wage and the people they'd "rescued" would be able to go wherever they liked.

"I'm sending a message to Yané," Sabé said. "She'll meet us there and take care of those blasted tracking chips they've been forced to carry."

She was carrying the control ring on her belt, and it felt like it was burning her. The navicomputer indicated that its calculations were complete. Tonra opened the comm to make a shipwide announcement.

"We're about to go to hyperspace," he said. "Please prepare yourselves."

Sabé counted to twenty-five, one second for each newly freed soul on board, and then made the jump.

The governor of Karlinus was a short young woman with warm golden-brown skin, whose round face was framed by thick hair that frizzed in the humidity and whose wide smile was instantly welcoming. She met them on the landing pad herself, with a dozen unarmed guards. Sabé appreciated the gesture on the governor's part and was even more pleased when she spotted Yané in the crowd. Her charges were mostly adults, but there were two families – one Rodian, one human – with children, and Yané would be of extra help settling them.

Sabé went straight down the ramp while Tonra went to the passengers in the hold. Yané threw her arms around Sabé's neck as soon as she was in range.

"I'm so glad to see you," Yané said. "And Governor Kelma said you've brought twenty-five people. That's a good day's work."

It had been weeks of work, but Yané's enthusiasm was contagious.

"We're grateful," Governor Kelma said. Her brown eyes hardened. "As long as they are all here by their own choice."

"It's not much of a choice," Sabé said. She had, of course, enquired, but none of the people she had relocated had anywhere else to go. "But you'll pay them and you won't force them to stay."

Sabé and Padmé had agreed on Karlinus because, in addition to being in the Chommell sector, it was a planet that was used to a high turnover in its workforce. Artists and students would come from Naboo, spend a season monitoring the droids that harvested tea or wove silk, and then head home with enough credits to establish a studio or continue their

studies offworld. Governor Kelma was in a position to welcome workers and pay them – well – and then send them on
their way once they could support themselves. Unlike the min-
ing moons, which struggled to maintain the balance between
the rule of Naboo and their allegiance to filling their quotas,
Karlinus was a place where prosperity began.

"May I go on board and speak to them?" Kelma asked.

"Of course," Sabé said, stepping out of the way so that
the governor could start up the ramp. "Captain Tonra will
introduce you."

"You're not happy," Yané said when the governor had
gone. "Not even a little bit, with what you've done."

"We haven't done anything, really," Sabé said.

"You brought twenty-five souls out of slavery," Yané said.

"There are so many more," Sabé said. "On Tatooine,
throughout the rest of the Outer Rim, and I'm sure there's
more in the Republic than any of us want to think about. I
just don't understand how it happens, and that's probably why
I can't help to fix it. How can one person *own* another person
and live with themselves?"

She hated feeling this naive and this helpless.

"We know the galaxy can be an ugly place," Yané said. "Do
you think I don't wonder what might have happened to us in
that camp if the queen hadn't come back? Death is final, but it
can be delivered in so many terrible ways. And you've helped
to stop that, even if it's just a little bit."

"It isn't *enough*," Sabé said.

"No," Yané said. "But you're hardly giving up, are you?"

Sabé thought about the cramped little house back on Tatooine and the wretched heat and blowing sand. She thought about lakes on Naboo, and how much she missed her friends and family there. Of course there was only one way for her to go.

Governor Kelma came down the ramp, one arm around the Rodian female and the Rodian baby braced against her hip. Sabé nodded to the governor as she passed and then looked up at Tonra. It seemed cold not to let him even touch the ground close to home, but his face asked the same question Yané had, and Sabé knew the answer.

Yané kissed her cheek, and Sabé headed back up into the ship. Tonra clasped a hand on her shoulder and went to start the preflight sequence. Sabé looked out the viewport until after he had made the jump to lightspeed to head back to Tatooine.

"The senator will understand," Tonra said. He was adding something green to a stewpot that he'd been fiddling with while Sabé had been out checking on their ship. The pot whirred strangely, but the smell emanating from it wasn't entirely bad, and Sabé had to admit she was moderately impressed. "You had limited funds and almost no authority."

He was always careful with her, but she never felt patronised. And he was correct, but managed to not make her feel worse about it.

"I know she will," Sabé said. "That only makes it worse."

Tonra nodded, and then kindly changed the subject. "How is the ship?"

"It's fine," she reported. "There were some strange tracks in the area, but the ship itself remains hidden."

They had elected not to dock their primary vessel at the spaceport in Mos Espa, in case they ever needed to make a quick, unofficial getaway. Sabé selected a place not far from where they had set down the royal starship when they were fleeing to Coruscant almost half a decade ago, though she picked a spot with better cover. At the end of everything, that ship was the most important thing they had.

Tonra placed a steaming bowl in front of her and handed her a spoon. She knew better than to look at it before she took a bite.

"Any messages?" he asked, digging in.

"Padmé wants to talk," Sabé replied. "She sent a time and asked me to reply if it would work, so I did. It's going to be the middle of the night for her, but I suppose she's busy."

"Should we pack?" Tonra gestured to their single cramped room as though it was a palace.

"I honestly can't think of anything I've picked up here that I wouldn't mind leaving," she said.

Against all common sense, Sabé had hoped that coming back after their run to Karlinus would change something, but it hadn't. She wasn't accustomed to failure, but at the very least, she and Tonra could start over on a different part of the planet.

"I don't know," Tonra said. "I'm getting fond of that mouse droid that can't wheel itself in anything but a circle."

The mouse droid had come with the house. Sabé had done her best to ignore it, but Tonra wasn't given to contemplation the way she was: he had to be doing something with his hands. It was, she had decided, his most annoying quality, but she was graceful enough to admit that her pensive silences were probably more than a little unnerving, so it evened out.

"You are welcome to it," Sabé said. "Just keep it out from under my feet."

She passed him her bowl and waited at the table while he finished eating. The food was a marked improvement from when they'd arrived, but Sabé had no appetite in the heat, and so she ate as little as possible. Tonra seemed largely unaffected by the weather, at least in terms of his appetite, and if Tatooine had taught Sabé anything, it was that she was happy to give away what she didn't need to someone who might want it.

Tonra set his spoon down and reached across the table to take her hands. People didn't often touch Sabé, and she was never entirely sure how to react when they did, but she thought that not immediately jumping up from the table and striking a defensive stance was probably a good start.

"You didn't fail entirely here, you know," Tonra said. "We were able to do a little bit of good."

"I know," she said. "But this meant a lot to Padmé and it meant a lot to me."

"You have made at least six new plans for what comes next," Tonra said. "I know you have."

She smiled. "It's eight, actually."

"See," he said. "And next time we'll be more prepared."

He'd said *we* twice, which probably meant it wasn't an accident. Fool's errand or not, he would follow her.

"I'm going to start packing," she said. "I'll take care of the gear that ties into our identities, you decide what you want to give away."

It didn't take them very long to settle everything into packs or arrange things so that the scavengers would find them without bringing down the already precarious roof. Then they walked out into the desert. Sabé had plotted a circuitous route to where the ship was stowed. It was difficult to get bearings on Tatooine's surface without equipment due to the lack of landmarks, but Sabé had been on the planet before, posing as Amidala, and she had an excellent memory for stars.

"Not that Panaka let us get off the ship," she said. "And not that I could have in that black gown. The headdress was tall and covered with feathers. We would have ruined it instantly. But there were viewports, and there was nothing to do while we waited for Master Qui-Gon to return but worry and read."

Everyone on Naboo knew the name Qui-Gon Jinn – the long-haired Jedi who had risked much and lost all during the battle for the planet – but comparatively few had met him. Tonra had heard all of the stories before, and had been present for many of them, but the Tatooine parts of that particular venture weren't exactly a matter of public record.

"This is where the ship was," Sabé said, gesturing at the featureless rocks around them. "This is where we waited."

"The hardest part of that story to believe isn't the podrace or the bit about the little boy," Tonra said. "It's the part where Panaka let the queen off the ship in the first place."

"Have you ever been able to refuse her?" Sabé asked, and Tonra conceded the point.

They kept walking, staying on the rocks for as long as possible and then turning around and going back almost exactly the way they'd come, but far enough from their previous tracks that Sabé hoped they would befuddle anyone attempting to follow them. There was no evidence of anyone taking that much notice of them, but Sabé had learned a long time ago that excessive precaution was the better part of valour.

At last they reached their ship. It was a decent midrange cargo ship without any identifying markings to speak of. Sabé had acquired it after asking the advice of Naboo's royal pilot. Ric Olié had suffered an inner-ear injury after the Battle of Naboo that made it difficult for him to leave atmosphere, though he could still fly below the clouds. The new pilot,

Daneska Varbarós was a woman of moderate height with dark skin, the most electric eyes Sabé had ever seen in a human, and long hair she liked to bleach and then dye in an ongoing series of different colours. When they had met to discuss the ship, it had been the sort of purple that was visible from low orbit.

Varbarós had also provided intelligence about hyperspace lanes, safe havens on a variety of planets, and what to do if they attracted the wrong sort of attention, be it Republic or rogue. Sabé hadn't actually had to use any of that information, but she wasn't about to forget what she now knew.

Tonra made himself scarce on the pretence of securing their gear and performing the necessary preflight checks while Sabé checked the chronometer and waited for Padmé's incoming call. As punctual as ever, the chime sounded right when the numbers flipped over, and a moment later, Padmé's image filled the display in front of where Sabé was sitting.

"Sabé," she said, "it's so good to see you."

"Same to you," Sabé said, and it was true: she'd been surly and off-centre the past few days, but hearing Padmé's voice and seeing her, even as a holo, made her feel better instantly. She wished again that she had better news.

"Do you have anything new to report?" Padmé asked, and Sabé knew what information her friend was after.

"I'm sorry, Padmé," Sabé replied. "I couldn't find her."

On the holo, Padmé's shoulders rounded forwards as she slumped.

"Did she die?" Padmé asked after a moment.

"No," Sabé said. "Not from what I can tell."

She'd made Tonra check the cemeteries after she checked them twice herself. Enslaved people weren't allowed very much on Tatooine, but they were allowed to set up markers for each other when they died, and so they usually did.

"How can a person, even an enslaved one, just disappear?" Padmé asked.

"It was my fault," Sabé said. "We came at this all wrong and made mistakes from the moment we got here. The Toydarian was gone, and I spent too much time trying to talk to his cronies. I know there are beings on Tatooine who oppose slavery, but they don't trust me because I talked to the scum who profit from it, and frankly I don't blame them."

"I know you tried," Padmé said, and the absolution only burned.

"I know the junk dealer lost her," Sabé said. "I don't know if it was another stupid bet or if he actually sold her, but I know she's not here. I just don't know where she ended up."

There was a pause that was long enough that Sabé might have thought the transmission equipment had frozen, except Padmé was thinking, pacing in and out of the camera's range. Finally, she came to a stop back in the frame.

"You think there are people working against slavery on Tatooine?" Padmé asked.

"I am sure of it," Sabé said. That was what was so frustrating. She had missed an opportunity. "Do you remember Shmi Skywalker's house?"

"A little bit," Padmé said.

"Was there a symbol cut into the lintel above the door?"

"I don't think so," Padmé said. "Why?"

"There's one now," Sabé said. "A white sun. Small, but definitely deliberate. And new. It's not worn down."

Padmé spent another long moment considering it.

"Could you try again?" Padmé asked.

This was what Sabé had been asking herself for days, weeks, really, when her failure became apparent and she'd been forced to settle for that damn auction. And because she had been thinking about it, she had an answer.

"Yes," she said. "We'd have to leave and scrub the ship clean of any identifiers. Maybe even change its registration, if we could. We'd have to scrub our identities, too. We'd set up in Mos Eisley or some other spaceport. We wouldn't come back as smugglers next time. We'd be merchants. Someone disreputable for the scum to talk to, but not enough for them to trust. We'd need to set up a viable business to use as a cover, but maybe then the local liberation group would trust us, if only as a reliable way off-planet."

Sabé paused, and Padmé knew her well enough not to interrupt.

"Twenty-five souls, Padmé," she said. "Twenty-five out of *hundreds,* and they'll already have twenty-five more coming."

"I'm sure it makes a difference to those twenty-five," Padmé said quietly. This time, the absolution burned less.

"We didn't get the one you wanted," Sabé said.

"But you tried," Padmé said. "You tried when I couldn't. And maybe that doesn't mean very much, but it means a lot to me."

"It'll take me a few months to set everything up," Sabé said. "The hard part is the cover business, and we'll need more funding, which will have to come from you. I'll let Tonra be the public face this time instead of me, because people are afraid of him. Well, they could be, if he worked at it."

"People are afraid of you," Padmé pointed out.

"People who know me are afraid of me," Sabé said. She gestured at her small figure. "Strangers are not afraid of me."

Padmé paused again. The blue holo was grainy and shimmered in the display, but Sabé could see indecision on Padmé's face. Whatever was happening on Coruscant, Padmé's plans weren't going smoothly, either, and it was clear she'd done a lot of hard thinking of her own. At last she sighed, and it looked a great deal like defeat.

"I need you here," she said. "The others are working well with each other and with me. They're well suited to the Senate, and we're adapting together. But I need someone I don't have to ask to do things. I need someone who will just do what needs to be done."

Now it was Sabé's turn to wait while Padmé considered her next words.

"I can't get much more specific until we're talking in person," Padmé said. Her tone was deliberately light, which made Sabé pay close attention. "But there is a great deal more at work here than I expected. It's a bit like last time."

At this, Sabé straightened. Last time on Coruscant, the Trade Federation had been trying to kill her.

"Don't get too worried before you get here," Padmé said. "I'm well protected. And I'm visible enough now that there would be ramifications if something were to happen."

"That doesn't make me feel much better," Sabé said.

"Imagine what it's like for Mariek," Padmé said dryly.

In spite of everything, that made Sabé smile.

"Come to Coruscant," Padmé said. "I'll transmit coordinates for you. Will you need new identities?"

"No," Sabé said. "The ones we've established here will be good for something, at least."

"Excellent," Padmé said. "Sabé, I know that being cryptic makes it sound dire, but I promise you it isn't. It's just something I can't take care of myself."

"My hands are yours," Sabé said.

Padmé could deny it all she wanted, but Sabé had been trained by a man who always, always prepared for the worst, and he had lived long enough to retire, which Sabé considered was something of an accomplishment, despite their ideological differences.

"I'll see you soon, my friend," Padmé said, and terminated the connection.

Tonra appeared so quickly that Sabé wondered if he had been listening up against the bulkhead. Part of her didn't care – he was risking just as much as she was every time they took a new step on this venture – but part of her was jealous of having to share a conversation with her friend when they had been so infrequent in the past weeks. She pushed her ridiculous feelings aside and turned to look at him.

"Where are we headed?" he asked.

"Coruscant," Sabé told him. "I'll have more detailed coordinates for you by the time we land."

He nodded and took the pilot's chair. Their liftoff from Tatooine was smooth, the lights of Mos Espa glowing in the distance. Sabé decided that she hated the city a little bit less at night. The ship cut through the clear sky until it broke atmosphere, and then Sabé let the navicomputer do its work. When its calculations were complete, Tonra slid them into hyperspace, and they sped towards Coruscant, with unfamiliar stars streaking past the viewports.

CHAPTER 9

After the austerity of Tatooine, the Coruscanti nightclub Caraveg was complete culture shock. Sabé felt the music against the back of her eyes and rattling down her spine and amended the thought slightly: nothing on Naboo really prepared a being for this sort of thing, either. She couldn't imagine how Padmé had even found this place, let alone how Padmé could feel comfortable enough to set up a meeting here. They were undeniably at the right coordinates, though they were about half an hour early. The club noise would cover their conversation, and the booth would shield them from casual glances, but it wasn't at all secure. Sabé concluded that this was probably the only meeting place that Padmé knew of, and realised that scouting better locations was undoubtedly going to be one of her first tasks.

Half an hour was more than enough time to get into trouble. Sabé had adopted her customary defence in these situations: she ignored anyone who tried to speak to her. Tonra was having a bit more of a problem. A barely clad Rodian had already given him several not-so-subtle invitations, culminating in the presentation of some kind of narcotic and the unmistakable suggestion that Tonra should follow him into one of the club's several dark corners. Tonra remained in his seat, much to the Rodian's disappointment.

"I would get rid of that, if I were you," Sabé said.

"I really don't want to stand up," Tonra admitted, reluctant to show anything that could be construed as interest.

Sabé took the tube of narcotics from him and shoved it into the cushions behind the booth where they were ensconced.

"Do you even know what that stuff is?" Tonra asked.

"I have no idea," Sabé admitted. "And I am not in a hurry to find out."

Tonra regarded his drink with new suspicion and then pushed it firmly away.

"If you want to make yourself feel better, imagine Mariek's face if she knew what was going on right now," Sabé said.

"That won't work," Tonra said miserably. "I'm too busy imagining what she'll do to me *when* she finds out."

Sabé smiled and linked her fingers with his as a show of solidarity. Tonra squeezed back, but before Sabé could unpack the feelings that unfurled in her stomach, two more figures joined them in the booth. They were both hooded, but Sabé recognised Naboo fabric when she saw it.

"Where in the known universe does the captain think you are right now?" she said to Padmé by way of greeting.

Padmé's companion laughed and took off her hood. It was the pilot Varbarós, her hair now incandescently blue. Several things, including Padmé's source for the club's location, became clear.

"Mariek thinks I am at a reception for the Alderaanian delegation," Padmé said. "Typho does, as well, and he is even my escort for the evening."

"Who is he actually escorting?" Sabé asked.

"Cordé," Padmé said. "Dormé can do almost as well, but I doubt she'd fool Typho, and I wouldn't ask her to try."

"They are going to catch you," Tonra said.

"Of course they are," Padmé said. "But by the time they do, it will be too late, and Typho knows better than to make a fuss. It's a bit over the top, but you know how I feel about practise."

"I don't think I like Coruscant," Tonra said to no one in particular.

"Nobody likes Coruscant," Varbarós said gamely. "My lady, do you want me to hear this?"

Open secrets were new. Previously, if Padmé wanted to fool someone, they would never know it. To have the gambits openly acknowledged by noncombatants was a development.

"Yes, please," Padmé said. "We're going to need you to act as courier. You have the most freedom of anyone on my staff."

Varbarós had come with the J-type Nubian starship that Queen Réillata had designated for Padmé's use – along with a blue-and-white astromech they were already familiar with – since the new queen had a pilot of her own and a ship had been built for her. There was no limit to the number of royal pilots, really, so Varbarós's current assignment to Padmé's staff wasn't a demotion, and she preferred the adventure of being away from Naboo anyway.

A droid came by with a tray of smoking drinks. Varbarós took two for show, as Padmé clearly had no intention of drinking anything.

"All right, here's the thing," she began. "Keep quiet. At the end of my senatorial orientation, there was a strange attempt on my life."

Sabé had suspected as much, but still couldn't quite keep her reaction under control. She squeezed Tonra's hand – hard – and then immediately relinquished her grasp when he winced. She understood why Padmé hadn't disclosed this via holo, but she was not used to learning about threats so late in the game.

"I'm fine, clearly," Padmé said. "And it was clumsy. Our guard was already up, and even Cordé, who was Amidala at the time, wasn't in any real danger, because the attempt was foiled by a random bystander."

Padmé detailed the attempt, and Sabé jumped immediately to the same question she had.

"Why was Organa there?" Sabé asked.

"We never found out," Padmé said. "I've met him a few times since then. He's politely distant. I know politicians do this professionally, but I feel like if he wanted me dead, there would be something about it in his face. Versé has been reading the newsnets and trying to slice her way into the companies that broadcast them, but we are so busy with all the senatorial work that she doesn't have a lot of time for it. I was hoping you and Tonra, working outside the senatorial residence, would have more luck, maybe even an actual source instead of a digital one."

"There's something else," Sabé said. She knew Padmé wouldn't have called her all the way here just to send her on a chase through the holonet. It was far more likely she'd confront the problem in public.

"The newsnets have been targeting me," Padmé admitted. "Ever since someone told them about the attempt on my life – which they painted to look like my own incompetence, of course. They run stories about my youth, about my inexperience in galactic politics, and they're mostly true, but they're always framed around Naboo customs, like how I dress, to make me look willful and ignorant."

Sabé chose not to remind Padmé that many, many of their teachers had, at one time or another, also told Padmé she was willful. Ignorant never, but Sabé could understand the sting.

"And this gossip is harmful because?" Sabé asked. Padmé cared about public opinion as much as any elected official might, but Naboo's meritocracy was startlingly uncorrupt, and the truth had always come through for her.

"It's not like home," Padmé said, guessing Sabé's line of

thinking. "The senators don't care about the truth, even if they know it. If they think I'm a hopeless child from the outer reaches of the galaxy, nothing will make them want to work with me, even hard evidence to the contrary. At the party right now? I can all too well imagine the slights and patronising statements Cordé is enduring on my behalf, because I've been hearing them since I got here. We're lucky we're all practised at keeping our faces blank, although honestly I am starting to believe that's part of the problem, too. I have to get ahead of this, and finding out who is publishing it is the first step."

Sabé didn't say anything for a moment, the noise of the club filling the silence with a droning buzz. This Padmé was new, more calculating, more wary. This was what the Senate did to people, and Sabé was about to throw herself into it, even though she was likely to only stay in the shallows.

"Why are you fighting so hard to stay?" Sabé asked.

"I – " Padmé hesitated. "I was going to say that I didn't know, but that's not true. It's hard to describe, but there are moments when I actually enjoy it, when we do good work for the people of the Republic. And I want more of those moments, if we can make them happen."

"All right," said Sabé. "We don't need to convince the whole Senate. We just need to get a few of them to accept you, and then they will do all the heavy lifting."

"I agree," Padmé said.

Tonra shifted, and Sabé remembered he was there. She had fallen into her old rhythm so quickly.

"Yes?" she said, turning to look at him.

"I'm sorry, my lady," he said. "But what do you need me for?"

Padmé smiled at him, the smile that had won her the love of a planet and the loyalty of everyone at the table.

"I don't want Sabé to be here on her own, Captain," she said. "And Sabé has told me that you worked well as a team on Tatooine, adapting quickly as the situation changed around you. I know Coruscant is an uncomfortable place, but if you can stay, I would appreciate it."

"As would I," said Sabé. She set her hand down next to his and tried her very best not to manipulate him.

"I will do what I can," Tonra said.

"I've arranged for funds to be transferred into an account for your identity," Padmé said. "You won't be living in the upper levels, but you'll still be somewhere you can secure with relative ease."

"This is my personal comm frequency," Varbarós said, handing over a pair of comlinks. "You can get in touch with me from anywhere on the planet. I shouldn't be offworld without warning."

"Oh, no," said Padmé, and Sabé noticed that her hood had slipped back while they were talking, leaving her face less obscured than any of them would have liked.

Sabé followed her gaze and saw a young human male staring at her, his confused expression sliding into delight.

"Sena – " he started to say, but before he could complete the word, Padmé had jumped up, grabbed his arm and dragged him back to their table.

"Senator Clovis," she hissed, "I would appreciate you not shouting my name in this crowded public establishment."

"I saw you at the reception," Clovis said. "It was so tedious. I can't blame you for leaving, too, and I'd heard this place was interesting. You must have an even better driver than I do to have gotten here so quickly."

"I'm much better than your droid," Varbarós said, as though this sort of thing happened to Padmé every day.

"Senator, these are some friends from home," Padmé said. "They were part of a cultural exchange and they only had time to meet with me tonight before they head back to Naboo."

"Oh, how wonderful," Clovis said. "The senator has been telling me so much about Naboo. Is it true you're all artists?"

"My talents tend towards public displays of acrobatics," Tonra said with uncharacteristic poise. Usually Sabé spoke first. "I juggle."

"Incredible," Clovis said, completely missing Tonra's sarcasm. "Naboo sounds like a wonderful place. I hope to visit it someday."

"Would you give us a moment?" Padmé asked. "They have to depart soon, and I would like to say farewell."

"Of course, of course," Clovis said. "I'm so sorry for intruding. I was merely surprised to see you."

Varbarós walked him over to the bar in order to ensure that his curiosity about Naboo didn't overcome his good manners.

"Where did you find him?" Sabé asked.

"He's another new senator," Padmé admitted. "He's a terrible politician so far, but his family is powerful and I can't afford to burn any bridges."

"What do they own?" Sabé had a low opinion of people who exploited family connections instead of employing their own skills, and it brought out her facetious nature.

"He's a lower ranking member of the Banking Clan," Padmé said. Catching Sabé's look, she added, "He's adopted," to explain Clovis's human appearance. Most members of the Banking Clan were Muuns.

Padmé's wrist comlink chimed, and she activated a holo of Versé in her palm.

"Please come home before Dormé and Typho say things to one another that they regret," Versé said. The image repeated itself before Padmé shut it off, so Sabé knew it had been prerecorded.

"This was much easier when it was just one planet," Padmé observed.

"How many restarts do you think we're going to get?" Sabé asked.

"Hopefully one more than we need," Padmé said. "But I'll prepare for the worst, just in case. At least at this point, the only thing that will suffer is my pride."

Sabé thought she was being a trifle blasé given the attempt to murder her, but was willing to make allowances for the stress of her new job.

Padmé waved Varbarós back to the table, because there was no way Sabé and Tonra would leave her there alone, and when Clovis came trailing along behind, Sabé made a face.

"I knew you wouldn't like the Senate," Padmé said, leaning close. "I've missed you so much. Thank you for coming."

"I've missed you, too," Sabé said. "I know it's not the same, but at least now we're on the same planet."

"Be careful," Padmé said. She leaned back a bit to include Tonra. "Both of you."

"We will, my lady," Tonra said.

"In the future, you had better just call me Padmé when we're out like this," she said. "Senators are a dime a dozen on Coruscant, and being a lady doesn't get you very far."

"I'll practise," said Tonra. Sabé thought it entirely likely that Padmé's name would stick in his throat the first few times he tried to say it.

Senator Clovis apparently decided that he had given them enough privacy, because he returned to hover and couldn't keep the disappointment from his face when it became apparent they were all preparing to leave.

"Are you leaving now?" Clovis said. "Because there's going to be a concert – "

"Yes, I am leaving now. I recommend you do the same, Clovis. I am not sure this is an altogether safe place," Padmé said. Sabé managed not to roll her eyes as Padmé slipped into the persona Clovis was used to. Padmé stood up, Varbarós beside her, and looked straight at Sabé. "I wish you luck in your travels."

"The same to you," Sabé said.

As they took their leave, she heard Clovis say "Where are you headed to?" and Padmé begin to explain even more Naboo traditions to him. She wondered if his interest in the planet was genuine or if he, too, wanted something from Padmé. Sabé had all sorts of dark thoughts as to what that might be but was smart enough to know that it was none of her business unless Padmé was endangered, so she resolved to stay out of it. Frankly, if she never saw Clovis again, that would be just fine with her. Perhaps she was being unreasonable, but he peeved her.

Her wrist comm chimed, indicating a transfer of funds had been completed. The name she used on Tatooine and also here on Coruscant was the name she had been given when she was born, but it felt false and artificial to her now. She had been Sabé for all of the most important parts of her life. Tsabin was a stranger. Not even her parents called her that any more, and all of her official records on Naboo had been changed.

Still, if she had to be someone else, at least she was still a person that Padmé knew. Tsabin and Padmé had met when they were barely fourteen years old, when she applied to be a handmaiden, and by the time they were settled into Theed palace, they were an unshakable pair and Sabé had a new name to show for it. Padmé had been trained to stand out, and Sabé had been trained to blend in. She had never minded it. It was hard to be resentful of something that she was so good at.

And now Padmé was reinventing herself again, and by necessity, Sabé was not there to help as closely as she might have liked. Senator Amidala was clearly different from the queen, judging by how Clovis had acted, and Sabé didn't fully understand it, but she trusted Padmé's judgement.

If she was going to be Tsabin anyway, maybe it was time to *be* Tsabin. She would remain Sabé in her heart, but she could learn to be a new person, too, as Padmé was.

"This was much easier when it was just one planet," she whispered, repeating Padmé's words.

"No argument here," Tonra said. His was a steady presence beside her, and she leaned into him with no ulterior motives. He might have been a bit surprised, but he put an arm around her shoulders anyway.

They waited in silence, the pulse of the music throbbing

in their bones, for time to pass between Padmé's departure and their own. For once, Tonra didn't fidget, only tapped his fingers lightly on the table in time with the inescapable beat. When they deemed it safe, they went out in search of an air taxi and a quieter place where they could plan their next steps.

CHAPTER 10

The shouting went on for quite some time. Padmé let Typho speak his piece, figuring that the sergeant had more than earned it. Mariek would get her own in later, but it had been Typho they had taken advantage of, and Padmé owed it to him to listen to him now.

" – not to mention the danger Cordé was in if anyone had discovered her," he wound up his tirade. "And I do not want to know any of the details about where *you* were, my lady."

"I was meeting with Sabé and Tonra," Padmé said, though for the sake of Typho's blood pressure she didn't mention exactly where, only that it had been a nightclub. "I was with Varbarós."

"While an excellent pilot, Vararós is not a trained guard. And her choice of meeting locations leaves a great deal to be desired," Typho said. "I realise that politics is complicated and sometimes there are things you have to do yourself, but please, Senator, I beg you: tell me next time. I am a much better actor than you think. And I can help with the details."

"I'm sorry, Sergeant," Padmé said. "I had hoped tonight would be a practical test for us all, in addition to a necessary meeting. But I see now that I was practising the wrong thing. The decoy plan used to involve fooling the guards, too, but we should modify that the same way we're modifying everything else."

"He reacted with complete discretion when he realised who I was," Cordé said. "Though I fear he may have torn the fringe off the sleeve of the ocean-dark ball gown."

"I can fix that," Dormé said. "And I think Typho is correct about the planning, too. If he was in on it, he could have prevented Senator Clovis from leaving. Or at least warned you when the gathering broke up."

They had fallen into this pattern automatically, and Padmé liked the way it functioned. She would do something, Cordé would rationalise it, one of the guards would protest, Dormé would smooth ruffled feathers, and Versé would change the subject.

"I've picked up a story on one of the newsnets," Versé said, right on schedule. "It's about tonight."

"I hope it's about the scandalous relationship Senator Amidala has with one of her guards," Cordé said, her voice dripping with sarcasm.

"Speak for yourself," said Mariek. "I'm a happily married lady, and I wish for no such drama."

"It's about Senator Clovis," Versé said. "Apparently,

after he ducked out of the reception, he went to some incredibly dangerous nightclub and met with – "

Too late, Versé became aware that Typho was reading over her shoulder. Padmé resisted the urge to bury her face in her hands.

"Do you have any idea the sort of thing that goes on in those places?" Typho all but shouted, all of his mollification gone in an instant.

"Of course she does, she's a grown woman," Mariek said. "Nephew, you need to calm down or the Senator is never going to trust you. She has already admitted that you are right."

Typho mastered himself and nodded.

"Is there anything in that article that could be used to identify me?" Padmé asked.

"No," Versé said, scanning the rest of it. "It looks like they actually interviewed Clovis, and he only told them he was seeing some friends from home."

"Everyone will know that's a lie," Dormé pointed out. "The Banking Clan isn't exactly known for fitting in at Coruscant clubs."

"It's a message for me," Padmé said. "That's how I introduced Sabé and Tonra without giving their names. I said they were friends from home. He wants me to know he's covering for me."

"It would be the first solid political move he's made,"

Cordé observed. She had a rather low opinion of Clovis's dedication to galactic politics.

"I'm not entirely sure he's thinking politically," Versé said. "I've stayed behind the scenes almost the whole time we've been here, and I've watched a lot of recordings. I've seen the way he stands when Padmé is in his orbit, and the way he looks at her."

"We continue on as we are," Padmé said. "Only now we've got Sabé and Tonra working outside the political framework to help us."

"And me, to help you inside it," Typho said.

"Yes, Sergeant," Padmé said. "And I do apologise. We have changed a great deal about how Amidala acts in public in the last few weeks, but I still find myself thinking about her the way I did on Naboo. I have trouble remembering that the circumstances of secrets are different here. We won't cut you out of a decoy manoeuvre again."

"Thank you, my lady," Typho said.

A soft chime indicated the arrival of the next day's schedule, and they spent the next two hours strategizing about votes and trying to determine how the Senate would act in each case. This was also much easier now that they were working as a team.

Before, Padmé had taken two handmaidens with her into the Senate chambers to observe, but the truth was, there was nothing for them to observe. Now she took only Mariek or Typho, and occasionally Cordé if the situation demanded it. The others stayed back at the senatorial residence or in Padmé's office, watching recordings of Senate proceedings and trying to figure out who was allied with whom. It was easy enough to trace through a single motion but became infinitely more challenging when multiple agendas were tabled, and with the size of the assembly, there were always multiple agendas on the table.

"You have to get on one of these committees," Cordé said.

Padmé knew this all too well. She had been deliberating for days, trying to determine which committee was best suited to her talents and experience.

"Senator Bonteri heads a committee looking into educational reform in the poorer areas of the Core planets," Dormé said. "This bill was stalled because no one on the Core planets wanted to admit they had poorer areas."

"There's something about piracy, too," Cordé said. "It's new and I'm not even sure there's an official committee yet, but the topic keeps coming up in your briefs so I am sure there will be soon."

"And there's always the antislavery committee," Versé added. "It's not headed by anyone you know, but I am sure you could talk your way into it without relying on the Chancellor's reference."

"I know," Padmé said. "I know, I just can't decide on the best way to get a seat at the table."

"What is it you want?" Dormé asked. "From the Senate, I mean."

"Respectability," Padmé said. "I want my words and my efforts to mean something."

"And you don't have it because everyone thinks you are too new, too inexperienced," Dormé said. "They think you're not a serious senator."

"And they think you're too connected to Chancellor Palpatine," Mariek added. "Too connected to your own planet."

"There's a degree of truth to all of those arguments," Padmé said.

Her last discussion with Chancellor Palpatine had not gone well. She'd encountered him almost by chance after a Senate session, and at first, he had been his normal self.

"Chancellor," she had said. She laid a hand on Versé's arm to indicate that she was going to need some space for the conversation, and her handmaiden and guard fell back a few steps. "I'm glad our paths have crossed. I wanted to asked you about joining your transportation committee."

She still didn't much care for the layers of political speaking that had to be set on top of the antislavery legislation, but technically there was no slavery in the Republic, and so Palpatine had to be creative with his wording. The actual debate was about the transportation of goods, and the roundabout discussion made Padmé's skin crawl, even though she very much wanted to have a hand in shaping the legislation.

The Chancellor had stopped when she greeted him, affable as ever, but his face hardened when she mentioned joining the committee.

"I don't think that's a good idea, my dear," he'd said. His tone had an odd note of dismissal in it, one that she'd never noticed before. Beside him, Mas Amedda glowered at her.

"Why not?" Padmé asked. "I've already begun my own explorations into the situation, and I think – "

"Senator, you misunderstand me," Palpatine said, a modicum of his usual warmth coming through. "You are eminently qualified for this committee, but you have known ties to Tatooine and to me. If you join the discussion, your qualifications will undermine my authority."

There was something about the Chancellor's statement that didn't entirely ring true, but Padmé couldn't quite put her finger on what it was.

"Find another committee, my dear," Palpatine said. "I will do my best to keep you up to date on my progress and I will let you know if your help is needed."

He swept off, his retinue behind him, and Padmé was left with too many questions and no sure direction.

"Then you have two choices, I think," Dormé said, recalling Padmé's attention to the present. "Commit to being in Palpatine's shadow. Go to him and use his influence as much as you possibly can."

"Or?" Cordé said.

"The exact opposite of that," Dormé said. "Amidala is charming now. Use that. Find someone who opposes the Chancellor, not violently or extremely, but enough to put a wedge in the public's image of you and him, and then step on that wedge until you've carved out your own identity."

"That rules out Bonteri," Versé said. "She's not cosy with him or anything, but she never directly opposes him."

Padmé was a little disappointed. She liked Senator Bonteri quite a bit and would have been honoured to work with her. But she also knew that there was no question of being in Palpatine's inner circle. Even if he had allowed it, she wouldn't have wanted to limit herself that way.

"Don't worry," Padmé said. "I have just the senator in mind."

Senator Amidala was dressed for the occasion. She had left off the ornate reminders of home. There was no headpiece in her hair today, just looped coils pinned in place so well that Dormé had made the pins themselves seem invisible. Her dress was deceptively simple. She wore a light blue undertunic with a collar that didn't impede the turning of her head, and wide sleeves that were folded back over the dark blue gown she wore over top. The deception was in the dress's embroidery, in the same light blue as the tunic. It could have been done by any machine on a mechanised planet. Only someone who got close would notice that the stitches had been done by hand – Padmé's sole concession to Naboo. And she didn't intend for anyone to get that close.

During the session, Padmé was almost giddy with impatience. She had to force herself to pay attention. The votes on today's schedule were not of less importance simply because the senator from Naboo had plans. Still, it seemed like the voting would never end, and by the time Chancellor Palpatine called a halt to the day's proceedings, Padmé was more than ready to go.

Dormé intercepted her before she could exit the pod, doing a quick check that every part of her dress and hair was still in place, and then wished her luck.

Padmé took measured steps. There was no reason for her to make unseemly haste. Versé had pored over the recordings and done a little bit of slicing that Padmé was sure was an invasion of privacy, though this time she turned a blind eye. Cordé had helped her prepare her lines, couching theoretical arguments for Padmé to contest until both of them were sure they had covered every option. Her handmaidens might no longer shadow her every move, but Padmé was no more alone than she had ever been as the Queen of Naboo. Mariek had been correct, all those months ago on the steps of the lake house: everything was different, but Padmé was different, too. And she was figuring out what that meant.

At last, she spotted her target heading for one of the rooftop gardens, right where Versé's analysis said he would be. He was in green today, which Padmé noted only because Cordé said it appeared to be a favourite. His outfit was simple, though he had allowed himself the indulgence of an asymmetrical cape. Padmé got close enough that she wouldn't have to shout, and raised her voice.

"Senator Organa," she said. The voice was more vibrant than the flat tones Queen Amidala had used. It moved better over the syllables of his name. Senator Amidala drew near as Organa stopped to listen to her.

"Senator Amidala," he said. "How may I help you?"

She stepped closer, modulating her tone to accommodate for her proximity.

"I wish to join your committee on the transportation of construction materials to the planets in the Mid Rim," Amidala said.

Whatever Organa had been expecting, it wasn't that.

"What do you know about the transportation of construction materials?" he asked. She suspected he was stalling for time while he puzzled through her true motivations, though his tone remained polite.

"Nothing," Amidala admitted. "And if I do not join your committee, then I suspect that is all I shall ever know."

He looked at her for a long moment. People didn't usually look at her face. They saw the ornamentation of Naboo's handiwork in her hair, in her style, in her makeup. That was why the decoy policy had worked so well. Everyone knew what Amidala looked like, so no one ever thought about Padmé. She felt exposed without her usual methods of disguise-in-plain-sight, even though she had done it on purpose. She had never wanted someone to *see* her before, not like this. She might never let him in again, but she needed him to see her now.

"Walk with me?" he said, offering her his arm.

She took it and followed his lead into the gardens. She hadn't come here before, preferring to go back to the residence and study policy or rest. She saw immediately why he visited with enough regularity for Versé to track him. Alderaan wasn't quite as green a world as Naboo, but it still took great pride in its natural wonders. Coruscant must seem to him a lot like it did to her: crowded, noisy, and entirely lacking in plant life. The gardens were a poor echo of what the two of them were used to, but the smell was close enough, and when one took a breath, one could feel the difference in the air.

They took a full turn around the garden, stopping here and there while he showed her his favourite grove of chinar trees, where he liked to sit after the general session and think of home. It was, she realised, his way of letting her see him. The brusque professional was gone, as was the overwhelming presence of the queen, and instead they were two colleagues standing on common ground. At last they completed their circuit of the garden and stood in front of the door that would take them back to the Senate's stuffy halls and overcrowded workspaces.

"We meet tomorrow, after the general session," he said. "The room assignments haven't been designated yet, so I will send an aide."

It was polite of him not to send his NON unit, all things considered.

"Thank you, Senator," Amidala said. It was very, very close to Padmé's voice. He inclined his head and took his leave of her.

Padmé lingered in the gardens for a few long green moments before heading back to the residence. She was due to get an update from Sabé, and she knew the others would want to hear how everything had gone. Also, she was going to have to do some reading on permacrete and how one went about shipping it. She commed Mariek and Dormé and told them to meet her at the shuttle.

"Success?" Dormé said when she was close enough not to be overheard.

"Yes," Padmé said. "I'll tell you all when we get back to the residence. It's not so interesting that I want to go over it twice."

"It's interesting enough that you agreed to discuss it in committee," Mariek pointed out.

"We must all make sacrifices," Padmé said, but the truth was that she didn't mind what she had signed on for in the least. She would be helping to build something again, like her father had taught her, even if it was only indirectly. And she would be making an ally at the same time.

Sabé was happy to see her, but even just over a holo, but somewhat less pleased when Padmé announced whom she had allied herself with.

"Correct me if I'm wrong," Sabé said, "but am I not investigating him for involvement in your attempted murder?"

"I'm even more sure he had nothing to do with it," Padmé said. "He was just in the wrong place at the wrong time. Or the right place, I suppose."

"Please tell me that Clovis isn't on the committee," Sabé said.

"He's not," Padmé assured her. "He's bouncing around the money factions. It's only a matter of time before the Trade Federation takes notice of him, and I don't intend to be near him when that happens."

"I should think not," Sabé said. "Speaking of our favourite invading attempted murderers, I found something about the newsnets that published those first stories about you. The chain of corporations is extensive in every case, and most of the companies are no longer active, but they're all owned by subsidiaries of the Trade Federation."

"They were slandering me?" Padmé said.

"I'm pretty sure it's libel when it's in print," Sabé told her. "But yes."

"Nute Gunray's third trial is underway," Padmé said. "It started just before I arrived on Coruscant. I suppose I shouldn't be surprised."

"He certainly holds a grudge," Sabé said. "I'll keep an eye on the trial, both what's being reported and what people are saying about it out of the media. Gunray has it in for you personally, and I don't want him to get close enough to you to get lucky."

"He doesn't have to get that close," Padmé said. "But I appreciate the sentiment. How is Tonra?"

"Homesick, but very much in love with the food at this terrible diner thing down the plaza from the apartment," Sabé reported. "He keeps trying to get me to go, but I make it a personal policy not to eat at any establishment that produces that much smoke."

Padmé laughed with her, and for a moment, they might have been sitting in the royal apartment in Theed palace, discussing the events of the day. Something chimed on Sabé's end.

"I'm sorry, I have to go," Sabé said. "One of my new contacts wants to talk."

"Be safe," Padmé said.

"I will," Sabé promised.

Padmé terminated the connection and called up the background documents that Versé had prepared for her.

PART III

NAIVE SENATOR SPREADS WINGS, LANDS IN PERMACRETE

Pundits across Coruscant were shocked when Senator Amidala (Chommell sector) appeared on Senator Bail Organa (Alderaan)'s committee for transportation of construction materials. No one could have expected Amidala, who has been notoriously flighty and unpredictable since her arrival on Coruscant, to join such a drab-sounding operation, so theories abound as to her motivations or, rather, the motivations of whoever she is operating for.

Senator Organa, though thoroughly reputable in his service, is often at odds with the Chancellor. It seems unlikely that Palpatine has set Amidala on the senator from Alderaan to sniff out some scandal. It's possible that Amidala is seeking to curry favour by finding one. We can only speculate what folly her newfound "interests" will lead her to.

– TriNebulon News

CHAPTER 11

There were two main problems with permacrete. The first was that mixing it required a large quantity of water, which not all planets had in readiness and which was impractical to ship. The second was that the mix itself was bulky and required large vessels to transport the loads. This meant that many systems used their own local variations on the formula, and all of those were drastically inferior.

The third problem with permacrete was minor but an annoyance all the same: Padmé was pretty sure it was the most boring subject of discussion in the entire galaxy.

Yet discuss it she did. After the general session, which had been taken up almost entirely by the Malastare delegation giving speeches that the Chancellor would not or could not interrupt, Padmé had followed Senator Organa's aide to a tiny room in the Senate building. There, she took a seat at the table and settled in to listen.

Only senators were present, though Padmé knew that several of them were recording the proceedings to disseminate to their aides at a later time. A couple of them had brought droids to take notes for them, but Padmé dismissed that as an option because she didn't particularly trust any of the droids she'd encountered thus far on Coruscant. Then she recalled the blue-and-white astromech unit that travelled with Varbarós aboard the Naboo Royal Starship. That little droid had a recording device, and she knew it was reliable. She made a note to remind herself to think about it later and returned her attention to the table.

After an hour of talk with no measurable progress, the meeting broke up so that the senators could depart for other engagements. Padmé would have followed them out into the corridor, but Organa caught her attention and waved her over to where he was standing. She got up to see what he wanted.

"Senator," Organa said, "did you find our meeting of any great illumination?"

"I did," Padmé said. She hadn't learned much about construction materials that she hadn't already learned from her reading, but she had gained insight as to how topics were tabled and how the elements of negotiation were incorporated into discussion.

"Allow me to introduce Senator Mon Mothma," he said, indicating the red-haired human woman on his left.

"Senator," Padmé said, inclining her head. Padmé did not extend a hand in greeting, and neither did Mon Mothma.

"I am pleased to make your acquaintance." The senator's voice was light, but there was an undeniable presence to it. When she spoke, people listened. She knew it, and she was learning to use it. "I was very new to the Senate when you made your speech as Queen of Naboo. It has been interesting to watch your transition into galactic politics."

Years of practise kept Padmé's frustration from showing on her face. She was still not used to being thought less of because of her youth and hoped she never became so dismissive of a person just because they lacked her own experience.

"It has been something of an exercise," she said politely. "And I do miss the more personal connections that serving my own planet allowed me to foster. Knowing the names and faces of those you are working to help is a luxury, I suppose, but I do think the scale on which the Republic can serve its members has much to be grateful for."

"Of course," Mon Mothma said. "It is no easy task to put one's own home to the side in order to serve a greater purpose."

The piece clicked into place so loudly in Padmé's head, she was worried that Organa and Mon Mothma might have actually heard her thoughts. It wasn't her inexperience, exactly, that was causing them to be so cold to her. They thought she was more loyal to Naboo than she was to the Republic, and that she wasn't up to facing that kind of conflict of interest. Indeed, her past actions in deposing Chancellor Valourum in an attempt to level the playing field against the Trade Federation showed how quick she'd been to dismiss Senate protocol. Naboo was part of who she was, but it seemed they expected her to exorcise that part, or at least isolate it, before they would fully trust her. She wasn't entirely sure she was willing to do it.

"I look forward to that service," Padmé said, though she didn't enjoy dishonesty.

She couldn't tell from Mon Mothma's expression if the other senator believed her, but the look she exchanged with Senator Organa wasn't as dismissive as her initial survey of Padmé had been.

"I'll send word when we have scheduled the next meeting," Organa said. "Hopefully we'll have everything ready to go on the Senate floor before the session breaks up."

"I'll look forward to that, as well," Padmé said, and let them precede her out of the room.

She didn't go to her office or to her shuttle back to the residence. Instead, she found herself wandering the hallways. It wasn't quite aimless – in theory she could be heading for the garden – but she wasn't in a particular hurry, and she was deep in thought.

"Ah, Senator Amidala!" A voice permeated her musings, and she stopped moving. It was Mina Bonteri.

"Hello," Padmé said with genuine warmth. "It's wonderful to see you again."

This, Padmé found she meant with complete truthfulness. Senator Bonteri was at least willing to talk with her as an equal, even if there was something else she wasn't sharing.

It was fair enough: Padmé kept her own counsel on several topics anyway.

"Come and have tea with me?" Bonteri asked. "My office is right around the corner."

"I would love to," Padmé said.

Bonteri's office was decorated with paintings from her homeworld. Padmé was no expert, but some of the works seemed to be distinctly less refined than the others. Perhaps Onderon prided itself on utilising all materials for art, not just high-quality ones.

"My son's work," Bonteri said as Padmé contemplated a particularly awkward painting of . . . a speeder bike? "He's probably destined for other things, but he was four when he made that, and he enjoyed bright colours and making a mess. I'm fond of his work, so I keep it here even now that he's moved on to other hobbies."

"Oh," Padmé said. Then she laughed. "On Naboo, we encourage all children to experiment with artistic expression so that they can determine where their talents lie."

"Where were yours?" Bonteri asked. She poured hot water into a plain metal teapot and got two cups out of a cupboard.

"Oration and poetry," Padmé said. "Not skills commonly cultivated, I must admit. Most parents would prefer their children be good at making something besides words. I think my mother would have preferred it if I had gone into music, even though my aptitude there was not as strong."

"You were queen of a planet, and your mother would have preferred you to be a musician?" Bonteri said.

"Naboo is a unique world," Padmé admitted.

"And parents are never particularly good at letting their children make their own paths," Bonteri said. She looked at her son's paintings and smiled. "Yet they do."

"Indeed," said Padmé. "And my parents are proud of my accomplishments, even though they wish I had remained closer to home."

"Your father has several friends in the Senate, does he not?" Bonteri said.

"He does," Padmé replied. "That's how I was able to gain sponsorship to the junior legislative programme when I was eight. He does a lot of aid work, and Senate contacts are useful for that."

"You didn't wish to join him?" Bonteri asked.

"I think I am, in my own way," Padmé said. "If nothing else, I am another senator he knows he can trust."

"I suppose that's as much as any of us can hope for, these days," Bonteri said. "It just takes so long to get anything accomplished through official channels. Why haven't you sought your father's friends out?"

"Because I wanted to stand on my own," Padmé said. "I am already viewed as an extension of the Chancellor by some, and I have no wish to be viewed as an extension of my father by others."

"Yet you do not mind being viewed as an extension of Naboo's queen?" Bonteri asked.

"I was Naboo's queen," Padmé said. "I am always going to be part of that system, though I believe I can be something more, as well."

Bonteri poured two cups of tea and passed one of them to Padmé. The scent was unfamiliar. Bonteri took a sip, and Padmé followed suit. The flavour was more floral than she might have preferred but not entirely unappetising .

"There are a growing number of senators who feel that loyalty to one's own world first, regardless of procedure, is not a bad thing," Bonteri said slowly. She locked eyes with Padmé, but Padmé kept her face blank and took another sip of her tea.

"A senator should be able to maintain a balance," she said. "To love the world they are from but see the galaxy as a whole."

"Can anyone truly do that?" Bonteri asked. "See the whole galaxy and remain objective about it?"

Padmé considered her words. Bonteri was usually much more open than Mon Mothma had been, yet it was clear that Mon Mothma believed in the Republic first and foremost. What Bonteri was suggesting wasn't treasonous, but it was dangerous, and Padmé couldn't tell which side of the argument Bonteri came down on.

"I think that we should try," she said at last.

Bonteri drained her teacup, and Padmé couldn't tell if she

had passed or failed the test. She also wasn't sure if she *wanted* to pass or fail the test, but Bonteri didn't look disappointed in her, so she supposed she had done well enough.

"You'll have to try harder than others," Bonteri said. "You've already gone around the Senate once by displacing Chancellor Valourum and then hying off back to Naboo to solve your own problems anyway through the use of military force."

"I am aware," Padmé said. "It is hardest to maintain objectivity when your own people are dying, but I want to be part of a Senate that feels that way about *all* people."

"You are an idealist," Bonteri said. "That's not a bad thing."

"I know," Padmé said. "I have worked very hard on it."

"More tea?" Bonteri asked, holding out the pot.

"Thank you," Padmé said. "I would like to hear how your plans for educational reform are going, if you have the time."

Bonteri did, and so they spent a pleasant thirty minutes imagining how they would rework the system if they had unlimited money, time, and personnel, and then a somewhat less pleasant time hashing out what was possible with the resources Bonteri actually had.

"We could do so much more if people would listen," Padmé said.

"People are listening," Bonteri said. "They're just not paying attention."

Padmé's comm chimed, and she remembered that she had to get home to give Cordé and Dormé their briefings on the committee meeting. It was unlikely that either of them would ever have to fill in for her in the actual room, but they needed to know all the salient details in case they were doubling for her at an unrelated function and the subject came up. It was complicated and probably overpreparedness taken to the extreme, but Padmé had relied on her handmaidens for too long to give them up now.

"I must be going," she said. "Thank you for the tea."

"Any time, Senator," Bonteri said. "I am always available if you need to vent your frustrations at our parliamentary process."

Her own chime sounded, and she made a face. "Well, almost always available."

Padmé considered what Bonteri had said while she made her way back to the residence. Some senators would prize her allegiance to Naboo, while others would distrust her for it. Some appreciated her aloof persona, while others required her to be more gregarious. And some were always going to dislike her, no matter what she did, because they believed the Trade Federation's lies about her. Her objective had not changed: rather than alter herself completely to meet the restrictions her colleagues felt were appropriate, she would forge on as she was doing. She was going to need a faction to support her at some point, but she would decide what that would be when the time came.

Typho was waiting for her at the shuttle, clearly frustrated by the amount of time she had been out from under his direct supervision. No matter now often she reminded him that the senatorial guards were highly trained and exceptionally loyal, he still preferred it when the responsibility of her safety fell to him or to Mariek. It wasn't exactly the way that Captain Panaka had fumed over her protection but it was familiar enough to be a comfort. Padmé resolved to make sure Typho had an easier time of it in the coming days. They had taken advantage of him lately, and the strain was starting to show.

"Thank you for waiting, Sergeant," she said to him now. "I know you don't like it when I am off by myself."

"Your meeting ended more than an hour ago, my lady," he said. "Checking in by the remote isn't the same as a physical confirmation."

"I'll keep that in mind for next time," Padmé said.

"Next time?" he sounded resigned to his fate.

"Yes, next time," Padmé said. "There will be other meetings, and I'll want some time to think privately when they're done, too."

"Perhaps we can make arrangements for that," Typho said. "If you went to a fixed location, I could – "

"I've been thinking about bringing that astromech unit

with me," Padmé interrupted. "It's not exactly procedure, but plenty of senators have their own droids."

"Artoo-Detoo is not a defensive unit," Typho said.

"No, but he has recording capabilities and he can call for help if need be," Padmé said. "Also, he can electroshock anyone who gets closer than I want them to. It makes them think I'm a bit low-tech, being tailed by a mechanic, but – "

"We all have our disguises," Typho mused. Padmé could see him incorporating the astromech into their defence plan out of sheer habit. "There is an advantage to using droids for security. People are suspicious when there are guards around, but they're much more likely to dismiss a droid."

"There, you see?" Padmé said. "I can think about my own security if I have to."

"I'm very proud, my lady," Typho said dryly. "But I still have to run it past Mariek before we can let you try it."

"Of course, Sergeant Typho," she said.

Together, they boarded the shuttle, and Typho directed the driver to return them to the senatorial residence. Padmé looked out over Coruscant as they flew. The Jedi Temple gleamed in the evening sun, and Padmé felt a stab of guilt. She had stopped looking for Shmi Skywalker and it was because she didn't know how to continue. She felt like she'd broken a promise even though she hadn't made one, and she didn't know what to do but trust in the system Sabé had found evidence of on Tatooine itself. She didn't like letting go.

Padmé looked past the shining lights of Coruscant's wealthy upper levels and down into the poorer, more dangerous parts of the city-planet. She couldn't see very far. She had the idea that was how Coruscant liked it. Naboo had tried that once, dividing the population against itself, and the result had been almost world ending. Padmé resolved to pay attention, not just listen, and not just look but see.

CHAPTER 12

Sabé took a drink of her decidedly inferior caf and tried not to look impatient. This particular contact was chronically late but gave up reliable intelligence, so she hoped her time would be productive. Kooib-s Guvar was a holojournalist for one of Coruscant's most prestigious newsnets, but she moonlighted at a far more disreputable establishment, as well, writing for the tabloids for extra credits. Since she played both sides, she always had the best access. Tonra had made the initial contact, posing as a journalism student who was eager to do *anything* to break into the market, and passed her off to Sabé before things got too serious.

Their meeting spot was the place Tonra liked so much, a not completely awful diner called Dex's. Sabé had to admit that the food was decent enough. More important, the clientele was boisterous and fast changing, which provided good cover. Today, Sabé was in one of the booths: two hard plasteel benches with a table between them. Tonra preferred the counter, where he could perch on a stool and watch the multilimbed proprietor at work in the kitchen, but Sabé didn't like to have her back exposed.

"Tsabin," Kooib-s said, sliding onto the bench across from her.

Kooib-s was a hairless humanoid female who was only a little bit taller than Sabé. She had mottled purple skin, bright blue eyes, a wide nose, and pointed teeth. Her hands had seven digits, and Sabé assumed her feet did, too, though she could hardly ask her to take off her shoes. The top of her head was ringed with short red spikes that came to a needle-fine point two centimetres from her skull. It was rude to stare, but Sabé found herself mesmerized by Kooib-s's appearance. She didn't always go for nonhumans, but it happened on occasion, particularly with interesting females.

"What have you got?" Sabé asked, waving the service droid over and ordering two more cafs. They were deposited on the table immediately, and Kooib-s picked one up and sniffed it.

"Ugh," she said. She set the cup down. "The senator from Chandrila is having a party next week. It's suspected that she will use the gathering as a cover to discuss something with a few handpicked senators, but we don't know what."

"Why do you care what the senator from Chandrila does at a private function?" Sabé asked.

"Because it's not a private function," Kooib-s said. "It's going to be the first time she hosts a public gala, so the news-nets will be there in full force."

"How can she possibly expect to have a private discussion

then?" Sabé had been reading up on Mon Mothma, and the woman was hardly stupid.

"She plans to invite someone to be a distraction," Kooib-s said.

Sabé sighed. The list of possible distractions was very short.

"I'm going to figure it out, you know," Kooib-s said.

"Figure out what?" Sabé was new to this particular game but was well accustomed to keeping a straight face.

"What it is you want," Kooib-s said. "Why you're so interested in the Senate all the time."

"I like to know what the government is up to," Sabé said through her teeth. "I'm a concerned citizen."

"Of course you are," Kooib-s said. "And I'm a dancer at the Galaxies Opera House."

Sabé looked her up and down. "You could be."

"Why, Tsabin!" Kooib-s said, placing a hand over what Sabé assumed was the centre of her cardiopulmonary system. The journalist laughed. "You should leave the flirting to Tonra. He's much better at it."

"That's not particularly reassuring," Sabé said.

"You just need to see him in action," Kooib-s said, smiling. "I'm not the only one who could fit right in at the opera house."

She poured her caf on the floor underneath the table, much to the consternation of the service droids, and left. Sabé settled the bill but lingered over her own cup even though it was going cold.

She needed to find a new contact. If Kooib-s was investigating them, even just to keep them on their toes, she might get too close to their real purpose. She didn't like to lose Kooib-s as an asset, but it was better to play it safe. No one could know that Sabé's chief interest in the government was Senator Amidala. From now on, they would only utilise Kooib-s Guvar if they had exhausted their other options.

The droid was hovering, clearly hoping Sabé would leave and free up the table, so that was exactly what she did. She held the door open for a small boy with dark hair and dark eyes as he struggled under the weight of a large carryout tray. He looked up at her briefly and then at her wrist, where she wore the communicator that linked her to Tonra. It was expensive tech that she'd bashed around to look cheaper, but the boy clearly wasn't fooled for an instant. He met Sabé's eyes again, and she set her mouth in a hard line.

"Apologies, ma'am," he said, ducking under her arm with his tray and scurrying off down the street.

Sabé watched him go, making a mental note to further modify the communicator as soon as possible, and then made her way back to the apartment she and Tonra had rented. She used the tiny washroom, picked up a bag of dried durang fruit from the kitchen, and locked herself in the closet attached to her bedroom. She ran a sweep for listening devices and then activated the signal that would catch the attention of Padmé, or Versé if Padmé wasn't home.

"Sabé?" the holo of Versé appeared in front of her.

"I need to talk to Padmé when she gets home," Sabé said. "It's too important to mess around with setting up a time, so I'll just wait."

"She could be hours," Versé said.

"I brought snacks," Sabé told her.

"All right," Versé said. "I'll let her know."

The holo deactivated, plunging the closet into darkness. Sabé stretched as best she could and settled in to wait.

Padmé arrived home wanting nothing more than plain conversation with people she trusted. Her encounter with Mon Mothma was more unsettling the more she thought about it, and her cryptic tea with Senator Bonteri had only made her more paranoid. She was barely out of her senatorial gown and into her soft green lounging robes when Versé came in.

"Sabé wants to talk to you," Versé said. Seeing that Dormé and Cordé were occupied putting the dress back in the wardrobe, she began to take down Padmé's hair. "She said she would wait by the transmitter rather than going back and forth to set up a time."

Padmé sighed. "How long ago?" she asked.

"Just over two hours," Versé said. "She had snacks."

"Don't wait for me for dinner," Padmé said. "Just keep something warm."

"All right," Versé said. "Also, you received this."

"This" was a disposable holorecorder, the sort that could be programmed to play one message and store it but didn't have the capacity for transmission. Padmé activated it and was surprised when a tiny holo of Mon Mothma appeared in her hand.

"Senator Amidala," the figure said, "I would like to invite you, your three aides, and as many of your guards as you deem necessary to a gala event that I am hosting next week."

"All three of us?" Cordé said, but then fell silent as the message continued.

Padmé listened to the details and passed the device to Dormé, who would enter them into her calendar.

"I'll talk to Sabé first, and then we'll deal with this," she said.

The three of them bowed and left her alone. Padmé removed the transmitter that was linked to Sabé's apartment from her desk, and turned it on.

"What news?" she said when Sabé's figure appeared.

"Senator Mon Mothma is hosting a gala," Sabé said.

"I know," Padmé said. "I just got the invitation. It's for me, all three of my handmaidens, and a couple of guards."

"That's magnanimous," Sabé said. "My sources think that

Mothma will use the gala as a cover to have private talks with like-minded senators, though they don't know the topic the senators will be like-minded on."

"She can't do that in public," Padmé said. "Unless there's a – "

"Distraction," Sabé finished.

"And what better distraction than Senator Amidala," Padmé said. It was not a question.

"Will you go?" Sabé asked.

"I'll have to," Padmé said. "And they're expecting three handmaidens, so switching one out for me is too risky. They've all spent time in the Senate building as visible support for the senator persona. 'Padmé' doesn't have the anonymity she used to, especially if someone is counting hoods."

Padmé drummed her fingers on the surface of her dressing table, her mind whirring through possibilities.

"I can't be the focus of attention at the gala," she said finally. "I have to hear what they're actually talking about. I have to see it. Their tone and body language, not just a report about it. I had a very strange conversation with Mon Mothma today, and an even stranger one with Mina Bonteri afterward. They both wanted to discuss my loyalty to the Republic, but I think there's something larger at play, and I have to know what it is."

"How many guards can you bring?" Sabé asked. The

image flickered, and Padmé could tell she was writing things down.

"As many as I deem necessary," Padmé said, using the invitation's wording. "I have the standard complement of six, but I never use them all at the same time."

"I could go in as one of your guards," Sabé said. "And then we could change places after we all clear security."

"You want to do an on-site switch in an unknown location?" Padmé clarified. "We haven't done that in a while."

"We'd have a week to prep," Sabé pointed out. "That's approximately one hundred sixty-seven more hours than we had to prepare for the Invasion of Naboo."

"Do you think you can learn everything about the Senate in that amount of time?" Padmé asked. "You'll have to sleep at some point."

"I can do it," Sabé said. "I was the best at being your decoy because I was the best at pretending to be you. Even if I don't know all the details, I can say what you would say."

"I'd still be more comfortable if you came here for a week so we could brief you," Padmé said. "Will Tonra be all right on his own?"

"He'll be fine," Sabé said. "He won't be happy, but he'll be fine."

"I don't think Typho and Mariek will be happy, either," Padmé said. "Considering that Panaka trained us specifically with the decoy manoeuvre in mind, the guards get very upset when we deploy it."

"At least you'll tell them this time," Sabé said. "That will make them feel better."

"I hope you're right," Padmé said. "Versé will transmit the details of how we're going to get you into the residence as soon as we have them figured out. You don't need to wait around by the transmitter for them."

"Good," said Sabé. "It's a little cramped in this closet, and I can hear Tonra moving around outside. I think he's starting to get nervous."

"Go tell him the plan," Padmé said. "We'll be in touch."

Sabé nodded, and then her image flickered and disappeared. Padmé took a moment to gather herself. She looked in the mirror and realised that Versé had pulled out all the pins but hadn't had time to uncoil her hair. She looked bizarre, and wondered why Sabé hadn't said anything. Padmé took a few moments to fix the mess and then wove her hair into a simple braid down her back. She put on a pair of soft shoes and went in search of dinner.

The others were halfway through their stuffed Rodian peppers by the time she arrived at the table, and Cordé took the cover off the plate they had kept warm for her.

"What did Sabé want?" Mariek asked.

Padmé gave them the details about Sabé's intelligence regarding the party and the plan that they had come up with.

"Three handmaidens, three guards," Mariek said. "It will look very nice when the newsnets publish pictures of us. We'll have to wear the full Naboo version of the uniform with the hat, so we can obscure Sabé's face."

"That's your only issue?" Typho said.

"Of course not," Mariek said. "But they're going to do it, and this time they told us about it, so I am going to offer constructive criticism."

"Thank you, Captain," Padmé said.

"Look at the bright side, Typho," Dormé said. She put a hand on the sergeant's arm. "The senator will be dressed in blaster-repelling armour, and you'll be standing right next to her for almost the entire night."

"Until she runs off to overhear whatever it is she needs to hear," Typho said. "Though I am glad about the armour."

"I promise to stay as close to you as possible," Padmé said. She grinned impishly. "Though I'm assuming you'll give us some space during the changeover."

He actually blushed.

"How are we going to get Sabé in?" Dormé asked, gracefully getting them back on topic.

"Wouldn't a simple switch work best?" Cordé said. "I mean, what if one of your guards went out, met Sabé somewhere, and then Sabé came back?"

"I agree," Mariek said. "It can't be the apartment, obviously, but I am sure we can find a location."

"Who will you send?" Padmé asked.

"Corin," Typho said. "He's the only one short enough."

"I will alter a uniform so it fits you and Sabé both," Dormé said. "And start picking out what Amidala will wear. It'll have to be an elabourate dress to justify a headpiece and the makeup we'll need. And I'll have to make sure the makeup kit is transportable so I can do it again on-site."

"Twice," said Typho. "We might have to switch them back at the party, as well."

"Just like old times," Mariek said with a grin. "And much easier when the planet isn't about to be invaded by murderous Neimoidians."

"It does take a bit of the edge off," Padmé said. "Versé, I want you to find out as much about the venue as you can. We need to know what internal security is going to be like. If you need someone to actually go and look at it, send Tonra."

With that, Padmé finally began to eat her pepper. Versé had been tinkering with the kitchen droid's programming again. This pepper was significantly spicier than the previous attempts had been, as Versé tried to compensate for the droid's Coruscanti base code. She smiled, her mouth still full, and Versé responded with a wide grin of her own. The others finished their meals, and Padmé dismissed them to their tasks. Soon she sat alone, though Typho had not gone any farther than the door.

Her secret shame was how much she enjoyed the decoy

manoeuvre. It was dangerous, only used when they absolutely needed it. They had done modified versions of it
several times since arriving on Coruscant, but they'd only
done a true switch – one with both Padmé and the decoy
present – that time when the NON droid had malfunctioned
– a malfunction that still hadn't been explained, though
everyone knew the Trade Federation's affinity for droids.
Now they would do it again, for the sake of Padmé's curiosity and political ambition, and even though she was sure it
was the right thing to do, Padmé wasn't sure she could trust
her own judgement. The ploy put Sabé, whom she cared for
very deeply, in peril. So many things could go wrong; they
could betray themselves a thousand ways, and the damage
would be irreparable.

And she *loved* it.

She loved the thrill that accompanied watching someone
talk to Sabé thinking it was Amidala whose attention they
held. She loved the way people looked right through her,
Padmé Naberrie, as though she were nothing. She loved taking that nothingness and using it to her own ends. And yes,
it was for safety, and yes, her intentions were as noble as
they had been on Naboo. She still remembered how she had
looked at Captain Panaka over Sio Bibble's head and he had
nodded that it was time.

We are brave, Your Highness.

They were all brave. That was how the handmaidens

were chosen, or at least it was a strong part of it. That was why Saché had scars on every part of her body: because they were brave. Padmé would never let herself forget it, never let herself dismiss what her friends did for her because they trusted her and believed what she was doing was right. They had stood by her as queen, and they were standing by her now, and she would do everything she could to make sure that she was worthy of their loyalty.

She felt at her neck for the locket, forgetting for a moment that she no longer wore it. She had given it to Sabé as a token, two girls on a planet watching the sky above them fill with starships that blocked them in. It had been a childish gesture, though no less genuine for its innocence, and one of the last such gestures she had ever made. The Trade Federation had seen to that. Sabé had tried to give the necklace back to her after the Battle of Naboo, as Padmé had directed, but by then, Padmé had changed her mind and told Sabé it was hers to keep, the thanks of a planet that would never fully appreciate what she had done.

Now Padmé wore a different token, one that was personal and had nothing to do with the people of Naboo. It was handmade, like all the best treasures were, and stood for luck and remembrance. Padmé didn't like to rely on luck and she rarely needed help remembering anything, but it helped to have something on which to focus her thoughts.

She ate the last of her dinner, even though it had gone

cold. She checked to make sure that Typho was all right, and when he nodded, she went to the window and let herself get lost in the brightness of lights.

CHAPTER 13

Senator Amidala wore a gown that was so deeply red it was very nearly black. The sleeves were long, almost trailing on the ground when she walked, and the ornate collar had hundreds of tiny gold beads stitched on it. Her hair was gathered into dozens of braids, each looped tightly and pinned low along the back of her head. From them rose three interlocked metal circles, upon which iridescent threads had been woven into softly glowing webs. When she turned just so and the light fell on the folds of fabric, scarlet and crimson glinted from within, but if you looked at her quickly, you wouldn't notice any of that.

No one looked at Senator Amidala quickly.

As she and her party came down the wide terraced steps, all heads turned towards them. Padmé breathed deeply. If they were going to stare, she was going to make them do it on her terms. She made sure to hit every spotlight at the right angle, moving slowly as the heavy-looking skirt swished around her feet. It didn't actually encumber her much – Naboo design was far too good for that – but it looked like it did, and the look only made her more powerful in the moment.

She found Mon Mothma in the crowd. There was a satisfied smile on the Chandrilan's face as every recorder in the gardens turned to monitor Padmé's entrance.

I will show you, Padmé thought. *I will show you what we can do together.*

They were escorted by one of Mon Mothma's aides – who discreetly scanned them in the process – to a seating place in full view of every terrace, where they could refresh themselves before mingling. Versé was dispatched with their drink order. She returned after a few moments with a little droid behind her, a droid that promptly spilled a glass of Toniray wine on Amidala's hem. The senator retired to the powder room with two of her aides and a guard, though not before offering gracious reassurance to the very alarmed protocol droid who came over to see what the noise was about. Versé had already re-reprogrammed the server droid and sent it on its way.

Dormé had done incredible work, and she had done it twice already tonight. She had practised on Cordé for a week, trimming down the time it took to apply the makeup and construct the hairstyle, until she could manage the whole thing by herself in less than ten minutes. By the time she, Padmé, and Sabé had locked themselves into the powder room after clearing security, Dormé could have done the entire switchover in her sleep.

"You're a little bit scary," Typho had muttered in her ear when the senator, the handmaiden, and the guard had emerged and rejoined their party.

"I know," Dormé said. "That's one of the reasons you like me so much."

The gala took place in one of the public gardens on Coruscant's upper levels. By day, the space was a high-end market, with a circular central floor and wide tiered steps rising up on three sides. The gardens were on these tiers, each level supporting a different biome. The booths that usually lined the walkways had been hidden away, and in their places were comfortable seats, tables of refreshments, and the most well-connected residents Coruscant had to offer.

Senator Amidala was a popular target for anyone with a recording device, but Sabé noticed that a great many senators sought her out to say hello, as well. She was grateful for the cramming sessions with Padmé. She knew most of their names from reading reports, but connecting to faces was entirely new.

"Senator Amidala, how lovely to see you," came a voice from her right.

Sabé turned, quite an operation in the gown, and realised that they were all about to face the first real test of the night. She hoped Padmé had her hat pulled down.

"Senator Farr." Sabé spoke in the modified tone that Padmé had developed for Amidala to use at social functions. It was much more flexible than the queen's voice had been. The affection that now infused her words was not feigned: she was also fond of the Rodian senator who was one of Padmé's father's oldest friends.

Onaconda Farr was resplendent this evening in an irides-cent blue suit that made his eyes sparkle even more brightly than they would have done in the evening light. He was smil-ing, in the Rodian fashion at least, and he already held a glass in his left hand.

"It's so good to finally see you, my dear," Farr said. He stepped past what Sabé would consider safe range, but as an old friend, he was entitled to. "I had hoped we would meet before now, but I suppose you wanted to establish yourself a bit first?"

"Yes," Sabé said. The handmaidens and guards had moved to the side of the walkway to allow others to pass while the senators spoke. Padmé stayed at the back with Typho. "I'm glad that you understand. It's hard enough being new, and as much as I would appreciate your guidance and mentorship, I don't wish to be seen as dependent on my father's connec-tions, among other things."

"Quite so," Farr said. "It's a smart move, even if we both wish otherwise. I was, of course, quite close with Valourum. But you are doing all right?"

"Yes," Sabé said. "I'm beginning to feel quite settled."

Sabé was the best decoy for a variety of reasons, and chief among these was the fact that she could tell truths as Amidala that carried conviction because they were true of herself, as well. She *was* settled on Coruscant. It was complicated, over-whelming work, but she was finding the rhythm of it. Even standing here tonight as Amidala was part of her ruse, and she felt complete for the first time since she had stepped foot on Tatooine.

"Excellent," Farr said. "Please do not hesitate to call on me if you wish. I am sure we are past the window of suspicion, at least, and no longer need to avoid one another. Everyone will know you are your own senator by now, or they never will."

Someone called his name from another tier, and the Rodian politely took his leave of them. Sabé heard Dormé exhale loudly beside her, but no one else had any sort of reaction.

They continued to mingle. Amidala greeted Senator Bonteri and Senator Clovis, the latter of whom also stepped past Sabé's definition of a safe distance. Cordé stepped closer, as well, deflecting some of his attention, but Sabé only relaxed when he went on his way again. Padmé was going to have problems with that boy if she wasn't careful. Of course, Sabé also knew that Padmé could handle herself. It was more likely that Clovis was going to have problems with her.

There were recording devices everywhere, as Versé's analysis had suggested. In addition to the droids and security that were part of the park's design, Mon Mothma had included her own measures. Several of the senators and all of the holojournalists had brought personal droids. Padmé had left R2-D2 behind, deciding that this was not a good time for the droid to make his first public appearance. The handmaidens were also personal guards, even if almost no one was aware of it, and their memories were almost as efficient as the little astromech's.

At last Sabé reached a bench that was wide enough for her to sit on in her gown. They had decided that it made the most sense for Amidala to be stationary, but the place where they had originally been seated was too close to the entrance to be practical. People would come to her and make a crowd, and that crowd would inspire more attention. It would also provide cover for when two of her guards took themselves off for a walk. Sabé turned and held out her arms so that Dormé and Versé could help her sit without crushing the dress, and then she was installed, as she had been on the throne of Naboo, except this time she was much more a showpiece than she had ever been as decoy ruler.

Dormé and Versé sat beside her while Cordé remained standing – ostensibly to fetch anything they might need – and Mariek took up her place on the other side, standing at parade rest. Padmé and Typho moved to stand behind the bench, allowing the bulk of Amidala's hair and collar to obscure them from view.

Mon Mothma appeared, her own coterie ranged out behind her. Two or three holorecorders descended just inside listening range.

"Senator Amidala," Mon Mothma said. "It's wonderful to

see all of you here at once. There is much discussion about your companions, as I am sure you know."

That was Dormé's cue. She stood and bowed to the senator.

"I am hopeful that we will be able to answer any questions about our service to the senator, the Republic, and our own home planet of Naboo this evening," she said. "It is a wonderful opportunity for us, and our first chance to appear in public since we arrived with Senator Amidala."

"Thank you for including us in the invitation, Senator," Cordé said. She also bowed.

"Of course," Mon Mothma said. "You must excuse me. As hostess I am expected to greet everyone, and it feels like everyone is here."

"I look forward to speaking to you later, Senator," Amidala said. "Once you have fulfiled those obligations."

Mon Mothma swept away, and in her wake even more recorder droids and the like grouped around where Amidala sat. Sabé felt movement behind her, and knew that Typho and Padmé were heading out. Silently, she wished them luck, and then she focused all her attention and charm on the battlefield in front of her.

It was a remarkable relief to wear pants. Padmé easily kept pace with Sergeant Typho, the two of them moving fluidly through the crowded tiers as they scoped out where the best vantage point would be. No one got out of their way, as they would have done for Amidala, but Padmé didn't need them to. It was much more comfortable to turn corners without the need to have someone maintain her structural integrity.

"I'd forgotten how much of Captain Panaka's training went both ways," Typho said via the private comlink wired into the ceremonial uniform hat. "We spend so much time making sure the handmaidens can play you, we forget how many people you can play."

"That was probably part of his plan," Padmé replied. "I miss him, you know. The rest of you are excellent, and I trust you completely, but still. Your uncle was one of a kind."

"It was hard for you to lose him and your other hand-maidens, I think?" Typho asked. "I know it was for vastly different reasons, but it's still a loss, and you had to keep on with an entirely new support team."

"I always felt like I was taking Captain Panaka away from his family. He was so focused on me – on the throne – that he never did anything else," Padmé said.

"He was always like that," Typho said. "Mariek told me that his obsession with your safety was the best thing that could have happened because it gave him something to work on. Even with the way it ended."

"I try to give your family space, but you know if you ever need anything, you can ask, right?"

"I do," Typho said. "So do Mariek and Versé. And I think Quarsh does, too, on some level. I think it will get better after the ion pulse is completed and we've all had some time to adjust."

"It has been challenging for all of us, changing from queen's staff to senator's," Padmé said. "But I think we've risen to it well."

"I agree," Typho said. "Now, since I technically outrank you at the moment, why don't you sweep the desert biome and I'll go up one further and sweep the rainforest. Leave your comlink open."

"I'll have to clean Corin's uniform for him," Padmé said, sighing. She always seemed to end up dealing with a mess when she was in disguise. At least cleaning the uniform would be easier than scraping carbon scoring off a droid.

Typho grinned at her and began to climb up to the rainforest level. Padmé made her way through the desert biome tier, marvelling at how well designed the gardens were: even the air was drier. She walked purposefully between arrangements of succulents and gatherings of partygoers, scanning visually for Mon Mothma as casually as she could.

"I've got her," Typho said in her ear. "Rainforest level, third section."

"Cover?" Padmé asked, turning back to the staircase she'd just walked past and beginning her ascent.

"Mostly low-growing shrubs, but there are a couple of larger trees," he reported.

"I'm on my way," Padmé said. "See if you can find a good spot to hide."

"On it," Typho said. "She's got Organa with her, and your friend Farr, and a couple of others I can't see clearly."

"Bonteri?" Padmé asked. She had reached the forest level, and began making her way through the underbrush instead of taking the path.

"Not that I can see," Typho said. "I think they picked this level because the holorecorders would have to be right on top of them to record. I can hardly see a thing."

"How's the sound?" Padmé asked. Her breathing was a bit ragged from her rapid climb through the biome, though she jumped lightly over a log. She reflected that she should probably add some sort of physical activity and security training to her daily routine, if only to keep up with her own guards.

"Pretty good," he said. "Are you here?"

"Right behind you," said Padmé, still a bit breathless. To his credit, he didn't jump.

They shuffled around quietly for a moment, trying to find a good vantage point, but the tree cover was too effective a screen.

"This is no good," Padmé said. "The whole point of this" – she gestured at her disguise – "is to *see* them." She looked up with a contemplative expression on her face. "Can you hold me on your shoulders?"

"I can for long enough for you to grab those branches," he said. "Here, take a boost."

He cupped his hands and braced himself for her weight. She stepped into his hold and then scrambled up, using the tree trunk for balance, until she was standing on his shoulders.

"A little to your left," she said.

Typho took two shaky steps to his left, and Padmé reached out for the branch. She caught it and pulled herself up. When she was steady, she braced herself on the trunk again and looked down to where the senators were grouped. From the overhead vantage, she had a clear view of them. She scanned the area around her for cameras or security measures, and when she found none, she turned her attention back to the ground.

"I'm just not sure if she can be trusted," Farr was saying.

Padmé's feelings were hurt. She had thought at least her father's old friend would trust her.

"She's getting heavily encrypted transmissions from off-planet, and she won't talk about them," Farr continued.

Padmé frowned, puzzled for a moment. She wasn't getting transmissions from anyone but Sabé, and while Sabé was using an encrypted signal, she made no attempt to disguise the fact that they were coming from Coruscant.

"She's trying to recruit Senator Amidala to whatever it is she's doing," Organa said.

Clarity dawned on Padmé. They weren't discussing her; they were discussing Senator Bonteri.

"Should we let her?" Mon Mothma asked. "It might be easier to flip Senator Amidala."

"I don't think you should underestimate her," Organa said. "She won't let you use her, and she's too smart not to realise what you're doing if you try."

"Is she loyal?" Mon Mothma asked. "Is Naboo loyal?"

"I think she is," Farr said. "And I think Naboo is, too. They will follow her lead."

"I think we should risk asking her outright," Organa said. "Tonight, if we can get her away from her entourage."

Padmé's stomach dropped into her boots.

"Oh, no," she said quietly.

"What?" Typho asked.

"I'm coming down," she said.

"Climb, don't jump," Typho ordered, even though jumping would be faster. "The ground is too uneven for a decent brace."

"Are you connected to Mariek?" Padmé scrambled downward.

"Not on this channel," he said. He reached up to guide her feet back to his shoulders and grunted as her weight settled on him. "But I can switch over. Why?"

"Tell her to have Dormé and Sabé meet me back at the powder rooms," Padmé said. "Senator Organa wants to have a serious talk with Amidala, and he can't have it with Sabé for the same reason Sabé couldn't climb this tree. They're going to trust *me*, so it has to be me they talk to."

She leaned against the tree trunk and slid down Typho's back as gracefully as she could manage in a hurry, which was to say: not very. She didn't stick around to hear Typho relay the command, but headed for the staircase at the fastest casual speed she could manage. A guard in a hurry would attract attention, and she had to avoid that now more than ever. She walked down the stairs, past the desert biome, and all the way back to the circular case at the garden's centre. Halfway down, she got stuck behind a crowd of slow-moving Ithorians who refused to get out of her way, even after they saw her. It took her almost five minutes to politely shove her way through them, and by then she was sure that Organa would be ahead of her.

At last she reached the bottom. She saw Dormé and Sabé making their way to the powder room door, and risked a glance across the plaza to the staircase that Senator Organa was most likely to descend. He wasn't there, so she fell into place behind Amidala's right shoulder. They were almost there.

Senator Organa appeared from an entirely different entrance, right in front of them. He made to strike up a conversation with Amidala but just as quickly realised where she was headed and stepped aside to let her pass. He stepped to his left, not quite far enough to get out of the way of the guard, and looked Padmé full in the face.

He stopped.

She didn't.

She stepped around him, and followed Sabé the last few steps into the powder room. Before the door closed, she heard a quiet laugh.

CHAPTER 14

Senator Amidala did a full turn of the water garden on Senator Organa's arm. They looked at the elegant pools, each one held at various levels by intricate repulsor fields. They admired the flowers that grew on the surface of a pond that glowed with a dim purple light. They lingered under a tree that had bubbles instead of leaves and listened to the soft fizzing sound as the bubbles floated away from the branches and up towards the next tier. They were strangely unbothered by holorecorders, largely thanks to the signal jammer Senator Organa wore on his belt, concealed by the folds of his cape.

And while they walked they discussed a great many things.

"You're in select company, Senator," Padmé told him. They paused to let a larger group pass them by. Several of them bade Senator Organa a good evening, but none of them overstayed their welcome. "Only a few people know the full lengths my most loyal bodyguards can go to, and only one other person has ever figured it out on their own while we were in the middle of a deception."

"It was mostly chance, I think," he said. "If I hadn't

caught you at just that moment, in that light, and with that expression on your face, it wouldn't have occurred to me."

"I am usually much better at controlling my expression," Padmé admitted ruefully. "We were in a tighter spot than usual, though I suppose at least this time, the only thing at stake was my professional pride."

"Who is the other?" Organa asked.

"His name was Qui-Gon Jinn, a Jedi," Padmé said. As always, a feeling of almost overwhelming sadness threatened her when she thought of him. He had been patient and understanding of her, never asking for more than she was willing to give, and he had given all, in the end. "He died defending Naboo during the battle for the planet against the Trade Federation. The Jedi memorialised him there, and we honour him as a hero."

"I am sorry for your loss, but I must admit, I do enjoy that I am in such excellent company," Organa said. He paused, clearly considering how to phrase his next query. "Is your life truly so fraught with peril that such extreme measures are necessary, or is this some kind of paranoia?"

"A bit of both, I think," Padmé said. She knew it was paranoia that had spurred Panaka to embrace the old tradition so fiercely, but the success of the plan was undeniable. "But every time I think I am getting paranoid, something happens."

"Something like what?" Organa asked.

"Do you remember how we met, Senator?" Padmé asked. "The second time?"

Organa laughed. "You'd gone to the wrong door at the Senate building," he said. "And you were almost incinerated."

"We were sent there, Senator," Padmé said. She had been talking in her own conversational tone but slipped into Amidala's when she reached such a serious subject matter. "My NON unit was programmed to lead us there at that time. You actually spoke with Cordé. I was the handmaiden, and you didn't even look at me, but that is fairly common. In any case, the entire setup was an attempt on my life."

"You say that with remarkable calmness," Organa said.

"It wasn't a particularly good attempt," Padmé told him. "And it wasn't the first."

"See, that would just make me less calm," Organa said. "But I understand your need for such intense security now. All senators and politicians lead complicated lives, but yours seems intent on outdoing the rest of us."

"You thwart the plans of one galaxywide trade conspiracy and they hold a grudge forever," Padmé said sarcastically.

"You cost them an inconceivable amount of money," Organa said. "*Before* they started paying Nute Gunray's legal fees."

"There are times when that does make me feel better," Padmé said. "How did you come to be there that day?"

"Have you been suspicious of my intentions?" Organa replied. He did not seem offended.

"I've trusted you since the day in the Senate gardens," Padmé said. "But I employ any number of highly trained people whose job it is to be suspicious of strange senators I meet in dark corridors."

"I was leaving the building and I saw your speeder go down past the safety limits," he said. "I did wonder why the NON unit didn't notify you, but when it became obvious you weren't turning back, I followed you down. I couldn't comm you because I didn't know your private channel, so direct intervention was the only option."

"That will certainly make Captain Mariek feel better about you," Padmé said. "Now, I believe you had some questions for me?"

"In the Senate, loyalty is a subtle and shifting thing," Organa said. "But there are certain limits."

"Like attacking a sovereign planet and holding it hostage?" Padmé said. "No, wait, that is permissible so long as you can pay off your allies to vote in your favour."

"Loyalty to the Republic is paramount," Organa said. He managed not to make it sound patronising, which Padmé appreciated. "Loyalty to democracy."

"And what if democracy does not return the favour?" Padmé asked.

"Then you must work to restore the democratic process," Organa said. "I know the Senate didn't move quickly enough for Naboo, but your senator's nomination to chancellor stalled all discussion on every topic except that election. You can work through the proper channels."

"What makes you think I won't?" Padmé asked.

"Your actions as Queen of Naboo," Organa said. "Your actions now. You stay out of almost every committee, and you have no faction."

"My choice in allies has kept me alive on more than one occasion, Senator Organa. I take committing to a faction very seriously," Padmé said. "And to be entirely honest, I am strongly considering yours, only I didn't think you would accept me."

"We will accept you now," Organa said. "My word carries a great deal of weight, and Mon will be grateful for the distraction tonight once she learns you provided it deliberately. Between the two of us and Senator Farr, you will be given a place."

She did not doubt him for a moment.

"I won't spy on Mina Bonteri," Padmé said. "And neither will I give up on my friendship with her. I will admit, I am curious about her activities, too, but I won't report them to you unless I feel the situation merits it."

"We will be content with that," Organa said. "I would only ask that it is always you we deal with, never one of your doubles."

"That is fair," Padmé said. "We only took our security measures tonight because Mon Mothma invited me here to serve as a distraction for your discussion. There was no danger, I simply needed to be free to move around."

"I imagine you're about to become much less interesting to the newsnets," Organa said. "Mon Mothma might have a few contacts to help you get rid of them."

"Even the ones owned by subsidiaries of the Trade Federation?" Padmé asked. Four years as a senator couldn't give Mon Mothma that much clout.

Organa regarded her with some surprise. "Do you ever sleep?" he asked.

"Of course," Padmé said. She wasn't about to give up all her secrets.

"She'll get them off your back," Organa said. "Even the Trade Federation steps carefully around Chandrila."

"I'm glad to hear it," Padmé said, though she wondered what the cost would be – and who would pay it. "Will you take me back to my guards? Dormé did my hair in a hurry, and it's very tight. I'm starting to get a headache."

"I'm surprised you can move in that thing at all," Organa said.

"Years of practise," she replied. "Plus, you've got the jammer under your cape. Imagine the kind of tech I can conceal if I have to."

They didn't stay long after Organa returned Padmé to the others. Mon Mothma spoke to her briefly, promising an update soon, and thanked her for being so excellent a distraction for the newsnets. Padmé shook hands and did her best not to notice Senator Organa's smirk.

Sabé left them at the door to the gardens, but Padmé was able to get a quick word with her before she disappeared.

"Thank you, my friend," she said. "I think this will be the last time I call on you to take my place."

"It was almost fun this time," Sabé said. "The lack of mortal peril meant I could actually enjoy being in charge."

"I'm just glad everything worked out," Padmé said. "Take a few days off if you need to. Hopefully everything will quiet down a bit now that Mon Mothma has taken me under her wing."

"I will," Sabé said.

She kissed Padmé on the cheek and disappeared into the vibrant flow of Coruscant's neon-lit night. Padmé turned back to the waiting Typho and let him hand her into their shuttle.

"Thank you, everyone," she said, relaxing into their company. "Now let's go home."

Sabé felt like every one of her nerves was humming as she made her way back to the apartment. It was always like this when a switch was finally over. She could maintain her calm as long as she was the decoy, no matter the stakes. The moment

Sabé was free to be herself again, however, all of her feelings crashed into her at the same time, and that always made her jittery. She was hungry, too, since she'd been unable to eat for most of the evening, but decided to wait until she got home before she stopped for food.

She was on high alert, probably moving like some kind of stim junkie, and replaying all of the scenes from the party in her mind. She'd fooled Onaconda Farr! Who actually knew who she was, and who Padmé was besides. Then she'd held court amidst constant camera and holojournalist attention for most of the evening, without batting so much as an eyelash. She felt like she could do anything, be anyone, be Senator Amidala, be Queen of Naboo again. Her adrenaline surged, and she reflected that it was probably for the best she was headed home. She was worse than a junkie right now, and she needed something to ground her.

The apartment was dark when the door slid open to admit her, and she thought maybe Tonra was out. Then she noticed his boots, neatly lined up beside the space where hers went, and realised he must just be in bed. She took off her boots as quietly as she could and then tiptoed into the kitchen to see if there was anything to eat. She had just started to rummage through one of the cabinets when the light came on, and she jumped.

"Tonra!" she said, turning around to see him. "You startled me."

"First time for everything, I guess," he said. He was dressed for sleep, his tall frame leaning on the doorpost while he looked at her. "Are you all right?"

"Yes," she said. She gave up on getting real food and cracked open a ration bar instead. It wasn't very tasty, but it got the job done quickly. "I'm all right, Padmé is all right. Everything is all right."

"I'm glad to hear it," he said. "I missed you this week."

She hadn't contacted him. Not even once. It was procedure, of course, but now she wished they had set up a protocol to meet while she was gone. It must have been hell for him to wait and not hear anything.

"I missed you, too," she said. "It's so easy to get caught up in Padmé's orbit, but I missed the work we do here."

"She's been your friend for a long time," Tonra said. "It makes sense that you get caught up in her when you're with her."

"It's more than that," Sabé said. She finished the ration bar and wiped the crumbs off her hands. It was never easy to explain, even to the closest of insiders, the bond that all the handmaidens shared.

"You love her," Tonra said. Sabé froze.

"Of course I do," she said. She met his gaze. "It's a complicated relationship. She can order me to my death, and I will go. And she knows it. We've worked so hard to maintain a balance we will never truly have. As far as I can see, she will always pick Naboo, and I will always pick her."

"I'm sorry," he said.

She couldn't stand his pity. More important, she didn't need it.

"I'm not," she replied. "I'm the right hand of Padmé Amidala Naberrie, and I always will be, even if someday she decides to follow her path somewhere else. I wouldn't trade my relationship with her for anything in the galaxy."

"Not even for someone who would pick you?" Tonra said. He was a large person, but he seemed smaller when he said it and completely vulnerable. "Someone who loved you, or at least thought they might?"

There was a time when Sabé would have headed that sort of thing right off at the pass. Tonra had never been exactly secretive about his feelings, but hearing them laid out like this was an entirely new matter. Before, her service to the queen had made sustaining outside relationships difficult. Now, though, it was an altogether different situation, even if many of her own feelings remained unchanged.

"Well, that's the thing," Sabé said. She took a step towards him. "I never have to choose between you. The choice is already made. It's up to you to decide if you want to make yourself a part of what I am."

Sabé had never been quite this honest with a potential partner before, even though Tonra was already her partner in several ways that mattered very much. Perhaps that's why she was being so direct with him. She wanted him to know what he was getting into, and she had suddenly decided that she would very much like him to get into it.

Tonra hadn't moved, not even a little bit, so she crossed the floor to where he stood, well inside his reach, and waited for him to make up his mind.

"Well," he said at last, "I think I'd like to try."

"Good," she said.

Then she closed her hands on the collar of his tunic, pulled his face down close to hers, and kissed him.

She meant it as a sort of test, to see if this was really going to work, but it bloomed into something deeper almost immediately. His hands found her waist, then her back, and he pressed her against his chest even as she tried to pull him closer than he already was. His mouth softened, and he pulled away for a moment to breathe, and press gentler kisses against her neck. She couldn't help the noise she made when he kissed the hollow of her throat, right between the two sides of her uniform collar, and she felt as much as heard it when he laughed.

His mouth returned to hers, more demanding now, and since she also had a few demands, she let him push her back towards the counter. When she could go no farther, his hands tightened around her hips and he lifted her up until she was sitting on the edge with her legs wrapped around him.

"This is a much better height for you," he said.

"Shut up," she said. He was right, though. From here it

was much easier to reach out, grab the hem of his tunic, and pull it over his head.

He laughed.

"How much trying did you have in mind for the immediate future?" he asked. He started working on the various buckles that held her uniform in place. He knew where all of them were, of course, and his familiarity led him to be highly efficient, even though he seemed to find each newly exposed bit of her skin a sublime distraction.

She paused with her hands on his belt and smiled.

"I'll let you know if I want you to stop," she said.

That was the last complete sentence either of them said for some time.

PART IV

AMIDALA FASHIONS FRESH AIR FOR CONSTRUCTION CONUNDRUM

After a slightly uneven start to her career in galactic politics, Senator Padmé Amidala of Naboo seems to be settling in. Now a member of several prestigious committees, the former planetary queen has become a voice for people other than her own in the most commendable of ways: helping them build the very roofs above their heads.

Working alongside such renowned senators as Mon Mothma of Chandrila and Onaconda Farr of Rodia, young Amidala is helping serve the galaxy while still respecting her homeworld via her style and manner of dress, called "tasteful" and "traditional chic." Senator Amidala is a fresh new face that the Senate needs.

Any rumours of pirates in the sector are, at this time, unsubstantiated.

– TriNebulon News

CHAPTER 15

The next six-month span of Senator Amidala's service to the Galactic Republic ran a great deal more smoothly. Her new allies meant that she was invited to sit on more committees and that the motions she helped to write were actually given real floor time. She hadn't yet presented any motions herself, but she found that now that she was working with people she liked, she didn't mind taking a background role for the time being, particularly since more of the laws she supported seemed to be making it through.

She didn't agree with everything Mon Mothma stood for, and they often argued extensively in the privacy of their own offices. The Chandrilan senator was anti-aggression, which Padmé admired, but having had to defend her planet in the past, she found that she was more open to direct conflict. This was a matter she knew that not all Naboo would agree with her on. The Naboo prided themselves on their pacifism almost as much as they prided themselves on their artistic endeavours, but the Trade Federation's invasion – and the resulting alliance with the more militaristic Gungans – had caused a slight shift in Naboo policy. Mon Mothma disapproved of it, and she never passed up a chance to confront Padmé over it.

"Should we arm every cargo hauler, then?" Mon Mothma said at the end of a debate about piracy in galactic hyperspace lanes.

There was still no official committee, despite Cordé's prediction, but the pirates were a specific threat to any transportation legislation. They were choosy with regard to their targets, and seemed to take beyond-reasonable risks to attack any convoy with building materials, food, or other practical necessities. They didn't have the numbers to make the attacks they did, and yet they attacked all the same. Padmé was starting to have a few suspicions about the whole thing, but wasn't yet confident enough to voice them outside of a committee setting.

"If you'll recall," Padmé said coolly, "my proposal was to guard high-priority targets with Republic gunships."

Padmé could tell Mon Mothma was presenting an extreme argument, but in front of trusted witnesses and advisors, it was a luxury to argue more passionately than the Senate floor allowed.

"And when the pirates organise themselves into an even larger force?" Mon Mothma asked.

"Perhaps then we'll be able to catch them," Padmé said. "As it stands, their smaller attacks are too difficult to trace, even for our probe droids. A massed effort on their part might make it easier for us to track them down."

"There is too much risk – " Mon Mothma began, but Senator Organa cut her off.

"I think we're getting a bit off topic," he said. "If you'll recall, we were discussing how we could best incorporate the offer of fuel reserves from Malastare to ease the shipment of permacrete to Coyerti."

They fell back into a less heated discussion, and Padmé thought, not for the first time, that she detected the hint of a smile on Mon Mothma's face. She wouldn't be surprised. Unlike the ugly arguments about Naboo's ion pulse, Padmé rather enjoyed these debates. Arguing with someone who almost agreed with her on most subjects helped her hone her talking points, and she was learning a lot. Padmé had discovered that Mon Mothma's positions were extreme at the outset of most conversations and would almost always move towards the middle as they hammered out a compromise. It was a useful skill and one that Padmé knew she had to master.

It wasn't easy. She had a difficult time turning their debates into academic thought experiments instead of real topics affecting real beings. She didn't like saying something and meaning something else, even as a means to work out an agreement.

"I don't think that's a bad thing," Onaconda Farr had told her.

It had been a rare moment of vulnerability for Padmé, and she had confessed her insecurities to her family friend, not to her fellow senator. He was smart enough to see that and advised her as such.

"You are hardly naive," he'd continued. "Or at least, you're aware of the subjects that you are naive about, which is more than I can say about myself, I am sure. Being a good and honest person doesn't make you a poorer senator. You'll find your own balance."

"What if I don't do it fast enough?" Padmé asked.

"You have plenty of time," he said, but that was the one point on which Padmé wasn't sure he was right.

According to Sabé, Padmé's public opinion was on the rise. No one on Coruscant really cared about the Senate or senatorial procedure, but they did read the newsnets, and Amidala was still featured in them with some regularity. The tone had changed though. Before, where they had dismissed her elabourate style of dress as the frippery of a young aristocrat, they now discussed her in terms of honouring tradition and adapting Naboo customs while in the capital. They no longer used her personality to pull her down. It was frustrating because the newsnets were reporting on all of the exact same subjects as before; they were just writing about them from a different angle.

"Well," Sabé said, "at least it's easier for all of us with Mon Mothma calling the shots."

"It's so pointless!" Padmé argued. "The newsnets should be impartial, not controlled by biased investors, and yet instead they control public opinion of all of us and manipulate the truth. What if Mon Mothma and I had a falling out? Then we'd be right back where we started, though I don't think she is anything as petty as Nute Gunray."

"They have to make money somehow," Sabé said. "You could work towards controlling the holonews if you wanted, but I think we both know you have other plans."

It was something of a sore point. Chancellor Palpatine's motion to increase Republic work against slavery had failed to make it to the floor for months after he had promised her he was working on it. When it was finally presented, it was so toothless that Padmé could tell it wouldn't get anything done. And then it had not received enough votes anyway and disappeared back into the committee. Padmé kept abreast of developments but stayed off the committee herself at Palpatine's request.

"Naboo can't be seen as too involved, my dear," he'd reiterated when she had asked him again about joining the committee after the failed vote. "It is the price we pay for having chancellor and senator both. I am doing my best to represent your voice because I know how much this means to you, but if it becomes public knowledge that we are working together on such a potentially radical topic, I fear there will only be more obstacles thrust into our path."

She hadn't agreed with him entirely, but she respected his position and trusted him enough to acquiesce, at least for now. She didn't stop thinking about it, though, and often made notes on the subject for the day that she would be able to speak about it in public.

Even with those stumbling blocks, Padmé had established herself well among the various Senate dignitaries. Senator Clovis still dropped by her office – always unannounced, to Mariek's unceasing frustration – to talk with her, but they had no real overlap in their day-to-day operations. He had followed the Banking Clan's interests, and she couldn't tell if he had any of his own, or if Scipio's priorities ever diverged from the bank's.

"He's very smart," she told Cordé one afternoon after Clovis had departed. Mariek had seen him out and returned, grumbling about the politeness of calling ahead. "But I'm not sure if he's ever going to act independently."

"Not everyone has your communication style," Cordé said. "Someone has to follow along, or the Senate would do even more yelling than it already does."

"Maybe," Padmé said. Surely a senator was of little use if all they ever did was follow. Even the Trade Federation representative, Lott Dod – who was almost certainly a puppet for Nute Gunray – used his position to speak up now and again, although Padmé trusted the Neimoidian about as far as she could throw him.

Still, as the session drew to a close and the various senators prepared to return to their homeworlds for recess, Padmé was able to look at what she had accomplished since her arrival on Coruscant with some measure of pride. She didn't have the connections and influence that Palpatine had had as senator, but she was well on her way to making them.

She helped Dormé finish packing up the last of what they would be taking back to Naboo with them for the break, stacking the full cases on a hover pallet for R2-D2 to shuttle out to the vestibule, where Cordé was overseeing the loading process. It was soothing work, folding cloth and wrapping pieces of jewellery into packing crates. She had missed working with her hands, something all the Naboo were trained from birth to do and to appreciate.

It was the one thing that nagged at her, despite how well everything on Coruscant was going. Even though she'd only been senator about eight months, she found herself falling into the persona of Senator Amidala with much, much more finality than she ever had as queen. When she was queen, she had known that her time would end and that someday Padmé Naberrie would make her return to the general populace and have to build a life for herself. Now she realised that Senator Amidala could be who she was forever. There were no term limits on senators, and Padmé knew that she was good at the work she was doing. But she felt the position dragging on her. Every time she compromised her ideals. Every time she lied by omission for the greater good. She wasn't sure if that was the sort of future she wanted, building things with words instead of with actions or physical material.

She felt that this Amidala was another part she was playing. As always, she was happy to serve, and she did – selfishly – take great pleasure in the victories she was able to help win on the Senate floor. But she knew there was more, and for the first time in her life, she was starting to want it. She didn't know how many new identities she had left to her. It was no feat of slicing that allowed her to reinvent herself from citizen to princess to queen to senator, only force of will. This recess was just what she needed. It would be time to visit her family, to talk with the queen, and to really, really consider her future once again.

Her comm chimed just as Dormé finished with the last of the wardrobe, and Padmé dismissed her to take the call in private. She activated the holo, and Senator Organa appeared before her.

"Senator Amidala," he said, "I'm glad I caught you before you left."

"Has there been some emergency?" she asked. She tried to quell the surge of resentment she felt at the idea she'd have to stay. It was her job, after all.

"No, nothing like that," he said. "My wife, the Queen of Alderaan, apologises for the lateness of the invitation, but wanted me to ask if you would consider coming to visit us for a time before you return to Naboo. She knows it isn't on your way, but you and your companions would be very welcome, if you could come."

"I would be honoured," Padmé said. She fell into formality at the word *queen*, out of old habits. "May I have some time to address the subject with my people? They have been away from home a long time, and I wouldn't want to put them out."

"Of course," Senator Organa said. "I am not leaving until tomorrow."

They exchanged farewells, and Organa disconnected. Before Padmé could get up and leave, another message came through, with a code she could not ignore. She took a deep breath before answering.

"Chancellor Palpatine," she said. "I hope I have not kept you waiting. I was on another call."

"It's nothing, my dear," he said. "I can always make time for you."

This was patently false, as there were several aspects of the Chancellor's job that rendered him unreachable at all hours, but she appreciated the sentiment.

"How may I help you, Chancellor?" she asked.

"I had hoped you would convey some remarks of mine to Queen Réillata," he said. "Upon your return home."

"I am happy to do so," Padmé said. "But we are heading to Alderaan for a week before we go to Naboo, so you may wish to send a message separately from me, as well."

Palpatine often affected an air of general disinterest when

he spoke via holo. Padmé suspected it was because there was a constant flow of information circulating his office and his attention was always split. At her remark, though, his focus narrowed in on her completely, and she found she was suppressing a shiver.

"I wasn't aware you were so close with Bail Organa as to visit him at home," he said.

"The invitation is from the queen," Padmé explained, though she wasn't entirely sure why it mattered. "She wishes to speak to me as a former monarch, not as a senator."

"I see," Palpatine said. Padmé could almost see the computations turning in his head, though she couldn't have said what any of them came out to. "I will forward my message to Queen Réillata myself then," he continued. "Though, please do convey a greeting to your parents and your sister when you finally return to them."

"Of course," Padmé said.

The Chancellor flickered and disappeared without a further word. Padmé allowed herself one moment of pure, selfish anger, relishing in the feel of it boiling through her blood. She couldn't help enslaved people with money and she couldn't help them with policy. Those were her two largest areas of influence, and she had so little pull that the Chancellor hadn't even said a proper dismissal. She felt a brief flash of despair, the closest she ever came to giving up. Then she turned off the comlink.

Padmé took a breath and went out into the dining room. There were wide windows that looked out over the cityscape, but today it was so hazy that it was difficult to see much besides the usual lanes of traffic. She commed a general call, asking her handmaidens and guards to join her when they were able. Most of them appeared almost right away, though Cordé was delayed by her task down on the landing pad.

"We have been invited to Alderaan," Padmé said by way of introduction. "All of us, for a brief time before we continue home. I wanted to consult with you, because I know you are looking forward to the holiday as much as I am, and I don't want to keep you from your families for longer than I have to."

Padmé felt a sharp pang of guilt. As much as she wanted to accept the invitation, her own sister had been delivered of a girl only a few days ago, and Padmé ached to see them both. At the same time, she could not stop calculating the benefits of going to Alderaan. It seemed she would always be of two minds when it came to family and duty.

"I'm happy to fly you wherever you need to go," Varbarós said. "I've never been to Alderaan before."

"Thank you," Padmé said. She surveyed the people in front of her and spoke as their friend, not their senator. "Please be honest about what you want to do."

Cordé and Dormé shared a look, and Dormé put her hand on Typho's arm.

"We'll accompany you, Senator," Typho said. "Captain, perhaps one other guard?"

"I'm coming, too," Versé said before her aunt could speak.

Padmé and Mariek shared a look. It had been months since the captain of her guard had seen her husband.

"A short visit?" Mariek asked.

"Yes," Padmé said. "No more than a week."

"Very well," she replied. "We'll send all the guards but Sergeant Typho and myself to Naboo on a shuttle, and Varbarós can fly us and get to see as much of Alderaan as she wants."

"Thank you," Padmé said. She turned to Cordé. "Can we reorganise the crates on the way? I hate to make more work, but we'll be visiting a queen, so we may need to dig out some of the formal outfits, and I know those are on the bottom."

"We can manage," Cordé said. "I made an inventory list, so if we need to find anything, Artoo should be able to track down the crate it's in pretty quickly."

"Excellent," Padmé said. "Thank you all for being flexible. Senator Organa has been very helpful, and I think this invitation is as much from him as it is from his wife. I am glad that I am able to accept it, and I know it's because you are willing to let me."

Padmé made sure to talk to each of the departing guards individually. Then she went back into her room to comm Senator Organa and inform him of her decision. He relayed his pilot's travel plans and gave her the time for departure, then told her he would see her soon.

With that done, Padmé pulled out the private transmitter she used to contact Sabé and initiated a call.

"There's been a slight change of plans," Padmé said when her friend's face appeared. "Nothing disastrous. We've been invited to Alderaan for a few days."

"By the senator?" Sabé asked.

"By the queen, his wife," Padmé told her. "Though I imagine the idea was his. I can't imagine why she'd know anything about me if he didn't tell her."

"Does that change our procedure?" Sabé and Tonra were also returning to Naboo for the recess but had planned to travel on their own.

"I've been considering a few changes for when the next session begins," Padmé said. "We can talk about it in detail when we are back on Naboo, but I think if you wanted to, you could come to Alderaan with me. You and Tonra both."

There was a pause while Sabé considered it. Padmé knew she was smart enough to hear all the things she wasn't saying. Coruscant wasn't as dangerous as they had expected it to be, and perhaps Sabé's efforts would be better spent doing something other than posing as Tsabin and chasing ghosts and slicers through the newsnets.

"It would be nice to be myself again for a little while,"

Sabé said. "And I don't imagine that Tonra would complain about the stop, if he got to be a senatorial guard again."

"I don't know how much guarding there will be to do," Padmé said. "But I'm always glad to see him."

Sabé stepped to the side, and Tonra himself appeared on the holo-emitter. He must have been standing right beside her. Padmé knew that Sabé probably told him everything she said anyway, and she supposed it was more efficient if he just listened in the first place. It made the closet very cramped, but they clearly neither minded their closeness nor minded that she knew.

"I don't mind the stop," Tonra said. "May I use the royal ship to send transmissions to my family while we're on the way? I haven't been able to communicate with them very much, but I'd like to tell them about the delay."

"Of course," Padmé said.

Sabé stepped back into the frame, and Padmé relayed all of the departure information to her. They decided it would be easier if Sabé and Tonra arrived at the residence tonight, after it got dark, and then they could board the ship tomorrow with everyone else. The familiar feelings of paranoia crept up Padmé's spine as they made their plans, but she tried not to pay them too much attention. Quarsh Panaka had never been able to silence those feelings, even if there was no immediate threat, and while his dedication had saved lives, it had not come without cost. She would not want to blindly follow his example.

Once everything was settled, Padmé said her farewells

– with considerably more enthusiasm than usual, since they would all be reunited shortly – and ended the transmission. She notified the house droids that there would be two more for dinner and breakfast and that additional beds would have to be made up. Then she wrote to her parents and to the queen to inform them of her delay and the reason for it.

Dormé stuck her head into the room.

"Versé's going to teach us how to cheat at Sabacc. Would you like to come?" she asked.

"I would love to," Padmé said. She was already pretty familiar with the standard cheats, but it was possible Versé had picked up something new, and in any case, Padmé never liked to say no to time spent with friends.

CHAPTER 16

Alderaan was blue and green from orbit, with puffy white clouds in the stratosphere that obscured the view of the ground below. Though the general biome and ecological makeup were similar to that of Naboo, Alderaan had no moon and there could be no mistaking the two, even from this far away. The boomerang-shaped Naboo Royal Starship waited for landing clearance, giving all those aboard enough time to take a good look at the planet below. The world spun, and the ship passed into its night side. Now there was no possible way of confusing Alderaan with Naboo: the lights that indicated population centres gave them away.

"We're getting our landing clearance now," Varbarós said to Sabé and everyone who was in general earshot.

Sabé had spent most of the trip in the cockpit, watching the pilot as she worked the controls. She knew that Padmé would be happy to see her, but she still didn't know the new handmaidens very well, and she didn't want to get in the way of their routines as they prepared for a royal visit. She hadn't been in a J-class ship for more than a year, and she enjoyed having the time to refamiliarise herself with the controls, and with Varbarós.

She was telling the story of extricating Tonra from the clutches of their holojournalist source Kooib-s Guvar when the control tower at the Alderaanian capital of Aldera finally replied with their clearance orders. Sabé watched as Varbarós expertly navigated the descent to the landing platform. They landed at sunrise, which meant skirting the night side of the planet and coming down just across the light line. The platform was unmissable in the early morning light, even with the sun behind them, and Varbarós set the ship down so delicately that only Sabé's knowledge of the craft's operation indicated they were no longer flying.

"Thank you, Varbarós," Sabé said. "Don't get into too much trouble while we're at the palace."

"I'll do my best," Varbarós said. She would remain aboard in her quarters, though she was free to move about the cities on the planet's surface if she wanted to.

Sabé was dressed as a Naboo guard again, as much for simplicity's sake as anything else. She made her way from the cockpit to the debarkation ramp and met up with Tonra, also in his uniform, and Typho. The ramp descended, and they made their way down to take up positions at the bottom. As she was walking, Sabé heard the door hiss open behind her and knew that Padmé had arrived.

Padmé came down with Cordé and Versé flanking her while Dormé and Mariek walked behind. The handmaidens were dressed in blue and grey, and their hoods were down as a sign of respect to another world's monarch. Padmé's gown was purple, though Sabé knew that was an understatement of the complexity of the colours, since the skirt was made of dozens of layers of fabric, each a slightly different hue. It moved easily as she walked, even though it was quite a bit heavier than it looked, and didn't give her any trouble on the incline. The bodice was tightly fitted and the neckline was decorated to match the skirt, giving the impression that a well-behaved purple cloud had descended upon Padmé's shoulders. Her hair was down, but her curls were pinned here and there with white flowers brought from a Coruscant hydroponics unit. The handmaidens could have been wearing mynocks around their necks, and no one would have given them a second glance.

The party that waited to greet them on the landing pad did not include the queen. Padmé had not expected it to, as she had rarely greeted visitors anywhere but the throne room when she had ruled on Naboo. She knew that local customs would be different, but a bit of familiarity went a long way to making her feel comfortable here, and she appreciated it. This was, after all, meant to be a recreational visit, not a political one. Padmé was very much looking forward to the break.

Instead of the queen, it was Senator Organa who waited for them, with a small complement of guards standing around him. They appeared to be entirely ceremonial, and upon closer inspection, Padmé wasn't even sure that they carried weapons.

She knew Alderaan was peaceful, much like Chandrila, but she had expected a small show of force.

"Senator," said Organa when they were all standing on the platform. "Welcome to Alderaan."

"Thank you," Padmé said. "Your world is a beautiful one."

"Come," he said, smiling. "I know you didn't make the journey just to see me."

"To be fair, I see you with some frequency," Padmé said, and returned the gesture.

He spoke to her as he did when they met in his office to discuss Senate operations off the clock – easily and relaxed, and she met his informality in kind. She didn't know if it was just his nature or if Alderaan was more laid-back about this sort of thing. She had expected a hereditary monarchy to be *more* formal, not less, but she knew she'd find out soon enough what the common procedures were. She followed Organa into the airspeeder, and Cordé and Mariek came with her. Everyone else would follow in a second vehicle.

The speeders travelled at a brisk pace towards the palace, though not at the breakneck speeds of Coruscant traffic. In fact, traffic around the palace was quite light. Looking down, Padmé saw that there were wide avenues lined with trees, and it appeared that the most common way to get around was to walk on those paths. At this time of the morning, many people were out, and Padmé could see clumps of them, presumably stopped for friendly conversation, either standing along the edges of the paths or sitting down in any of the several little gardens that were plotted out along the way. This left the sky refreshingly clear.

"Air traffic picks up as you get further from the palace," Organa said when Padmé commented on it. "Especially when you go towards the shipping platforms. But we try to keep the view intact as much as possible."

"I can understand why," Mariek said. "It's an excellent view."

"It reminds me of home, a bit," Cordé said. "Only our mountains are gentler, and our capital is ringed by waterfalls."

"I have seen holos," Organa said. "Naboo is a lovely place, as well, but I suppose we're all rather partial to our own homes."

The airspeeder landed on a small pad, and everyone got off. Senator Organa escorted them into the palace via the main entrance, and they made their way towards the throne room.

The hallways of the Alderaanian palace were wide and welcoming. Nothing about them was built to intimidate or dominate. In a galaxy where those with power so often built upward, each layer covering over the sins of the one beneath it in a blind reach towards the stars, the sprawling layout spoke of honesty and ownership and, moreover, of stewardship and responsibility.

Before long they reached the great double doors that led to the throne room itself, and beyond that a blue-carpeted pathway that stretched towards a pair of thrones, though only one of them was occupied.

"Senator, assembly," Organa said, "allow me to introduce the Queen of Alderaan, Breha Organa."

Padmé's check of protocol on the inbound flight had indicated that a former monarch need not bow to the Queen of Alderaan, but she inclined her head to be polite. She knew that behind her, her retinue would flawlessly execute the protocols they had been assigned.

"Your Majesty," Bail Organa said with a profound sort of affection that made Padmé's heart flip, "it is my honour to present my colleague from the Galactic Senate of the Republic, representing the sovereign system of Naboo and its sector, Senator Padmé Amidala."

Padmé took a step forwards, and Breha made eye contact with her for the first time. The Queen of Alderaan was older than Padmé by more than ten years, but she had an ageless look to her that Padmé recognised was the result of an excellent team of stylists. She wore a high-necked gown of silver and blue, with a wide skirt and a flat reinforced bodice to cover the pulmonodes that Padmé knew kept her alive. Her braid was twisted up on the top of her head, with the crown of Alderaan woven right into it, and she wore a veil down her back that covered the rest of her dark hair.

"We are pleased you could come and visit us," Breha said. Her voice was vibrant and pleasant to the ear, and she spoke as one who was accustomed to drawing attention to herself. "Planetary politics do not leave me much time for travelling offworld, and I am always glad to welcome my husband's colleagues here instead."

"I recall those limitations," Padmé said. She had left her planet only at gravest need, and even then under protest. "A senator has a bit more free time, but the difference is only recognisable because I have seen the schedule from your side, as well."

"Indeed," Breha said. "I know you have come straight from your ship, but you have arrived in time for a late breakfast on the terrace, and if we go right away, we will see the last bit of the sunrise on the lake."

If they went back to their rooms now, they would never be oriented to the right time. Padmé would just accept the invitation and hope that Alderaanian caf was effective.

"That sounds marvellous," she said.

Breha came down off the terrace and took Padmé's arm. She quickly introduced a few of her assembled ministers, and Padmé introduced Mariek, nearly tripping over "Captain Panaka," because to both of them, that name still belonged to someone else. After a quick check to make sure their skirts were not about to tangle – both of them were professionals – the queen led them all towards the back of the throne room and through the door there. Padmé looked back at her handmaidens and realised that Bail had contrived to walk next to Sabé while Tonra followed with Typho by his side. She supposed she should have expected as much. It wasn't as though Sabé was going to give away any trade secrets.

It was a short walk to the terrace, and Breha still pointed out several different pieces of art that Padmé wanted to come back and take a longer look at later. She might have lingered by a particularly intricate water sculpture, but her traitorous stomach betrayed her and emitted a quiet rumble.

"Here we are," Breha said, leading them under a high arch and back into the sunlight.

The view was breathtaking. A lake, much like she might find on Naboo, spread its fingers out between differ-ent mountains, its glassy surface reflecting the sun, just as Breha had promised. The differences from Naboo's terrain began almost at the waterline, where the steep green peaks of mountains sprang up in place of Naboo's gentler hills. They were tall and snowcapped, and one of them was wreathed by clouds like the ones Padmé had seen from orbit.

"That's Appenza Peak," Breha said. She placed a hand on her chest when she spoke, and Padmé thought the ges-ture looked automatic. "It's the most famous mountain on Alderaan."

"It's beautiful," Padmé said.

"And treacherous." Senator Organa came close to draw out his wife's chair and hand her into it. His fingers rested in hers for a moment longer than was truly necessary.

Breha directed them all to their chairs, and food was

brought. The caf was, as hoped, effective, and Padmé felt her mind clearing a little bit as the chemicals recharged her brain.

"That mountain is the one that took my lungs and heart," Breha said quietly once her husband was safely out of earshot and engaged in a discussion with Sabé and Mariek.

"From everything I have heard of you, your heart was not the mountain's to take," Padmé said.

"Oh, I am sure there are songs about it," Breha said. "How I gave my heart to Alderaan. Only this time the poets are being literal. And a bit gruesome. Though I suppose I am the one who decided not to regrow my skin."

"We all show our dedication in separate ways," Padmé said. "The office of Queen of Naboo requires a certain suspension of self. Sometimes I feel like I am still pulling my individuality back in, though there are of course many who would argue that I was too personal in my actions as monarch."

"It is refreshing to know that elected monarchs and hereditary ones share similar critiques," Breha said. "When I refused the skin grafts, they said I was being too showy."

The minister of culture, sitting to Padmé's left, was turning a little green, so Breha changed the subject to spare his stomach.

They spoke of the intricacies of being queen, delighting in the aspects of their rulerships that were the same and dissecting all the ways they were different. Senator Organa interrupted at one point to tell the story of the first time he was presented at the royal court, and Mariek responded by telling hers. By the time everyone was finished eating and the tables were cleared off, Padmé was even more glad that she had come.

"We have nothing else planned for the day, if you and your people would prefer to rest," Breha said, leaning back in her chair and holding up her face to Alderaan's clear sun. "There will be concerts and tours of Aldera's galleries, as well as a trip up one of our gentler mountains to look forward to."

Padmé looked down the table and saw Cordé link her fingers in her lap, which was the sign that indicated splitting up would be all right.

"If you could show anyone who would like to rest to their rooms?" Padmé said. "For my part, I would like to return to some of the artwork we passed. I get the feeling I could spend a lifetime looking at pieces here and never see everything."

"I would be happy to walk with you," Breha said. A minister – Padmé thought of finance, but she looked a great deal like the minister of agriculture, so Padmé wasn't sure – made as if to protest and then decided against it.

They made their way back to the water sculpture, and Padmé lost herself in contemplation of it. Incorporating shape, aesthetic, and sound, the sculpture was fascinating from every angle and equally interesting when Padmé closed her eyes.

"I have been thinking about what you said about suspension of self," Breha said when Padmé opened her eyes again.

Clearly, she had not wished to interrupt, but now they walked again. "It is almost the opposite for me. Being queen required my entire self, treacherous mountain or no. Maybe that is the greatest difference between our styles of government."

"Well," said Padmé. "I don't have much say in my successor. In fact, I am encouraged to be as neutral as possible in public."

Breha laughed. "You're correct about that," she said. "Bail and I have talked about it extensively. My mother gave birth to me, but my father was onworld for her entire pregnancy and for several months afterwards. Bail doesn't have that kind of flexibility, and we're reluctant to rely on certain ministers to give up power if we have to cede it to them for a brief period."

Padmé recalled the minister of finance – or agriculture – and agreed with Breha's thought process. Maintaining a rulership, whether inherited or elected, was a balancing act, and giving power away was much easier than taking it back. Breha could trust her husband to be selfless, but others might give in to temptation.

"What will you do?" Padmé asked.

"We haven't made that decision yet," Breha said. "As long as there is continuation of the name Organa, the old houses will accept it."

"My sister just had a baby, her first," Padmé said. "That's the only reason I hesitated before accepting your invitation. It's put me in a mind to think about the future in a different sort of way than I usually do."

"My mother told me that she had a similar shift in her thinking after I was born," Breha said. "And I imagine that I will, too, however my child comes to me."

"Sola has no interest in a partner," Padmé said. "It's normal enough on Naboo. I think I would like what my parents have, though. Or some version of it. I'm not sure I want to mix politics and family, but I suppose it depends on a great many things."

"That's one benefit of a nonhereditary monarchy," Breha said, a smile in her eyes. "Your children aren't bound to politics the way mine are."

They paused for a moment in front of a landscape painting. It was Appenza Peak, but the colours were bleak and dangerous, and the lake was dark and cold-looking beneath it.

"Come," said Breha. "If you liked the water sculpture, you should see and hear the air work the artist has done."

Padmé let the Queen of Alderaan take her arm again. She followed Breha's easy pace and was led out onto a new terrace, though this one was much more sheltered than the one where they'd breakfasted. The reason was immediately apparent as soft sounds reached Padmé's ear. Before she realised the full scope of the air sculpture, she could hear its gentle music, soaring under the bright new morning of clear blue skies and unceasing Alderaanian winds.

"Naboo and Alderaan have a great deal in common," Padmé said. "We both place high value on arts and good government."

"And we're both pacifists," Breha said. "Though I have heard that Naboo is installing defensive weaponry."

"An ion pulse," Padmé said. There had never been any attempt to keep it a secret. "The Trade Federation has a long memory and a seemingly infinite number of droids."

"I suppose it is easy to stand here, on a world that hasn't seen conflict in generations, and judge you," Breha said. "And yet I will not."

"Naboo did not make this decision lightly," Padmé said. "I lost one of my dearest advisors because he wanted firmer measures and I would not allow them, and my parents are still furious that we're doing anything at all. But we had to do something."

"I don't know what we would do," Breha said. "But I must confess: I have begun to think about it."

Padmé didn't ask for details. There were some things each planet – each planet's ruler – had to tackle on its own.

"My only advice is to prioritise that which your planet holds the most dear," Padmé said. "For Naboo, that was art and our own lives, so we reached a compromise." She remembered Quarsh Panaka and added: "Just don't get so fixated that you forget to be flexible."

"Alderaan is old, and bound by a great many traditions," Breha said. "But we can change if we have to."

Padmé didn't answer, and the two of them stood silent, listening to the wind.

CHAPTER 17

The week on Alderaan was almost a true holiday. There was no danger to speak of and no set schedule, though both of the senators had to block off time to go over their correspondence, and the queen had to maintain the smooth operation of her government. Outside of those times, however, a feeling of almost indulgent idleness overwhelmed Sabé, and she wasn't entirely sure she liked it. Hers had been a busy life since she'd passed the first of Captain Panaka's tests all those years ago, and for the past year, her mind had been almost constantly at work. To stop all of that now was, to say the least, unsettling. At one point, during an evening concert in one of Aldera's many music halls, she linked fingers with Tonra for a whole minute before he looked at her and she remembered they were in public. Sabé was not a particularly reserved creature by nature, but she had cultivated a certain persona, and breaking out of it was very strange.

"Are you trying to make something up to me?" Tonra asked a bit later, catching her hands and holding them above her head.

"No," she said, then: "Maybe? I don't know. I am not embarrassed."

"I know that," Tonra said. He laughed.

"Stop laughing at me," she demanded.

"You said you weren't embarrassed!" he said.

"Well I am now!" She pulled out of his grip, squirmed out from underneath him, and sat on the edge of the bed.

They were in his room because she was sharing with Dormé, but since they were all guests of the queen, Tonra rated a suite on account of his rank. No one had bothered to correct the rather staid room assignments given out by the protocol droid that served as Breha's chamberlain. Compared with the apartment on Coruscant, it was unspeakably luxurious. Tonra let her have some space. He was very good at this, and usually she was, too, but with the decrease in tension everywhere else in her life, she barely knew how to handle herself, let alone someone else.

"I like you like this," he said. "The part where you have feelings and let me see them right away."

"It won't last," she said.

"I know," he said. "You can like something even when you know it's not going to last."

Sabé thought about queens and terms of office and criminal trials for credit-obsessed despots, and then realised that might not be what he was talking about.

"I'll be fine," he promised. "Come back."

"You have terrible timing, Captain," she said, sliding between the sheets. "You should have waited until I was finished figuring everything out."

"Probably," he conceded.

By the time the sun came up, Sabé was feeling almost like her old self. It was their last day on Alderaan. Due to travel times and orbital mechanics, they were leaving just after Alderaanian sundown to arrive on Naboo at midday. They'd be tired, but that was normal for interplanetary travel, and Sabé was looking forward to finally getting home.

She slid out of bed and got dressed, then went back to her room. Sabé went into the washroom and finished her preparations for the day. She had selected a long ivory tunic with a wide blue belt to wear over leggings in the same colour, and her regular boots. By the time she came back into the bedroom, Dormé had returned and was already clad in a set of green robes. Since she didn't have to wear the hood up, she took a bit more time with her hair, but long practise had made her efficient.

"Padmé would like you to have breakfast with her," Dormé said. "It will just be the two of you."

Handmaidens were the souls of discretion, which meant that Sabé and Dormé didn't have much to gossip about. She missed the ease of the relationships she'd had with her cadre, but she respected Dormé and the others too much to make a fuss.

"Thank you," Sabé said. "Do you need help packing while you see to the senator's things?"

"I'll be all right, thank you," she said. "The robes make travelling fairly easy."

A handmaiden's travel case was usually about the size of one holding a single outfit of Padmé's, thanks to Naboo's unique style, which Sabé knew quite well, but there was never any harm in being polite.

She went down the hall to the suite where Padmé was staying and knocked. A droid opened the door and admitted Sabé after a brief moment of mechanical contemplation.

"Good morning!" Padmé hadn't dressed for the day yet, indicating that this breakfast was quite informal.

"The same to you," Sabé replied.

"Come and sit," Padmé said, indicating the table where two steaming bowls were waiting.

Padmé's suite was one room bigger than Sabé's because it included a receiving room, which was where they were to eat. Like every other room in the palace – and on all of Alderaan, as far as Sabé could tell – it was elegantly decorated in a minimalist yet beautiful style. The windows looked out over the city, but even that view was pretty.

Sabé sat down and waited for Padmé to do the same before she began to eat. Padmé sprinkled some of the sour berries that were currently in season into her bowl, but Sabé passed on them when offered.

"I know I said we would talk on Naboo," Padmé said. "But I thought here might be better."

It would be hard for them to arrange a private conversation when they were home. Sabé had seen Padmé's schedule, and it was already stacking up.

"Are you going to go back to Coruscant?" Sabé asked.

"I am, for at least one more session," Padmé said. "Working with Senators Organa and Mon Mothma, I have seen what it takes to be good at this. I've learned that I can be that adaptable, but I don't know if I want to be. They can reduce policy to ideas, and I have trouble forgetting the people who will be affected. At the same time, I also don't know who Naboo would send in my stead. The queen might think I am the best choice, but I am not so sure."

"We could always steal the ship," Sabé said. "I am sure we can talk Varbarós into it, and then we could go wherever we liked."

"When you're serious about something, you always start with the most ridiculous premise," Padmé said. "Does it have anything to do with the report I get from Artoo every morning about you sneaking back into your room?"

"I was hardly sneaking. That chamberlain droid did offer to switch us all on the second day, but everyone had already unpacked," Sabé told her. She paused thoughtfully, and Padmé braced for something ridiculous. "Though I suppose if we did take the ship, it would undermine all the work you've started to put into your antipiracy legislation."

Padmé made a face. She hadn't been able to form her own committee, since the official position of the Senate was that the piracy wasn't a single issue. They refused to acknowledge the pattern of attacks that indicated to Padmé that the problem was larger than a few strikes against convoys carrying food or building supplies. All she could do was continue to argue hypotheticals with Mon Mothma, and hope that when the time for real action did arrive, someone would listen to her.

"I think you might be the only person on Coruscant who reads all the Senate news," she said.

"You do it," Sabé said, as if it were obvious. "So I do."

"Do you ever wish we'd never met?" Padmé asked. Sabé froze. "I mean, do you ever wish you hadn't taken Captain Panaka's offer and just lived a private life on Naboo?"

Anyone overhearing them might be surprised at their formal manner, mistaking it for a lack of affection. In truth, the very foundation of their friendship – not to mention their personal safety on more than one occasion – nested in that formality. It was difficult to explain, particularly because they were equally good at teasing each other, but it was no less genuine just because outsiders found it unusual.

"And become third best halliket player in my family?" Sabé said. "Not for a moment."

"Your brothers are famous," Padmé pointed out.

"And I would have always been in their shadows," Sabé said. "Your shadow is much nicer, trust me."

"No matter how long I go back to Coruscant for, I think we might want to reconsider your role," Padmé continued as if there had been no diversion.

"How do you mean?" Sabé poured herself a cup of tea and added more sweetener than usual. She found the tea on Alderaan to be stronger than she preferred.

"I'm not sure that level of security is called for," Padmé said. "The newsnets have backed off, and there's been not so much as a whiff of danger since that first attempt, and that was months ago. We can think of something else for you to do, but I feel like I sent you into exile, first on Tatooine and then on Coruscant, and you could come back."

"We were going to go back to Tatooine after Coruscant," Sabé reminded her. "Tonra might have changed his mind – though I doubt it – but I haven't."

"I remember," Padmé said. She made a face like it physically pained her to continue speaking. "But I'm still hopeful the Chancellor's motion will have a better chance in its next round, and if word gets out I'm meddling on Tatooine directly, I'll be right back where I started: too much of an independent for anyone to trust. I hate having to make this kind of choice."

"I don't envy you, certainly," Sabé said. "But at the same time, I also think you should have me remain undercover for a while longer, and Tonra with me. Gunray's trial will be winding down soon, and depending on which way it goes, that will change the threats to you. If I'm at large, I can maintain my newsnet sources – and my other sources that we don't talk about – and find out what's going on."

"I hate Neimoidians," Padmé said grimly, stabbing her spoon into the bowl. It was rare for her to visibly indulge her feelings, even with Sabé, when they were offworld. "And I hate how much I hate Neimoidians."

"They've been responsible for a lot of death and suffering," Sabé said. "I think you're allowed to hate them."

"I shouldn't dismiss an entire species," Padmé said. "That kind of thinking almost tore Naboo apart, and even though it was a long time ago, it's taken forever to patch things up again."

"I don't know why anyone ever thinks they can't trust you," Sabé said. "You're so honest it hurts."

"Honestly, I think that's *why* they don't trust me," Padmé said. "They keep waiting for me to turn."

"Politics makes me tired," Sabé admitted. "It never used to, but it does now. And I still like it for some reason."

"Possibly we're too close," Padmé said, so seriously that Sabé knew it was a jest. "We've been in too long, and there's no escaping."

"Now who is being ridiculous?" Sabé asked. She drained her tea and took the last bite of her breakfast. Their stolen moment was nearly done.

"Do you like him a lot?" It was a shy question, and it didn't come from the senator but from Padmé Naberrie. "Tonra, I mean?"

"Yes," Sabé said.

"Do you like him enough?"

"I don't know," Sabé said. "We've talked about it, so it's not like I'm leading him on. And I warned him. A lot. And he's known me, us, for a long time."

"You're protecting him." It wasn't quite a question. As usual, they walked the line of their peculiar bond with perfect symmetry.

"I don't want to be callous," Sabé said. "So in a way, I am protecting myself, too."

Padmé finished her own breakfast and looked out the window. It was going to be another glorious day.

"I don't know what I'd do," Padmé said. "I've guarded my heart against everything for so long, always aware of the dynamics and the flow of power. I've been lucky to find so many people who understand that and give me that space. I'm afraid that if someone breaks through, I'll let them, and it would be catastrophic."

"It's not a reactor leak," Sabé said.

Padmé never spoke to her about matters of the heart, largely, Sabé suspected, out of respect for privacy. She wondered who Padmé was thinking of that made her do it now, or if Padmé was merely intrigued by the prospect of whatever she imagined Sabé was getting up to. She wasn't the jealous type, but she'd always been curious, and Sabé rarely did anything first.

"Maybe you should let someone break through a little bit," Sabé suggested. "To see how it goes."

"Do you really think that would work?" Padmé asked.

"It'll have to be someone who understands you," Sabé said. "Which will be a challenge to find, but if you wanted to, you could at least look."

"I might." Padmé rolled her shoulders, and the Naberrie fell away from her. "Will you help me dress?"

Sabé breathed in, completely comfortable.

"My hands are yours," she said.

It was a simple outfit for the last day, with limited jewellery and hair that was so straightforward Padmé could almost have done it herself. Sabé laid out the travelling dress, as well, for Padmé to change into when evening came. Then Cordé and Versé came in to pack. This time Sabé didn't leave. She both did and did not have a place among them, but she was going to take advantage of proximity to the senator while she could. She put a brave face on living in that apartment on Coruscant, and Tonra had always been excellent company, but she missed her friend and the feeling of self-possession Padmé always managed to conjure in her. Dormé joined them.

"Varbarós says that the ship is ready whenever you are," she reported. "She took the time to refit a few of the components that had been annoying her over the past few months, and yesterday she went on a quick trip around the system to shake everything down."

"And your guards have everything squared away." This was from Mariek, who had entered the room without knocking, because they would have missed the sound in all of their bustle.

"Excellent," Padmé said. "I hope you have all enjoyed our time here, but I must admit, I will be so happy to see the waterfalls of Theed again."

Sabé dismissed herself and went to finish her own packing. Dormé's half of the closet was empty, and it took Sabé almost no time at all to stow her own things. She hauled the carrying case out into the hallway and saw the little astromech unit coming out of Typho's room, pushing the sergeant's case on a hovercart.

"Hey," she said to get the droid's attention. He turned to aim his photoreceptor at her. "You can take mine to the ship, too, you little blue snitch."

The droid beeped something that translated vaguely to "All's fair with standard programming," and Sabé placed her case on top of Typho's.

"Thank you," she said, because she was still polite, and also because the droid had saved her life once and also helped save the entire planet on a separate occasion.

The droid chirruped and went on his way.

The day was quiet, with Padmé and Breha spending most of it in close conversation. Senator Organa sought Sabé out once again, and she didn't mind his company, either. He knew when to stop talking and when to explain every minute detail of whatever artwork she was looking at.

"Everyone who has ever seen you has underestimated you, haven't they?" he said. It was the most direct thing he had said to her all week, but she was expecting it.

"I encourage them to," she replied. "I am small. I carry only a single blaster. And I'm usually wearing something much less practical-looking than these."

She gestured at her tunic and leggings.

"The Trade Federation has ugly priorities," Organa said. "I don't talk about it much on Coruscant because it would cost me too much political capital for no good reason, but here I can be a bit more honest. I don't like the way they operate, and their willingness to use droids to kill sentient beings is unsettling."

"I'm not entirely sure what you're saying, Senator," Sabé told him.

"I'm glad she has you to protect her," he said. "I'm glad they'll always underestimate you, if they are even smart enough to figure out you exist. I'm glad she has you."

"It is my honour to serve," Sabé said, and she knew he understood.

As the day drew to a close, the last dinner was eaten and the last toast was said. They witnessed a glorious sunset over lake and snowcapped mountain peak, and then the queen and her husband escorted them to the platform where their ship awaited. Varbarós stood at the bottom of the ramp to welcome them aboard. Their farewells were brief but heartfelt, and then Senator Amidala took her formal leave of Queen Breha Organa of Alderaan.

"We thank you again for your welcome and hospitality," Padmé said. The senatorial voice was much warmer than the royal one, and Sabé knew that developing it for situations like this had been worth the effort. "We look forward to our continued joint efforts with both you and your world's senator as we work together to create and preserve a legacy of peace in the galaxy."

"We look forward to it as well," Queen Breha replied. Senator Amidala gave the smallest of bows and then boarded the ship.

As the ship climbed into orbit, Sabé took a seat in the cockpit once more and stared out into the emerging stars. They sang to her of home, and soon they were racing past her as she flew along her way.

CHAPTER 18

The covered walkways that led from Theed's royal spaceport to the palace doors had never seemed so welcoming. Each step Padmé took was farther into the familiar, and as she looked around at the much-loved architecture of the capital, she felt better than she had in months. Alderaan had been a wonderful place to visit, but it wasn't hers, and she was glad to be back on Naboo. Soon she would truly go home.

First, though, there was her meeting with the queen. Réillata had been quite gracious in her response when Padmé informed her of the invitation to visit Breha, but she knew that the Queen of Naboo was even more eager to speak with her than the Queen of Alderaan had been. Padmé understood. Her relationship with then-Senator Palpatine and his successor had been calm, save for the Invasion of Naboo, but whenever they returned to the planet, she was always ready to hear their reports.

Mariek and Typho had both begun their leave, so it was Tonra who served as their official escort to the palace, though of course Queen Réillata had sent her own guards, as well. Versé had gone with her aunt, and Varbarós had stayed with the ship, as she usually did. So they were a smaller party than they might have been, and Padmé couldn't help feeling that something she couldn't quite describe was ending.

At last, they reached the palace steps, and from there Padmé could have found the throne room in her sleep. With Cordé and Dormé trailing behind her – and Sabé even farther to the rear – she entered the bright room and bowed to the woman who waited there.

After months on Coruscant, Réillata's age no longer seemed as strange to Padmé as it had before. She assumed meeting Breha had helped with that, as well; a queen who was nearing twenty-three was young for most places in the galaxy. Naboo's culture couldn't be completely changed so quickly of course, but Breha had given Padmé a great deal of perspective on the subject. The pair of them had had lengthy conversations about experience and preparation, and while Padmé still didn't think that the system that had produced her was inherently flawed, she was more sympathetic to Réillata's idea of a second term later in her life.

"Senator Amidala," Queen Réillata said, "we are happy to receive you home and to hear what you have accomplished. Please, come and take your seat."

Padmé moved to the empty seat on the queen's right-hand side, and Dormé and Cordé flanked her. After a moment's hesitation, Sabé took the second seat on the queen's right. Together, they faced Sio Bibble across the room, and Saché was seated next to him. It was almost like old times, except no one was concealing her face.

"Governor," Padmé said politely to Bibble. She made sure not to speak with any of Queen Amidala's inflections.

"Senator, I have asked Representative Saché to speak on behalf of the planetary government along with the governor and myself," Queen Réillata said. "I understand that your rapport with her might prove beneficial. We have a lot of ground to cover, and since I denied you a true visit to your parents before you left to take up your Senate seat, I am hoping we can move quickly through our discussions."

"Thank you, Your Highness," Padmé said. It was a thoughtful gesture on the queen's part.

"Please begin," Queen Réillata said. She leaned forwards, giving all evidence of an attentive listener, and though Padmé couldn't see their faces, she knew that the queen's handmaidens were listening even closer.

"I will admit, I did not have the cleanest start to my term as senator," Padmé said. "There were a great many differences to be learned and mastered, and the orientation was long and onerous."

"I would have thought that your inclusion in the junior legislative programme might have hastened that along," Sio Bibble said.

"Alas, no. Though it did make several of the informational tours something of a rehash," Padmé said. "In any case,

I joined several committees, the better to incorporate myself into the governing body, including one headed by Senator Bail Organa of Alderaan. I like him immensely and respect him even more, but my initial motivations for working with him were a bit self-serving: he had allies that I wanted."

It felt like an eternity had passed since that first meeting, and yet in the grander scheme of things, it was almost no time at all.

"In any case, I was moderately successful in that regard," Padmé continued. "In my first year of service as senator, I have positioned myself so that my voice is respected by senators who control well-placed factions within the voting body. I am hopeful that I will continue to work well with them, though I don't know that I would be suited to leading such a faction myself, nor am I sure how it would serve Naboo's interests. Most of the factions are headed by senators from the Core, or have the backing of wealthy corporations."

"I do not envy you that position," Saché said. "It sounds terrifically complicated."

"Nor do I," said Queen Réillata. "But Naboo is grateful for your service."

"Thank you, Your Highness," Padmé said. "The motions I have helped pass deal mostly with arming convoys to deal with a wave of pirates preying on systems near hyperspace lanes in our part of the Mid Rim. These topics are not easy ones to discuss in the Senate at all. My colleagues are either

pacifists, as I would like to be, or they are in favour of prolif-
eration, and there is very little in the way of middle ground.
Furthermore, our official position is that the pirates are all
acting independently, which means that every time we deal
with them, we need new legislation."

"I am not comfortable with wide-scale arming of anyone,"
Queen Réillata said. "But I agree with you that our ideals and
our practises may not always line up. The Gungans saved us as
much as our own N-1 fighters did, and if we were true pacifists, we would have supported neither."

"That is usually the argument I make, as well," Padmé
said. "But to someone who has not been invaded, I imagine it
is difficult to picture, and I wouldn't wish it on anyone. I do
have an idea, but it will require something from Naboo, and I
would need your full support."

"Please explain," the queen said. "If we can help, I believe
we should. Do you agree, Governor?"

"I do," Sio Bibble said. "If it is within our measure."

"Naboo's recovery from the Trade Federation's invasion
was slow because we did not seek much in the way of outside
aid," Padmé said. "At the time, we decided it was the most reasonable and sustainable course, and we were proved correct.
However, we have now recovered almost fully, and I would
like to start using a portion of our food stores for charitable
ventures."

"Who are you proposing to feed?" Réillata asked.

"We don't know very much about the pirates who are currently plaguing ships in Republic hyperspace lanes," Padmé said. "But we do have some suspicions about where they originated from, even if they have left their home planets behind them. If we focus on sending aid to those planets, perhaps fewer of them will be desperate enough to turn to piracy, and those that do will be less well protected."

"Starvation was the primary cause of strife in the camps here," Sio Bibble mused. "People did all sorts of things they would never normally consider because it was the only way they could think of to feed their children."

"I agree," Saché said. "Senator, our yields may soon be even better than they were under your reign as queen. Eirtaé's early experiments have been very encouraging. She has increased the amount of blue-algae, and the farms in the south are already utilising her harvest. They've almost halved the growing season."

"That's remarkable," Padmé said. "She wrote to me about it, but it was highly technical, and I'll confess that I had so much on my mind, I didn't ask the questions I should have."

Eirtaé's letter had arrived around the time of her attempted assassination, and Padmé had forgotten about it entirely until just this moment.

"I'm sure Eirtaé won't mind explaining it to you in person," Saché said. "She's already presented her preliminary finding to the legislation, and she does it with her art, so we who aren't botanists can understand her."

It was, Padmé reflected, remarkable to hear Saché so at ease speaking her mind. She'd never been shy in private, but part of her job had involved staying out of the spotlight. Now that she was in it, she was flourishing. Padmé had never imagined her running for Queen of Naboo, but now she could see it quite clearly. If Saché wanted it, she would have Padmé's full support.

"I will have the ministers go over the exact numbers," Sio Bibble said. "But I am sure we can come up with a plan that will satisfy Your Highness and give the senator some room with which to work."

"Thank you, Governor," Padmé said.

"Your name is Sabé, is that correct?" Queen Réillata said, addressing Sabé directly.

"Yes, Your Highness," Sabé said. She showed no surprise that the queen knew her name, but Padmé knew from personal experience how good her bluff was.

"Are you here to talk about aid or arms?" the queen asked.

"Only in a manner of speaking," Sabé said. She leaned forwards so that she was in Padmé's line of vision. "Senator, with your permission?"

"Of course," Padmé said.

"I have been working as part of the senator's security detail on Coruscant," Sabé informed the queen. "Along with Captain Tonra, I have been undercover in one of the capital's seedier neighbourhoods, gathering intelligence on the public opinion of Senator Amidala."

"Is the public opinion of Coruscant so important to the senator from Naboo?" Queen Réillata asked.

"It is when it involves an attempt on the senator's life," Sabé said bluntly.

"Not the Trade Federation again?" Sio Bibble burst out. He could rarely control his emotions on the subject, but Padmé didn't blame him. He had remained on the planet when she'd gone to ask for help and, in doing so, had essentially supervised a massacre.

"We're reasonably sure it is," Sabé said. "Though our investigation is ongoing. When they realised that killing the senator might be impractical, they settled for character assassination instead. The holonews eviscerated her on every imaginable topic, and then none of the other senators would take her seriously."

"I assume this was part of the reason you needed Senator Organa?" the queen asked.

"It was," Padmé said.

"There has been a decline in threatening activity since Senator Amidala began to work so closely with Senator Organa and Senator Mon Mothma of Chandrila, but with Nute Gunray's fourth trial drawing to a close, I am reluctant to say the matter is resolved," Sabé said. "Furthermore, we don't know what will change when the trial is concluded, no matter how it ends."

"I agree," said the queen. "We must do what we can to

ensure your safety. Senator, will you walk with me along the terrace?"

"Of course, Your Highness," Padmé said, rising to her feet. Everyone else rose with her, the queen and her handmaidens a beat behind. "Governor, it was lovely to see you again," Padmé said.

"Indeed, Senator," he replied.

He bowed to Queen Réillata and strode out of the room. Saché crossed to Sabé and took her arm.

"Come," she said. "We have so much catching up to do."

She sounded so much like the enthusiastic twelve-year-old she once was, that Padmé almost believed she had no political motivations for talking with Sabé. They bowed to the queen and left.

Padmé went to the queen's side, and the two of them began the careful trek down to the terrace. The queen's dress was stiff and not the easiest to walk in.

"I sense that you are not eager to return to Coruscant," Queen Réillata said when there was no one to overhear them but their handmaidens.

"I do not wish to shirk my responsibility," Padmé assured her. "It's only that I am not sure if I am the right person for the job."

"You have given every evidence that you are perfect for the job," the queen said.

They stepped out onto the terrace, and Padmé took a

moment to enjoy the beauty of her own sun, which she had missed.

"I was viewed as something of a wild card," she admitted. "Everyone in the Senate knows that I called for the replacement of Chancellor Valourum, and because my own senator replaced him, it looks like a setup. I had to distance myself from Chancellor Palpatine to prove my own autonomy, even though he has several projects that are important to me on a personal level."

"It is this sort of dedication that I think makes you an excellent choice," the queen said.

"The perception is that I am too loyal to Naboo," Padmé said. "I went around the Senate to liberate us from the Trade Federation. There are strange undercurrents in the Senate right now. I fear that there are those among us who are starting to doubt the effectiveness of the Republic, and I am doubly afraid that unless I take great care with my actions, I will be labelled as one of them."

"They fear that if you forced the Republic's hand before, you would do it again," Queen Réillata said.

"And they are correct," Padmé said. "But I would do it for any planet, not just Naboo."

They walked to the edge of the balcony and looked out on the fields and waterfalls that surrounded Theed. There were flowers in the meadows and birds in the sky.

"I think you must return," Queen Réillata said. "You must

go back and show them that Naboo has the political maturity to do what needs to be done. As you said, I do not wish disaster on any planet, but if you can show the Senate that you will go to extreme lengths for anyone, then perhaps they will understand Naboo's loyalty remains unchanged."

"To tell you the truth, I had already decided to return," Padmé said. "I don't like backing down from a challenge or shirking my duty when I am needed. I wanted to be sure you understood the full scope of the situation."

"I do," Réillata said. "There are others I could send, but it would be another year before they were able to get results. You have done so much work already, I know, and it has been a burden to you, but you have the thanks of a grateful queen."

Padmé looked out over the vista and considered Réillata's words. She knew that she would do the exact same thing in the queen's position, though she had never faced such a dilemma during her reign.

"Do you know why I ran for a second term, Senator?" Réillata asked.

"No," Padmé said. "Though I admit I have wondered."

"I was nervous the whole time I was queen, the first go-around," Réillata said. "But I liked it. I liked helping people. By the end of my term, I had convinced myself that I wasn't helping enough. My greatest strength was my singing voice, and I thought that was a silly thing for a queen to prize. So I didn't run again, because I wasn't perfect for the part. Years

later, in the middle of a performance, I realised how ridiculous that was. I could sing arias in front of hundreds and
empathise with every person in the room. I could listen just
as well as I could speak. So I talked with my family, and I ran
again. You have been a large figure to measure up to, but I'm
not afraid any more. I hope you will continue to serve Naboo,
and I hope you will continue to enjoy it."

Padmé let the queen's words turn over in her mind. It
meant a lot, though she could not have articulated exactly
how, to hear that Réillata hadn't only been thinking of Padmé's
youth when she ran for her second term. Padmé knew she had
been a good queen and that she would have been an even better one if she'd stayed in office, but that wasn't how Naboo
operated. She had been the queen Naboo had needed her to
be. Now, it seemed, she was to be senator for the same reason, and it was up to her to compensate for any lack that she
perceived, the way that Réillata had done and continued to
do. No single system could be perfect; one method was not
inherently better than the other. Politics was not a game of
absolutes, except that those who served must never stop working as long as they held their office.

And Padmé was going to hold.

"Thank you, Your Highness," Padmé said after a long
moment of golden silence. "And thank you for hurrying
these meetings so that I could get back to my family as soon
as possible."

"It was my pleasure," the queen said. "I have heard the news about your sister. I know you must be eager to get to them."

Padmé was indeed eager. Her sister had sent a few holo-images, but that was hardly the same thing.

"I am, Your Highness," she said.

"We have discussed all we need to, Senator," Réillata said. "I have much to think about and so do you, but there is little point in your waiting around the palace for answers when a simple holomessage can reach you. Go to your family."

"Thank you, Your Highness," Padmé said.

She bowed one last time and then turned to lead Cordé and Dormé back into the palace. She commed Sabé to tell her that she was setting off, and then Tonra led them to the speeder Queen Réillata had provided for their use while they were on Naboo. Padmé was too excited to send a holo to her mother, so she typed a note instead and let her parents know that she'd be home in time for dinner.

CHAPTER 19

The house that Padmé Naberrie had grown up in was far from the capital of Naboo. Like most Naboo houses, it was made of stone and capped with domed roofs. Her father, Ruwee, had built it himself, before he became a lecturer at the university, and her mother had imbued the cold stone with that sense of place and time and belonging that true homes were founded on. It was large enough for the entire family, which had recently expanded, but small enough that Padmé didn't feel like she was stepping into another grandiose residence every time she crossed the threshold.

It was home. She had never lived anywhere else that was as warm and as filled with love. She was grateful for the official residences that Naboo had provided for her, but they were never hers. This was the house she had dreamed of when she was lonely on Coruscant as a member of the junior legislative programme, and this was the house she wanted to always return to, for as long as she could.

The courtyard was empty when Padmé, Tonra, and Dormé arrived. They each brought only a small case with them and didn't wear anything that marked them as in service to the government. Tonra still carried his blaster openly, and Padmé could only assume that Dormé had hers tucked away somewhere as she did herself, but Naboo was at peace and she didn't think there was a real need of it. Padmé intended to leave her weapon in her room for the duration of her stay. R2-D2 had come with them and remained on the ground while they took the stairs towards the front door. Jobal Naberrie waited there with a big smile on her face.

"Hello, Mum," Padmé said, and whole months' worth of frustrations melted away.

"Padmé," Jobal said, and pulled her daughter in for a hug. "Oh, it's wonderful to see you. Come in, come in."

Padmé brushed her fingers against the piece of carved wood that was attached to the doorpost as she crossed the threshold and stepped directly into her father's arms.

"Dad," she said as he hugged her, and that was all the greeting either of them needed.

Jobal led the way into a sitting room that was lined with tall windows. The walls were painted blue, and bowls of red flowers decorated various architectural flourishes. There were chairs and a table under one of the windows, with a steaming teapot and a tray of little sandwiches. But Padmé had eyes only for one thing.

"Sola," she said, and crossed the room in a flurry of rustling fabric to kneel before her sister.

"Hello, Padmé," Sola said. She smiled and turned the

blanket-wrapped bundle in her arms so that Padmé could have a clearer view. "This is Ryoo."

"She's beautiful," Padmé said, reaching out to touch her niece's face.

"She screams for two hours in the middle of the night for no logical reason," Sola said. "But yes. Would you like to hold her?"

Padmé did, and carefully took the sleeping baby from her sister's arms. She sat down on the sofa next to Sola and stared into her niece's face for a moment before she heard her father give a soft cough. Belatedly, Padmé realised that she needed to make some introductions.

"Mum, Dad, you remember Captain Tonra?" she said. "He fought in the Battle of Naboo and has been with me ever since."

"Congratulations on your promotion, Captain," Ruwee said.

"And this is Dormé," Padmé continued. "She is my wardrobe mistress, among other things."

They all knew what those other things would involve.

"Thank you, for staying with our daughter, both of you. Please, sit down. We try to keep the formalities of politics at a minimum here, or no one would ever get anything done," Jobal said. Tonra and Dormé did as they were told while Padmé suppressed a laugh. "We had hoped the danger would be less on Coruscant, now that Padmé was no longer queen."

"It is," Dormé assured her. "But we are still being careful."

"I'm glad to see Captain Panaka's legacy continues," Ruwee said. "I didn't always agree with his methods, but he kept everyone safe so that they could keep my daughter safe, so I came to understand him."

"He visits for lunch, sometimes," Sola said. "I try to be out of the house before they start shouting at each other."

Noticing Tonra's confused look, Padmé said, "My dad and Captain Panaka like to debate the necessity of military action. The Royal Security Forces grew in size under my term, and I don't think my father has ever forgiven me for it."

"It was necessary, sadly," Ruwee said. "And it saved us, I know. But surely we can scale back again?"

"Ruwee, let them sit for more than two minutes before you start," Jobal said.

"It's all right," Dormé said. "Occupational hazard."

"And Dad is much more reasonable than most of the senators I work with," Padmé said. "But don't worry. All of my friends are pacifists."

She'd meant it as a joke, but as soon as she said it, she realised how comforting it was, even when she was butting heads with Mon Mothma. It reminded her of where her aim was set and of the sort of senator she wanted to be. In her arms, the baby cooed, and Padmé looked down. Ryoo had woken up but hadn't started crying, so Padmé made faces at her in an attempt to make her smile. There was a lot to be said for this form of negotiation, as well.

"Did the queen give you any indication of how long you would be needed in the Senate?" Sola asked. She stood up and went to the table where the teapot was sitting. "Tea, anyone?"

"No," Padmé said. "Just that she wants me to go back. And yes, please."

Sola poured for everyone, having long ago learned that when Padmé brought home people she worked with, they tended to follow her lead regardless of what Jobal declared about informality. It was one of the most common Karlini teas and didn't need any additives to improve or change the flavour. Although it wasn't Padmé's favourite, it was rarely exported, and therefore drinking it was one of the quiet rituals that confirmed she had come home.

"Will you?" Jobal asked.

Padmé hesitated. She looked at her mother and father, at the walls of the house – still her most comfortable place in the galaxy – and felt the weight of the baby in her arms. Ryoo had worked an arm free of her wrappings and was grabbing at Padmé's necklace. She tucked the piece into her collar – it was too precious for babies – and offered up one of the baubles from her hair instead. Ryoo put it directly into her mouth, and Padmé retrieved it quickly. She was not up to speed on this, clearly. Her sister laughed and provided one of the baby's toys.

"Yes, though I don't know for how long," Padmé said. "The queen has given me her trust, and I have many projects underway on Coruscant. I miss home of course, but . . ."

"If you like, we won't bring it up again," Ruwee said. "You can help me in the gardens instead."

"Well it's far too nice a day to spend indoors," Sola agreed. "Let me get Ryoo's sun protection, and we can all go out. Even if Dad doesn't conscript any of us, he can lecture us while he does things, and we all know he likes that almost as much."

"I'm a builder and a lecturer," Ruwee said. "What did you expect?"

Padmé handed the baby off to her mother and went to walk with Dormé as they all went out to the gardens.

"Are you all right?" she asked, speaking with enough volume that Tonra heard her, as well. "I know my family visits can be a little awkward, but they really do mean to be inclusive. I meant to warn you, but once we arrived on the planet, everything happened so quickly."

"It's fine, my lady," Tonra said. "Sabé did let us know what to expect."

"It's just an adjustment," Dormé said. "And frankly, it's nicer than the Senate's idea of inclusion."

"All right," Padmé said. "But if you want to go, you can

just go. Mum will have prepared guest rooms for you if you need to get away from all this Naberrie family charm."

"Why, Senator," Dormé put a hand to her chest as if she were in the deepest shock. "What a thing to say!"

The visit went well. As promised, Padmé's parents didn't bring up her senatorial future again, and all it cost her was two hours of sanding down beams for the new greenhouse that Ruwee was building so that the local school could have flowers to study and draw during the cold season. She brought R2-D2 over to help, but the droid was immediately distracted by the baby, and instead of contributing to the building project, he spent his time entertaining Ryoo with a variety of noises and, until chastened, displays of controlled lightning.

"Why do you have an astromech unit?" Sola asked, once R2-D2 was playing with her daughter in a way less likely to result in electroshock or a short circuit.

"Artoo is a hero of Naboo," Padmé said. "He repaired our hyperdrive when we were running the Trade Federation blockade, and he was an important part of the battle to retake the planet. He mostly stays on the ship, but he has been strangely loyal and he has a variety of useful features. Also, sometimes he just makes me smile."

"Well, Artoo," Sola told the little droid, "you need direction as a babysitter, but I suppose you'll do."

The droid chirped at her and then returned his full attention to Ryoo.

"You're not really in favour of arming civilian traders to help them fend off pirates, are you?" Sola asked, her voice quiet. "That's almost exactly how the Trade Federation blockade began."

"No," Padmé said. "The other senators I work with are entirely anti-aggression, to the point of non-defence. But they're mostly from Core Worlds. They're smart and experienced, but I think this is a place where I outpace them, and I haven't found a way to gracefully pull them up on it yet."

"So you're ungracefully playing the other side of their arguments?" Sola said. "That could be dangerous."

"It's not as serious as that," Padmé said. "We keep those debates off the floor, so there isn't a record of them beyond what we ourselves make. It's more like a dress rehearsal, so that when Mon Mothma or Bail Organa takes the matter to the rest of the Senate, they're aware of how the discussion might go."

"Don't you ever take the matter to the floor?" Sola asked.

"Not yet," Padmé admitted. "It galls me, I'll tell you that, but I've decided to wait a bit longer before I address the Senate directly over a motion I've written. They all remember what happened the first time I addressed them, and that sort of government shake-up isn't easily forgiven."

"You saved us," Sola said. "That's what happened."

"I know," Padmé said.

"You had better go and rescue Dormé before Dad adopts

her," Sola said, looking across the garden to where Ruwee was loudly proclaiming that Dormé was the best carver he had seen in ten years. "Your friends are always so talented."

"That's how they end up with me," Padmé said. "It seems mercenary to surround yourself with people who are good at things that you are not with such intention, but it does keep life interesting."

She got up and went to see if Dormé needed rescuing. Her handmaidens could usually handle themselves, but expert assassins and cunning politicians were one thing, and Padmé's parents were something else. Dormé held a small vibroblade and was carving scrolling vines into the parts of the beams that would be visible from inside the greenhouse.

"She has such steady hands," Ruwee said. "And she can see a whole pattern in her head and then make it fit where she needs it to go."

"What do you think the wardrobe mistress does?" Padmé asked. Dormé smiled.

"Well, when my daughter is finished with galactic politics, you won't have any trouble finding something to do here," Ruwee said.

"Thank you," Dormé said. "My great-grandmother taught me how to carve. It's easier for her now that she is older, and sewing makes her joints hurt. I'm looking forward to seeing her when Cordé and I switch places in a couple of days."

Dormé finished carving the vine and went back to add leaves and flowers to it.

"I meant to ask," Ruwee said. "How is Sabé? We were hoping she might come with you, but I suppose she has her own visits?"

"She is well," Padmé said. "And yes, she does. Saché took her off to see the others, I think, and then she'll go home."

"Your friends are doing marvellous work here," Ruwee said. "In the legislature, with those children, with music, and I've read the initial reports of the blue-algae project. It's very heartening."

"I'm proud of them," Padmé said.

"You know," Ruwee said, "no one has to be amazing forever. It's perfectly all right to save a planet or two and then retire to being normal for the rest of your life."

Padmé took up the sander again. It was easier to think on her father's terms when she was helping him with his heart's work.

"It is strange to see my friends go on to do such wonderful things without me," Padmé said. "And Sola, too. Ryoo is wonderful, and I think just as much a part of Naboo's future as Eirtaé's blue-algae. But I don't know what I would do, if I came back now. I want a family, but not yet, and the only skill I have truly cultivated is politics."

"You are an excellent aid worker," Ruwee pointed out.

"And that's what I am doing in the Senate now," Padmé said. "Or trying to."

"You're always going to go back," he said.

"Yes." Padmé felt oddly energized. "I know it's not the life you wanted for me, and I know it's not the life I want for myself – at least not forever – but it's still good, and I still need to do it."

"You always have our support." Ruwee said as Jobal appeared with more tea.

Padmé took a cup from the tray and let the smell of it bring back memories of a thousand cups that had come before it. Hopefully, there would be more than a thousand cups in her future. They continued to work on the greenhouse, so that the young artists of Naboo would have flowers when there were no flowers to be had.

CHAPTER 20

Padmé spent her last night on Naboo back in the royal palace. The queen had been so understanding of the time Padmé needed with her family that when Réillata asked if she would spend the last few days of her furlough in the capital for further discussions, Padmé could not refuse her. Now the time for talk was ended, and Padmé was ready to face the Senate again. She had the full backing of her planet, the support of her queen, and almost all of her own confidence.

She was packing again, but this time she packed with certain intent. Sabé was with her, along with the others, and together they were curating a new collection of gowns that would fit the image Senator Amidala was trying to project. Padmé had banished most of the bright colours regretfully, save for a few accent pieces she couldn't bear to part with, but it was with a certain amount of relief that she sent all the larger headpieces into storage, along with the most ornate of the gowns.

With Dormé's eye for line and function, they constructed a wardrobe based on darker shades of blue, green, and maroon. All of the dresses were still heavily embroidered with Naboo designs, and many consisted of multiple layers, but they were easier to sit in and easier to walk in. Padmé would be able to turn her head and turn a corner on her own. The practicality of Dormé's designs extended to support garments and footwear.

Cordé had begun sketching new styles for Amidala's hair that relied less on structural aids and more on discreet pins. The pins – designed and made by Cordé's jeweller sister – could, in a pinch, double as weapons or tools, yet they were small enough to make it through most security scans. Versé and Sabé had worked together on outfits for even more mobility: jumpsuits and the like that could be combined with dramatic capes to remind everyone of Amidala's status without getting in her way.

"It'll move better than the battle dress," Padmé said, holding the white trousers up in front of her.

"And it's probably easier to climb in than the guard uniform is," Sabé added. She kept a straight face, but her eyes were shining. Typho had been sworn to silence, but they all would have given a great deal to have seen Padmé come down out of that tree.

Sabé was addressing her own clothes. They had given her a guard uniform, as well as two sets of robes in case she was needed as a handmaiden. She had commissioned a new pair of boots – carefully scuffing them once the cobbler was gone so that they didn't look so pristine – and a utility belt, in addition to the one that went with her uniform. Her clothes ranged from practical trouser-and-tunic combinations that were scarcely embellished at all to three higher-end outfits in case she required them.

"Are you sure about the gowns?" Sabé asked. "I can't exactly wear them in my neighbourhood."

"We might need you at short notice," Padmé said. "I know it's unlikely, but we have the cargo allowance for it, and this way, you will be prepared for all eventualities."

"Fair enough," Sabé said.

There was a knock on the door, and Mariek came in. Padmé had barely seen her while they were on Naboo, and she was glad that the captain of her guard had returned.

"Are you about ready to send all this down to the ship?" she asked.

"Yes, Aunt," Versé said.

Cordé set the last few fragile pieces in their boxes, and Dormé checked the seal on the crates. When everything was secured, the crates went onto repulsorlift sleds, and Mariek left to supervise the loading. She had only just stepped out when there was another knock on the door and Saché stepped in.

"Hello," Padmé said warmly. She had seen her friends during her furlough, at their concerts, homes, and art shows, but it was never too much.

"I came to ask if you are having dinner with the queen tonight," Saché asked.

"I'm not," Padmé said. "She had a previous engagement with the trade ministers, and I didn't want to infringe."

Also Padmé had eaten with the trade ministers often enough already.

"Well, then I have an invitation for you, for all of you," Saché said. "I am hosting a dinner party. I have the southwest hall, with the windows you like. It's just going to be us, so you can come down whenever you are ready."

"That sounds wonderful," Padmé said. "Let us finish up here, and we'll be right down."

The southwest hall was Padmé's favourite because it was small and simply appointed. Its glory was in the wall of ceiling-high windows that let in so much light and the balcony beyond that, where all of Theed and much of the surrounding landscape was visible. As queen, Padmé had read there and had taken audiences with the closest of her confidants. It seemed a more than fitting place for a farewell dinner, and she was glad that Saché had remembered.

"Just us" turned out to be all of the handmaidens, except for Yané, who had cancelled at the last minute because the set of twins she was fostering had fallen ill and she was staying home to tend to them. Saché was visibly disappointed but put her best face on it.

"They're sweet kids, most of the time," Saché said. "And I'm so proud of her for what she does."

"I met them when we visited," Padmé said. "It wasn't very

long, but it was enough to get to know them a bit and to see Yané again. I can't imagine having twins, but she's so good at it."

"She really is," Saché said.

Padmé's attention was caught by the new stained-glass window. She had commissioned several after the Battle of Naboo, to replace the ones damaged during the occupation, but this was not one of hers. The window depicted a royal procession wherein a tiny glass figure of herself walked the streets of Theed under a canopy while her attendants surrounded her. Rabé followed her gaze and laughed when she saw the window.

"How many of us do they think there are?" she said. There were a great many flame-hooded figures in the scene.

"Is one of them holding the canopy?" Saché asked, squinting. "I don't think the artist understands what it is we do."

"Good," said Sabé, and they all giggled. "That's how it's supposed to be."

Rabé performed for them while they waited for the dinner hour to approach, and Eirtaé gave more details about her time in Otoh Gunga than she had given to the legislative assembly. She had also brought several of her pieces for Padmé to see, and Sabé insisted on buying one of them, even though she currently had nowhere to put it.

"I'll ship it to your parents' house," Eirtaé told her.

Padmé went out onto the balcony after sunset, with Sabé giving her some distance as she followed behind. For once, there was no security issue to be considered. The entire trip had been without incident, and Padmé was deeply glad of it. She knew it was their job, and she knew it was her position, but she hated it every time people risked themselves for her, especially when it was her friends.

It was quiet on Naboo in a way that Coruscant could never be. The city-planet had a constant hum: generators, traffic, the buzz of millions of simultaneous conversations. Naboo's hum was much quieter, but it was still there if you knew what to listen for. Padmé had loved Theed's waterfalls since the first time she had laid eyes on them, and being away from the planet had only made her fondness grow stronger. She stood still, leaning out over the city that her heart loved best, listening to the far-off sound of rushing water.

"We'll come back here, you and I," she said to Sabé. "We'll do what we need to do out there, and then we'll come home."

Sabé rested her head on Padmé's shoulder – felt the press of Padmé's cheek against her hair – and neither of them doubted it for a moment.

PART V

PIRATE THREAT GROWS, UNCHECKED

Shipments throughout the Mid Rim have come under attack by vicious pirates set to steal anything that's not welded to the hull. Millions of credits' worth of investments have gone missing as stripped ships are left to make their way back to the Core. How much longer will the Senate ignore the Mid Rim's plight? How much money will investors like the Trade Federation be forced to risk? And will Chancellor Palpatine convince the galactic government to intercede before it is too late?

– TriNebulon News

CHAPTER 21

Coruscant was loud and crowded, and the air smelled terrible, even as high up as the balcony of Padmé's senatorial residence, but she found that some small part of her had missed it, in spite of her best efforts. She acknowledged that she enjoyed the intellectual challenges that came with being a member of the Galactic Senate, and she quietly reminded herself not to get so caught up in the theoreticals of power that she would forget how her actions – or inaction – affected other beings.

They had returned a day early in order to settle into the apartment and unpack, but no sooner had the carry cases been stacked in her room than her official comm chimed, demanding her attention. Padmé went to read the message and then sat down as she realised what was about to happen.

"Dormé!" she called. The handmaiden appeared in seconds. "Dig up something senatorial that we don't have to press, as quickly as you can. I have to go to the Senate floor immediately."

"What's happened?" Dormé was already moving. She knew

exactly what case she was after, and before long she had assembled everything she would need.

"There's been an emergency session called," Padmé said, beginning to strip out of her travel clothes. "Something about the planetary aqueducts on Bromlarch. There aren't many details in the report, but it must be important to call everyone in a day early. I'm glad we made it in time. What do you want me to do with my hair?"

"Leave it for now," Dormé said. "And keep that undersuit on. It'll be fine for under this."

Padmé let Dormé dress her in one of the new outfits. The brown undergown was topped by a ruffled green overdress that wouldn't get wrinkled, and then a brown tabard went over top of that, in place of a cape or cloak. Dormé took the braids that were hanging down Padmé's back and coiled them around her head in a manner reminiscent of Queen Breha's crown, though Padmé's hair was only held in place with pins.

"That will have to do," Dormé said critically.

"Thank you," Padmé said. "Please tell Typho and Mariek to meet me on the platform. Everyone else can stay here and try to recover from the trip."

Dormé left, and Padmé took a moment to collect herself. A thousand what-ifs crossed her mind, and she ruthlessly dismissed them all. There was no point in planning anything or worrying too much before she knew what the issues were and how she could best approach them. She took one more deep breath and headed out to her guards, becoming Senator Amidala to her fingertips.

Typho drove the speeder himself because there wasn't time to wait for senatorial transportation to arrive. Amidala's office had the clearance to fly off the main city routes, so it didn't take them very long to get to the Senate building. Typho dropped off Mariek and Padmé, and promised to meet them at the pod.

Padmé didn't stop at her office but went straight out to the floor and took her seat. She turned on her translator in case she would need it and settled in to listen.

" – potential for tragedy looms," the senator from Bromlarch, a spindly humanoid male named Caelor Gaans was saying. "We had no way of predicting the seismic activity would be that severe. Our aqueduct system is capable of withstanding considerable pressure and stress, but this was far beyond anything the planet has ever experienced."

"What of your houses and population centres?" Mon Mothma asked. Padmé was relieved to hear her voice.

"They fared a little better, Senator, thank you," Gaans said. "The houses are made of a more flexible material and they are lower to the ground. We build our houses to be replaceable, and we thought the aqueduct would endure."

"It sounds as though you have done what you could," Mon Mothma said.

"It won't be enough," Gaans said. "Without the aqueduct,

our agricultural system is all but annihilated. We can get water to less than ten per cent of our fields, and the shaking has caused many private wells to run dry. We don't have time to dig new ones while we figure out how to rebuild. We just finished planting season. If we can't get water to the crops, the whole planet will starve."

At this dire prediction, Gaans took his seat. It was almost as though his legs would no longer carry him upright. Padmé's heart went out to him. She knew what it was like to stay on Coruscant while her planet suffered.

"Can the citizens of Bromlarch be relocated?" asked the senator from Malastare.

"There are millions of us," Gaans said, struggling to his feet again. "It would be impractical. And many have nowhere to go."

"Senators, senators," Chancellor Palpatine finally made his voice heard. Silence, or the nearest thing to it, fell over the Senate chamber. "We must move as quickly as we can to allay the suffering on Bromlarch. Relocation will only be considered as an absolute last resort. The chair now recognises the senator from Scipio."

Padmé sat up straight. She felt the sharp and unfamiliar stab of jealousy coursing through her at the idea that Rush Clovis would make a solo address before she would, but she quickly squashed the ugly feeling. She did wonder what he could possibly offer, though. She hadn't come up with anything beyond basic food aid yet – an obvious and short-term solution at best.

"Senators," Clovis said, "I propose that an auditing team be sent to Bromlarch. They can assess the damage and provide a cost estimate of the repairs. I understand that Bromlarch is too overwhelmed to conduct the survey themselves right now, but this body can handle the task, and then once we have the reports, we can make further decisions."

Credits, of course. Clovis wanted to know what everything was going to cost. Still, it wasn't a bad plan. Padmé's only hesitation was that she knew from firsthand experience how long this sort of survey could take.

"Onderon seconds the motion," Mina Bonteri said. Padmé was surprised. Bonteri hadn't spoken up very often towards the end of the last session. Perhaps her furlough had revitalised her.

Palpatine conferred with his advisors, which still included Mas Amedda. Padmé had no love for the Chagrian councilor and wished Palpatine had chosen someone else now that he was more established as chancellor. She had not been consulted of course, but Palpatine knew of her dislike. As with so many other topics, he had dismissed her opinion the moment it failed to align with his. As Mas leaned forwards again to speak, Padmé felt the chill of history repeating itself.

"Very well," he said. "We will send the survey team. I will

ask our friends the Jedi if they will also send someone. They are excellent ambassadors during humanitarian crises and often provide a less policy-driven point of view for any proposed solutions. Senator Clovis, Senator Bonteri, you may bring whichever of your colleagues that you like."

Padmé's comm chimed, and she knew it would be Organa before she even looked down. The message was only one word:

"*Go.*"

Padmé was on her feet with Typho and Mariek on her heels as Chancellor Palpatine began to say the formulas that wound down the session. She walked briskly, heading for the spot where Mina Bonteri's pod would dock. Hopefully, she would be able to talk the Onderon senator into letting her come, even though they had drifted apart since Padmé had begun taking meetings with Mon Mothma. If she was desperate, she supposed, she would approach Clovis, but she would rather take her chances with Bonteri first.

"Senator Amidala," Bonteri said as she stepped into the hallway, "I am not at all surprised to see you."

"I would like to accompany you to Bromlarch, Senator," Padmé said. "My past experience with disaster relief makes me – "

"Yes, my dear, I know," Bonteri said. "That's why I am not surprised to see you. Walk with me?"

Padmé fell into step beside her. At least Bonteri wasn't

moving slowly. They went down the corridor to an alcove in the wall where a small bench was tucked out of the path of foot traffic. Bonteri sat, and so did Padmé.

"You were one of the first people I thought of, Senator," Bonteri said. "I knew that the Senate's first act would be to send people to observe the damage. They cannot trust reports, even when visuals have been provided. They must see everything with their own eyes."

"I remember," Padmé said. She felt the old familiar bitterness swell in her stomach.

"You will ensure a speedy trip, I am certain," Bonteri continued. "And I will be able to give your observations the weight they need to move the Senate. But I warn you, we may not carry the day, in the end. Even after your recommendations, the Senate may still do something you do not approve of, and since you submitted the report, you will almost surely have to vote for it."

Padmé was digesting that when Clovis arrived.

"Senator Bonteri, Senator Amidala," he said. His eyes widened and he smiled despite the severity of the situation. "Do we have our first volunteer?"

"It would seem so," Bonteri said coolly. Apparently, she appreciated Clovis's attitude as much as Padmé did.

"Excellent," Clovis said. "I will put my ship and its crew at our immediate disposal. Will you be bringing anyone else?"

"I have a droid," Padmé said. Mariek was going to be

furious, but as Clovis was in charge, she could hardly bring her guards.

"My secretary can take care of the rest of the recording," Bonteri offered. "And we will have Senator Gaans with us, of course. I think that is a sufficient number."

Clovis might have proposed the survey, but Bonteri was making it very clear who was in charge, and Padmé appreciated that. She had not been looking forward to a week or two of doing whatever Clovis deemed appropriate. Bonteri was a much better leader for the venture and someone Padmé was much more comfortable working with and taking orders from.

"All right, then." If Clovis was offended, he didn't show it. "Will you be ready to depart tonight? Say, four hours from now?"

That would give Typho enough time to yell at her, Dormé enough to repack, and Padmé enough to comm Sabé with an update.

"Yes, it is," she said.

"I will send my shuttle for you both," Clovis said. "Now if you will excuse me, I have my own preparations to make."

He departed, and Bonteri sighed deeply before getting to her feet.

"He's a strange boy," she said. "But he's honest."

"Do you think?" Padmé said. That wouldn't have been the first word she came up with to describe him.

"I meant that he has no guile. You know exactly what

you're getting with him." Bonteri looked at her shrewdly. "You are very similar, in that regard, though the manifestation of your honesty is different."

"Thank goodness for that," Padmé said quietly but loud enough for Bonteri to hear. The older woman laughed, and Padmé smiled. Perhaps they had not grown so far apart after all.

"I have some messages to send," Bonteri said. "And I imagine you do, as well. I will see you in a few hours, Senator."

Padmé got to her feet.

"Thank you for including me, Senator," she said. "Causes like this mean a lot to me."

"I know," Bonteri said. "I will do my best not to take advantage of that."

While Padmé considered the oddness of that remark, Bonteri walked back to her office. Eventually, Padmé turned and made her way back to where she had left Typho and Mariek.

"You're going." Mariek did not present it as a question.

"I am," Padmé said. "Come on. We need to go back to the residence so that I can pack, and it's going to take some time for you both to finish yelling at me."

"Why are we yelling at you?" Typho asked.

"Because you can't come," Padmé said.

"Now, just a minute," Typho began.

"At the residence, Sergeant," Padmé said. "I need a united front here, but when we get home you can yell at me all you want."

In the end, it took Padmé only an hour to change and pack. Dormé had organised the closet so that all her offworld clothes were together, which simplified the whole matter. Padmé commed Sabé, but she was out, so Padmé was forced to leave a message. Typho expended his vocabulary over the course of thirty minutes, while Mariek took another fifteen. By then, Varbarós had arrived to drop off R2-D2, and Padmé was ready to go.

As she boarded Clovis's shuttle, she felt a thrill of excitement that she was more than a little ashamed of, given the circumstances. This would be the most alone she had been in a very, very long time.

CHAPTER 22

From orbit, the aqueduct system that sustained life on the planet of Bromlarch looked like unusually straight rivers branching out across the surface of the planet. Clovis's pilot had set their ship so they could watch the planet spin beneath them, and as the night side came up, the rivers disappeared completely. Only the lights of the settlements were visible. At least the planetary power grid had been partially restored.

"You should still be able to see them," Senator Gaans said sadly. He put a long-fingered hand up to the viewport, each of his nine digits splayed along the transparisteel as though he could reach through and hold the pieces of his broken world. "Their lights should be viewable from here. It was always one of my favourite parts of coming home."

"How much of the system sustained damage?" Padmé asked.

"Almost eighty per cent in total," Gaans said. "The critically affected areas were right by the epicentre of the quake, but the damage radiated out, just like the water usually does."

Jedi Master Depa Billaba joined Padmé at the viewport. Padmé had known her by sight, as she was one of the Jedi who had come to Naboo for the funeral of Qui-Gon Jinn, but they had not spoken very much on the journey so far. Padmé liked her well enough, but it was strange to interact with a Jedi again after so long. Padmé knew better than to expect all individuals within a culture to be the same, but there were stark differences between the way Qui-Gon had carried himself and the way Billaba did, and Padmé found it distinctly strange in a way she couldn't quite identify or explain, except to say that Qui-Gon had looked at her – too deeply sometimes – whereas she got the impression that Billaba was looking *through* her.

"I sense fear and pain on your planet, Senator Gaans," Billaba said. "But not in any specific concentrations. Your world is hurting, but the hurt is not yet critical."

"Thank you, Master Jedi," Gaans said. "It is cold comfort, but it is still comfort."

Clovis came into the room where they had gathered to watch the landing. His ship design was quite different from that of Padmé's silver craft, but the Naboo prided themselves on making everything look beautiful as well as serve a function. Clovis's ship was blocky, its dull grey exterior betraying none of the absurd luxuries contained inside it. Everyone had their own quarters, which explained why they were limited as to whom they were allowed to bring with them. R2-D2 had accessed the ship's blueprints almost as soon as they came on board, and Padmé didn't need to understand binary to understand his low opinion of the layout. It was nice not to be crammed in on top of one another – even the Naboo ship felt that way sometimes – but the ship presented itself as a target to anyone who got close enough to scan them.

"We should be landing as soon as our clearance comes in," Clovis said. "My pilot is double-checking to make sure the coordinates haven't changed due to an emergency shipment or something. We'll be on the ground shortly, if you would like to get ready."

Padmé went to fetch R2-D2, but everyone else remained behind to watch the landing procedures. Clovis's pilot was almost as good as Varbarós, but no one could land as smoothly as she did, and Padmé felt the jolt as they made contact with the ground. R2-D2 whirred dismissively.

"I know," Padmé said. "But they did fly us all the way here, so maybe be polite?"

The planetary council was waiting on the platform when they debarked. They all looked absolutely exhausted, and Padmé couldn't blame them. Recovering from a natural disaster was enough work, without taking into account the concerns over the aqueduct. She followed Bonteri and Gaans down the ramp. Clovis tried to fall into step beside her, but with R2-D2 there, he had no choice but to walk by himself. Master Billaba brought up the rear.

"My friend," the chief councilor said to Senator Gaans, and the two embraced. She was slightly taller than the senator, with light brown skin and short-cropped hair that had a light greenish cast to it. "It is so good to see you. I wish only that it was under better circumstances."

"And I wish I had been here when it happened," Gaans replied. "Though I don't know what I would have done."

"You were where we needed you to be," the councilor said. "Because of you, the Senate's response was swift."

"I hope so," Gaans replied. "Allow me to introduce Jedi Master Depa Billaba, Senator Mina Bonteri of Onderon, Senator Rush Clovis of Scipio, and Senator Padmé Amidala of Naboo. They have come to help assess the damage so that we can be specific with what aid we ask of the Senate. This is Councilor Eema, the chair of our planetary government."

"I am afraid we can't really accommodate you," Eema said.

"Please don't worry on our account," Clovis said, stepping to the front. "We are going to stay on the ship, and we can move around wherever you need us to be. Moreover, I know it isn't much, but I purchased what relief supplies I could before we left Coruscant. The hold is crammed full of ration bars and medical supplies. It's not a lot, but I hope you can use it."

Padmé thought about how much space there was in her quarters, of how many more supplies could have been made to fit in if she and Bonteri had shared, and ground her teeth together. Clovis was trying, but she was good at this and could have given him advice had he asked. At least he brought useful supplies.

"Thank you," Eema said. "We can only spare one liaison, but we do appreciate your help."

The councilors waited while the supply crates were offloaded, and then rode back into the city with them packed into several of the shuttles that were waiting on the landing pad. The liaison remained behind, standing awkwardly as she watched the process unfolding. She had clearly never seen a Jedi before and didn't quite know how to act around one. Padmé went over to stand beside her.

"The first time I saw a Jedi, I was running for my life," she said. "It gets a bit easier when you remember they're still sentient beings, like us. They just say strange things from time to time."

"Someday, I would like to hear that story, Senator," the liaison said. "Excuse me, my name is Ninui."

"I'm sorry we have to meet under these circumstances, Ninui," Padmé said. "Now, where would you like us to begin? Is it easier if we take the ship back into orbit so that you can use this landing pad?"

"It might be," Ninui said. "I'm sorry, I am thinking of a million things a minute."

"Let's go back on board," Clovis said. "You'll have some quiet to think, and we can get you some food. I imagine you've been on the move a lot."

Ninui looked up at Clovis and smiled. Padmé was impressed. So far, he'd been almost tactful. They went back into the ship. R2-D2 stayed behind to introduce himself to the docking computer, and Depa Billaba stared out over the landscape, though Padmé couldn't imagine what she was doing. She led Ninui into the viewing room. Clovis brought her a tray of food and a caf, and Bonteri and her secretary joined them after a few moments.

"I think the simpler we can keep this the better," Bonteri said. "It will be easier for you, and it will certainly be easier for the Senate."

"I agree," Padmé said. "Ninui, can you tell us what your people need right now, what they'll need in a month, and what they'll need in a year?"

"Well," Ninui swallowed her last mouthful of caf, and Clovis refilled the cup. "Right now we need water. In a month, we'll need food, and in a year, we'll be back to needing water."

"And to get water, you need the aqueduct fixed," Bonteri said.

"It's more complicated than that," Ninui said. "It's raining in Dravabi Province. Without the aqueduct to carry that water to other parts of the planet, there will be flooding."

"So what you need is water *control*," Padmé said.

"That still means fixing the aqueduct," Clovis said.

"Yes, but I think Padmé is right to make the distinction," Bonteri said. "Shipping water is hard, but there's plenty of moisture in the air here if we needed to set up temporary moisture farms. Only that wouldn't solve anything, because the problem is where the water is."

"What do you need to fix the aqueduct?" Padmé asked. "We saw it from orbit, but the details on its construction were pretty scarce."

"We need permacrete," Ninui said. "We don't have the necessary chemicals to make our own here, not even one of the knockoff versions, so we usually import it. But now we need a lot of it."

Padmé leaned back in her chair.

"One of the committees I serve on deals with the transportation of permacrete, and we've made the shipment process a bit less onerus," she said. "It will still take me some time, but I think I can at least get the supply lines running again."

"That would be good," Ninui said. "The dealer we use can't get enough of it for us."

"Can you have someone draw up an order of repair?" Bonteri asked. "If there's flooding, we should repair those regions first, and then move down the line."

"That's actually already a part of our disaster planning," Ninui said. "We just haven't got as far as implementing it yet."

"Excellent," Bonteri said. "Don't worry about remembering all of this, by the way. My secretary will send you their notes."

"Oh, thank goodness." Ninui put her head on the table, and Padmé reached out to pat her on the back. "I have never been so tired. I'm afraid if I stop, I'll never get moving again."

Clovis was looking at her with a strange expression on his face. Padmé knew that his personal history was not free of tragedy – losing her parents was one of her deepest fears, and Clovis had lost both of his when he was quite young – even though his story had a happy ending with his adoptive father. Perhaps this was the first time he had ever witnessed suffering on this scale. Padmé was glad he was becoming aware but frustrated that it took the near-complete destruction of a planet's eco-financial system to do it. Maybe this was why Naboo encouraged its children to go into public service at such young ages: it ensured they were awake.

"Can you give our pilot coordinates to anything we need to see?" Clovis asked gently. "The bridge has comfortable seats, so you might get a bit of rest there while you keep working."

Ninui picked her head up and cracked her neck.

"Yes," she said. "I can do that."

"I'll go get Artoo and see if Master Billaba wants to come," Padmé said.

She went back down the ramp and sent R2-D2 inside. Billaba hadn't moved from the spot where they had left her. Padmé went over, making as much noise as possible as she walked. Billaba turned around when she was no more than a few paces away.

"Senator?" she said.

"We're going to do an aerial survey," Padmé told her. "Would you like to come along? I would appreciate if you could give the Jedi Council a firsthand account."

"Of course," Billaba said.

They had only taken a few steps before Billaba stopped and, for the first time, looked directly *at* Padmé. She did her best not to squirm. It was more than a little disconcerting.

"You have not changed very much since the first time I met you," Billaba said. Padmé wasn't entirely sure what to make of that, and it must have shown on her face, but the Jedi Master continued. "You have grown, of course. You are wiser. You are more balanced. But you haven't changed. You are still the person who took on the Trade Federation, and I think you always will be."

It was probably the oddest compliment Padmé had ever received, including the time a small boy on a desert world had assumed she was an angel, but she was pleased by it nonetheless. She had been wondering about herself. About the path she would take. Jedi could see things that no one else did, and Padmé trusted in their vision, as much as any non-Jedi could.

CHAPTER 23

The trip back to Coruscant seemed endless. All Padmé wanted to do was get to work, and instead she had to content herself with writing down her plans to make sure she didn't forget anything when it was finally time to go before the Senate. It was determined that Senator Bonteri would make the official report, and then they would decide their next move based on the reaction. Padmé was cautiously optimistic.

Clovis came to see her just before the ship dropped out of hyperspace. She was less frustrated by him now, but she still didn't enjoy his company the way he seemed to enjoy hers.

"Senator Amidala," Clovis said, "may I come in?"

"Please," she said, and waved him towards one of the empty chairs.

"I wanted to thank you for coming on this trip," Clovis said. "I don't know what I was expecting, but I do know I was overwhelmed by it. I couldn't have done anything without you around to clear everything up."

"You did well with Ninui," Padmé said. "She needed support, and you could see that clearly enough."

"It's a little easier when it's just one person," Clovis admitted. "You could look at the whole planet and not flinch."

"I do have a certain amount of practise," she reminded him.

"It's not just the queen part, is it?" he asked. "There's something else."

Padmé took a deep breath. It was a painful memory, because it contained so many good and terrible things. But she was going to have to keep working with Clovis, and telling him would cost her nothing.

"My father did a lot of relief work when I was very young," she said. "Before he confined himself to only building on Naboo, he built houses and so many other things everywhere you can think of. When I was old enough, I went with him.

"I was seven, and the planet we were evacuating was called Shadda-Bi-Boran. The sun was dying and we managed to relocate the entire populace, but we couldn't replicate the environment properly. Whatever nutrients they got from their sun, they couldn't get anywhere else."

"What happened?" Clovis asked.

"They died," Padmé said. "All of them. I have a few pictures, and there was a monument built afterward, but that's all that's left."

Clovis searched her face, looking for something, though she wasn't sure what.

"You would do it again," he said.

"Of course I would," Padmé said. "Maybe next time, one

of our scientists would figure it out soon enough to save some-one. Maybe next time, there would be survivors. I would try a thousand times, Clovis, even if I only ever saved one being. I would try ten thousand times."

She could tell he believed her.

The ship dropped out of hyperspace, and the pilot came on the comm to tell them all to prepare for landing. Clovis didn't say anything else until they were on the ground.

"I know we came to the Senate for different reasons," he said, standing up. "You had your expectations to fulfil, and I had mine. But I think we could do all right together, if you wanted to."

"I'll keep that in mind," she said.

"I'll look forward to it, Amidala," he said.

"It's Padmé," she told him. "I don't mind if you call me Padmé when there is no one else around."

She had no idea what had led her to say that. Almost no one outside of her family and inner circle had permission to use that name.

"I've always been partial to Clovis," he said. "It's the name I shared with my parents."

"On Naboo, we call people by the names they wish to be called," Padmé said. "The previous captain of my guard was called Panaka, but his wife chose to go by Mariek to avoid confusion, though she is still Captain Panaka if we are being formal, or if a stranger is talking to her."

"What if someone wants to change their name?" Clovis asked.

Padmé picked up her carrysack and hoisted it over her shoulder.

"Then you call them by their new name," Padmé told him.

He nodded, and walked with her to the top of the ramp, where Padmé said her farewells to Master Billaba. Bonteri was waiting for her at the bottom, and Padmé hurried down so as not to delay her. It was vital that Bonteri get herself onto the speaking schedule as soon as possible.

"I'm not too hopeful," Bonteri admitted as their speeder pulled away from the landing pad. "I know we kept everything as simple as possible, but I just don't know if the Senate will pull together."

"I know you will do everything you can to help Bromlarch," Padmé said. "And I will, too."

"Will Clovis?" Bonteri said.

"You know," Padmé mused, "I really think he might."

"At least we'll have that," Bonteri said.

The speeder dropped Senator Bonteri off first and then took Padmé back to her apartment. She let Dormé and Cordé dress her in something that wasn't covered with the dust of a fractured world and then requested that anyone who was free to eat with her join her for dinner. All three handmaidens, Varbarós, Typho, and two other guards were sitting at the table when she arrived. Mariek was on duty but drifted in to hear the salient points of Padmé's summary.

"I'd like to volunteer our ship as part of any convoy that goes," Padmé concluded. "Even if we're only ferrying people. Is that doable?"

"The ship will be ready whenever you need her," Varbarós said.

"I'd like to request two Republic patrol ships as an escort," Mariek said. "With our pilots."

"Sabé and Tonra can do it," Padmé said. "Then Typho can stay close to me, and Mariek can organise everyone else."

She paused thoughtfully.

"I would like to ask Master Billaba to accompany us, as well," she said. "She can fly her own ship from the Jedi Temple, or one that we provide her with."

"I like that idea, my lady." Typho nodded. "If this becomes a regular thing, we should call up some N-1s from home. We have the space to dock them, and I think we'd all prefer it if the fighters were flown, stored, and maintained by our own people."

"I agree," Padmé said. "I'll sign the requisition after you write it."

"There's still very little in the newsnets about Bromlarch," Versé said. "But I imagine that will change when the Senate debates start."

Padmé yawned.

"Please excuse me, I'm exhausted," she said. "It was a non-stop few days. Thank you, Versé. We know better than any how the newsnets prefer a scandal, so I'm not really surprised."

"Do you want to give them a scandal?" Versé asked. "I've sliced in enough now that I'm sure I could."

"Let's try the Senate first," Padmé said. She could hardly believe she was giving Versé's proposal any consideration in the least. "Though we can always hold a scandal in reserve. This is politics, after all."

The next morning, Padmé dressed for a fight. It was a subtle variation on the actual battle dress Sabé had worn during the Battle of Naboo, only without the headpiece or face paint. The underdress was black, with wide sleeves. Over it went a deep yellow dress with shorter sleeves, which left the black fabric free for Padmé to theoretically conceal things in her hands if need be. Over that went a black tabard, held in place by a wide belt that would accommodate her blaster if she were carrying one. Dormé twisted her hair into the coronet of braids again, and then Padmé was ready.

She arrived at the Senate building as early as she could and went straight to Senator Bonteri's office. The door was open, and Padmé could hear her talking to someone, so she hesitated before she knocked. It was an unfamiliar voice – deep and commanding of attention – and Padmé couldn't help overhearing.

"Do as you must," the mysterious speaker said. "But if you cannot control the situation, I will step in and control it for you."

"Yes, my lord." Senator Bonteri did not sound happy about whatever it was.

Padmé heard nothing further and assumed the conversation had ended. She was curious about what she had heard – both Bonteri and the unknown contact had seemed deadly serious – but more than curiosity, a strange dread settled in her stomach, and she was eager to dislodge the feeling. She counted to fifteen before she took the last few steps and knocked on the door.

"Good morning," Bonteri said cheerfully. It was a completely different tone of voice.

"Hello," Padmé said. "I came to see if you needed anything?"

"No," Bonteri said a bit curtly, despite her lighter countenance. "I was able to get us on the schedule right away. It should go well."

"Excellent," said Padmé. She decided to let it go and focus on the main goal. "I'll be in the gallery if something comes up."

Padmé walked to her seat and waited for Typho to meet

her. The Senate chamber was so large that she didn't like being by herself in the pod, even though she was sure the room was one of the safest places in the entire galaxy. Also, she was too excited to sit still, and she didn't want anyone to see her fidgeting. At last the time came, and with Typho behind her, she took her seat.

"The floor recognises Senator Mina Bonteri of Onderon," Chancellor Palpatine said. He sounded almost bored.

"My friends," Bonteri said, "I have returned from our survey of the damage sustained by the planet of Bromlarch due to recent seismic activity there. You should have received my report in your morning information packet, but I know it is still early, so I will summarize it for you now."

While Senator Bonteri talked, Padmé scanned the gallery. It wasn't easy to see anyone's face, but she was learning to tell a lot about a senator's manner by how they sat in their pod. Looking around, she saw far fewer beings leaning forwards, listening intently, than she'd hoped. Instead, they reclined or chatted with their associates. Padmé swallowed a surge of resentment and focused on Senator Bonteri, who concluded her summary by giving the details of the plan the Bromlarch Council had submitted.

"It is always wisest to trust those people on the ground," Bonteri said. "The plan presented by the citizens of Bromlarch is straightforward and will result in the fastest and most efficient repairs."

Bonteri's pod floated back to its port, and the Chancellor spoke again.

"The chair recognises the senator from the Trade Federation," Palpatine said.

Padmé stiffened. This could not mean anything good.

"What Senators Bonteri and Gaans propose is too much," Lott Dod began. "We can ask citizens of the Republic to contribute small amounts of their own credits and materials to reconstruction, but the idea of a planetwide rebuild is ridiculous. If Bromlarch requires so much help, they must be able to pay for it in some manner."

"Senators," Senator Gaans said, "my people are doing the best they can. I don't think you understand the scale of the destruction – "

"We do," Lott Dod interrupted. Padmé looked down, but Palpatine made no sign of interfering. "We also understand the economics. The Trade Federation is happy to come to a private arrangement with the citizens of your planet, if that is something you are willing to consider, but you cannot expect galactic intervention for an internal problem."

Padmé felt angrier than she had felt in a long time. She would not sit by while the Trade Federation bought a planet out from under its people's feet.

"We will vote now," Chancellor Palpatine said.

The voting screen appeared on Padmé's monitor, and

she quickly voted in favour of Senator Bonteri's motion.. She held her breath.

"Motion failed," Chancellor Palpatine said.

Padmé collapsed back in her seat. She saw defeat slump Bonteri's shoulders. Senator Gaans had floated close enough that she could see the absolute despair in his face. Lott Dod floated his pod back to its dock and waited.

Padmé was done waiting. Waiting to be seen. Waiting to speak. Waiting to serve. She was going to make something happen if it was the last thing she did as a senator for the Galactic Republic.

CHAPTER 24

Padmé sent Typho to retrieve Senator Gaans and bring him to her office, where she installed him, distraught, in one of the chairs that faced her across the desk. Cordé poured him a caf and then retreated to her usual place behind Padmé's shoulder. He didn't drink it.

"Senator, I know it is bleak," Padmé said. "But you cannot sign that treaty. And you cannot let anyone else sign it, either. The Trade Federation cannot be allowed to buy your planet and your people out from under you. You must resist."

"I know," he said. "But how can I resist when the Trade Federation could save them?"

"Save them?" Padmé said. "Senator, the Trade Federation once offered to save my people, too. They put them into camps and starved them, trying to force my hand. This situation is different, I realise that, but you must avoid an outcome that can only favour them."

"There isn't even a treaty yet," Gaans told her. "They'll need two days to write it, and I'll get one day to look it over and see if it's plausible."

"Plausible?" Padmé thought of fifteen things to say to that and as a result said nothing at all.

There was a chime at the door, and Senator Organa came in. Padmé waved him into a chair beside Gaans.

"I'm sorry, senators," he said. "We tried."

"We need to try again," Padmé said. "You told me that if democracy failed us it was up to us to restore democracy. That's what I intend to do."

"They'll stall you," Organa said. "I know it's a horrifying situation, but you can't fight every evil in the galaxy."

"Evil?" Padmé said. "I've fought evil and it was easy: I shot it. It's apathy I can't stand."

"You may be in the wrong profession," Gaans said darkly.

"We have three days," Padmé said. "Surely there's something."

Clovis burst into the room and skidded to a halt when he saw that Padmé already had guests. "Senators," he said. There were no chairs left by the desk, so he remained on his feet.

"What is it, Clovis?" Padmé asked.

"Earlier, what I said about us making a good team?" Clovis said. "This is what I meant. You know people and I know credits, and we have both been trained to negotiate. I know I can help. Please let me."

Padmé considered it and realised she wasn't exactly in a position to turn anyone down.

"All right," she said. "Three days, Clovis. And we can't

just reintroduce the motion. We have to be smarter than that. What do you suggest?"

"We need to focus on the votes," Clovis said, pacing in front of the window. "The content of the motion is still important, but I think we need to pay more attention to who we're courting."

"That's not how my faction of the Senate is supposed to operate," Organa protested, but his tone was resigned. He knew as well as she did that his age and experience afforded him greater privilege than she had, and that was before their planets were taken into account.

"And yet here we are," Clovis said. "The Trade Federation allies just voted down a bill that would save millions of lives because Lott Dod made them blink over it."

Organa was clearly unhappy with the argument but did not refute it.

"All right," Padmé said. "There are more systems in the Core represented than there are in the Mid Rim, and a few of the Core Worlds voted in favour of the bill anyway. We need to flip Mid Rim senators, get them to vote with us instead of their allies in the Core who support them."

"We need to target certain systems," Clovis said. "There are senators that always vote in blocs. We need to turn the leaders of those blocs, not the members."

"Malastare," Padmé said. "They'd bring more than a dozen systems with them, all at the expense of the opposing bloc."

"You'll never convince them to change their minds." Gaans leaned forwards and put his head in his hands.

"I'm not going to convince them to change their minds," Padmé said. "They're going to do it themselves because they want what I have."

"What do you have?" Clovis asked.

"I'm working on that," Padmé said. "We can't just reintroduce the motion as a relief operation, but what if we introduced it as something more general? If it benefited more than one system, those systems would vote with us. They would bring their allies, and the motion would pass."

"A motion for Mid Rim cooperation?" Organa said. He was skeptical, but Padmé could tell she had nearly convinced him. "In the wake of the recent run of piracy, you'd certainly have public opinion on your side, and you'd make the Chancellor look good, so you'd have him, too."

"We might call it something else," Padmé said. "But yes."

"What does Malastare want?" Gaans asked.

"They want political power," Padmé said. "Their senator was not elected chancellor when Valourum was unseated, and they have been backsliding ever since."

"We can't give them power," Organa said.

"No," Clovis said, and Padmé knew that he was keeping up with her. "But we can give them credits, which is almost the same thing."

"You're going to buy their fuel reserves?" Gaans asked. "For what purpose?"

"It's the Mid Rim Cooperation motion," Padmé said. "Someone else is going to buy the fuel. We just need to figure out who."

Padmé stood and went over to the more comfortable seats in the other corner of her office. There were low tables where they could work and the light was good. Clovis followed her and sat down. He reached into the bag he carried for several datapads and a stylus. Padmé looked back at Organa, who got to his feet.

"My schedule is full today, so I can't stay here and help," he said. "But I'll have my comlink with me if you have any questions. And I'll try to come back later."

Padmé knew that there were other crises in the galaxy right now, and tried to tell herself that he wasn't abandoning her because he thought she was working on a lost cause.

"I need to go talk to Eema and the other councilors back home," Senator Gaans said. "We have a lot to discuss."

"Please take care of yourself," Padmé said. "They're going to need you, and so are we."

He gave her a weak smile, and then he and Senator Organa left the room. Padmé sat next to Clovis, for the first time completely interested in what it was he was going to say.

"All right then," she said. "Malastare for credits and fuel. Where do we go from there?"

The next three days were draining in a way that Padmé had never experienced. She thought she'd known exhaustion after the Occupation. Constantly moving to planets with different diurnal cycles and enduring the mental challenges of maintaining Sabé as her decoy for that length of time while coping with the stress of the military situation on Naboo had been the hardest things she had ever done. This was more like chasing a thread across a room that was carpeted with other threads, some of which she needed but most of which would only tie her down. It required her to pay attention to details and to move quickly, but not *too* quickly, lest she unravel the whole thing.

She was aware that Cordé, Dormé, and Versé had all come and gone, switching places to ensure that some of them were well rested while Padmé drove herself on. Typho, Mariek, and the other guards rotated through, as well. She had no idea if Clovis's security was in the corridor, but if they were they never came into the room. Food was brought, and Padmé could not recall eating any of it – though the fact that she didn't pass out indicated that she probably had. They slept sitting up, when their weariness overcame them, usually to be awakened the next time one of them made a breakthrough.

In the end, the Mid Rim Cooperation motion involved more than a dozen key systems, a variety of different resources, and the heads of every bloc they needed to sway in order to lure sufficient votes away from the Trade Federation. Padmé was scrambling to finish her speech as the chronometer ran down.

"All we have to do now is sell it to them," Clovis said. "I think this was actually the easy part."

"I'll get us on the schedule," Padmé said. "I haven't called in a single favour from the Chancellor since I got here, but this is worth it."

"I'm going to my office to change," Clovis said. "I'll see you out there?"

"Yes," Padmé said. "Thank you, Clovis."

"We'll have to do it again sometime," Clovis said, and yawned. "But later."

When he was gone, Versé helped Padmé to change into a fresh dress that Dormé had delivered the previous afternoon. Then she contacted the Chancellor's office to make her scheduling request.

"Senator Amidala," Palpatine said, "we have missed you in the gallery these past few days."

"I've been working on a motion I think the Senate should hear immediately," Padmé told him. "It benefits Bromlarch, but it also grants advantages to several other Mid Rim worlds, and it might help the Senate deal with the piracy issue, as well, if we can line everything up. I think it has a good chance of passing."

"Wonderful," the Chancellor said. "Though I must

caution you to tamper your optimism. I have seen all manner of motions fail, even when I thought they were sound."

"I know," Padmé said. "But I think this motion will garner support across faction lines. It could unify the Senate."

"Or circumvent it," Palpatine said. He looked pensive, and Padmé knew he was considering all of the options. He might see something she had not, some opportunity or pitfall. He smiled. "But I have faith in you, Senator. Your course of action is always for the good of the Republic."

"I just need time to present it, Chancellor," she told him. "As soon as possible."

"I'll have you scheduled first for today, if you will be there?" he said.

"I will, Chancellor," Padmé said. "And thank you."

"Of course, my dear, of course," Palpatine said, and ended the call.

Padmé stood and stretched as much as she could and then put her shoes back on to head out to the floor. She paused in the centre of the room as something occurred to her. In all the flurry, she'd barely kept track of anything but the datapad in front of her nose, but she was still aware of who had and had not been in the room at any given time.

Mina Bonteri had not come to help them.

"Senators of the Galactic Republic," Amidala said, "the last time I spoke to you, it was to ask for aid to be given to my planet. I stand before you now with a similar request, but for systems that are not my own. Our service here is done in the name of our homeworlds, but we represent all the citizens of the Republic, and it is by virtue of this coalition that we are able to undertake greater tasks than we would as individuals."

Senator Amidala's pod hovered in the middle of the assembly, and every eye was on her. Dormé had done her makeup in a new way, so that each brush stroke highlighted the uniqueness of her features rather than overwhelming them. It had taken a while to perfect, and she'd had to practise the technique on anyone she could get her hands on, since Padmé was busy, but the overall effect was undeniable: Padmé Amidala stood before her colleagues with her own face, as open and genuine as she could be.

Padmé had dressed for the part, as well. The outfit Cordé had designed had wide blue trousers, cut in a Coruscanti fashion but embroidered with Naboo designs. Over a smocked white shirt, Padmé wore a sharp jacket that came down below her knees and was open at the front to show the details sewn into the lining. Her shoes were plain and comfortable, in case she had to remain standing and take questions when the speech was done.

Versé had embedded fabro-refractors of her own programming into key parts of the outfit. They ensured that

Padmé was always lit from a perfect angle. There would be no shadowed, unflattering pictures in the holonews when the session was over. Every part of Naboo that Padmé had brought with her was on display right now but made over so that the Galactic Republic would accept her as a senator, not a queen.

"The planets of the Mid Rim have been under siege by pirates and we have not acted against them," she continued. "I understand your hesitancy, for it is mine, too: I am reluctant to arm the galaxy any more than it needs. But my friends, we do have some need. Our shipments are being taken, and the pirates who take them are only looking for security and enough food to feed their own. We must act swiftly."

The recorders buzzed around her, and Padmé knew that she had finally captured everyone's attention for the reasons she wanted. The other senators, even her allies – who more or less knew what she was going to say – were shifting towards her, hanging on her every word.

"Appearing on your screens now is the Mid Rim Cooperation motion," Padmé continued. "You will note that a number of systems benefit from the proposed trades and acquisitions."

She gave them a moment to start reading. There was quite a bit of detail, given the number of planets involved, but she didn't want to lose too much momentum.

"Not only are we able to send necessary resources to Bromlarch," her voice rang through the speakers, "Bromlarch will be able to pay for the supplies without going into debt, and the whole of the Mid Rim will benefit."

She paused again. There were hushed whispers now, not out of rudeness but because the senators and their staffs were discussing the terms. Padmé took a deep breath and launched into the final section of her address.

"But we cannot continue to send such valuable resources to star systems without adequate protection," she said. "Since this is a Republic exercise, it must be guarded by Republic ships. Only then can we guarantee the safe passage of the Wookiee labourers to Bromlarch. Only then can we guarantee the safe trade of credits for fuel between Malastare and Sivad. Only then can we guarantee that the ships carrying food from Thiafeña and Naboo to Bromlarch will arrive intact.

"And perhaps, in working to maintain this guarantee, we will turn those who have fallen to piracy to better paths," she concluded. "I know they have called me idealistic and naive, and you, my friends, have agreed with them. I do not hold it against you, and I do not apologise for my faith in democracy and what this body can achieve when it acts together. Let us act together now. For Bromlarch. For the Mid Rim. For the continued safety of the Galactic Republic."

Lott Dod was frantically trying to get the floor to recognise him, but his attempts went unanswered. Instead, Palpatine acknowledged Malastare.

"There is wisdom in this motion." Aks Moe had a reedy

voice, but the amplification system ensured everyone heard his words. Padmé could almost see them calculating how many credits Malastare would make in profit as a result of the trades. "The Congress of Malastare seconds."

There was a loud crowing noise a few levels above where Padmé's pod was floating as the Wookiees, never much for procedure, added a third supporter to the motion.

"We will vote, then," Palpatine said. He still did not acknowledge the Neimoidian senator, who was fuming in his seat as a result.

It was to the divine powers that looked over Naboo and Gungan alike – and whoever else might be listening – that Padmé addressed a quiet "Please" as she voted in favour of her plan. It only took a few seconds for the votes to tally, but she felt like it was an eternity.

"Motion passes," Palpatine announced.

Cheers went up all around as Padmé's pod returned to its dock. When she was absolutely sure the recorders had been distracted, she allowed herself a satisfied smile. Palpatine continued with the day's schedule, but she was almost too elated to pay attention. It seemed like hours passed before the session finished and Padmé could finally get back to her office. Clovis arrived shortly afterward and cheered as soon as she admitted him.

"You did it!" he said.

"We did it." Padmé was more than willing to share the

credit. "I couldn't have gotten everything finished so quickly without your insights."

"I could sleep for a week," he said. He stepped past what her brain would usually consider a safe distance, but she was tired, and it took her a moment to catch up.

"Me too," she admitted. "But we're going to have to keep going to get everything organised and sent to – "

He kissed her, and her exhaustion faded immediately.

"No," she said, and pushed him away.

"I thought – " His hands cradled her elbows, as though to pull her close again.

"No," she said.

"But you – " He took a step back. He looked angry, and her own fury flared.

How dare he presume what their relationship was without asking her consent? She'd been warming up to him, that much was true, and she'd thought that their newfound friendship had potential to develop beyond what they had built over the past three days, but he had *no right*.

"No." She said it in the queen's voice. "We are colleagues, Senator Clovis."

"I take my leave then," he said, and stalked out.

"What was that?" Padmé said as Versé appeared beside her, rapping her fan against her palm. She had been present the whole time of course, and Clovis's attention had slid right past her as he charged for the goal.

"I don't know," Versé said. "But I'm glad he listened. I like this fan, and I'd hate to break it on his hard head."

"Things were just starting to make sense," Padmé said.

"They'll make more sense when you sleep," Versé told her. "And since we both know you're not going to sleep until you've organised the first round of shipping containers, let's get started on that."

Padmé called up the first of the proposed manifests and did her best to focus on what was right in front of her.

CHAPTER 25

It took nearly a week of shuttling materials around the Mid Rim, but at long last all the credits were in the right append-ages and Padmé had the first shipment of permacrete ready to head out to Bromlarch. The permacrete had been purchased with credits given to Bromlarch by Joh'Cire, a desert moon with a burgeoning moisture market and a growing popula-tion, in return for irrigation technology. If it had been as simple as that, the Mid Rim Cooperation motion would not have been necessary and Naboo could have simply filled the gap in Bromlarch's food supply privately. But it wasn't that simple. They needed the votes. Malastare didn't care about Bromlarch, but the Congress had voted in favour anyway because of what Padmé had offered up, and along with the other systems, they ensured Republic support for the whole effort.

Republic support meant Republic protection, and only three of the convoys had been attacked. All of the cargo had made it to its destinations intact, but one Sivadian pilot and fighter had been lost. The pirates had almost disappeared after that, perhaps fearing a galactic-level reprisal. The

Chancellor was credited with restoring the peace, and Padmé almost didn't mind.

Padmé would be ferrying herself, Senator Gaans, and Senator Yarua of Kashyyyk aboard her own vessel, along with as many emergency food supplies as she could cram into every available corner.

Mon Mothma was joining them after the initial run, to report back to the Senate on their progress, while Senator Yarua would be overseeing the beginning of the construction along with Senator Gaans. The Wookiees had been hired to do most of the actual building as part of the deal, in return for logging rights to a particular kind of hardwood that Bromlarch produced and Kashyyyk did not. The inclusion of the Wookiees had been a bonus, since they had voted in favour of providing aid in the first place, and Padmé was happy to spend more time with them.

Once the permacrete was loaded and everyone was aboard the royal ship, Padmé, with Typho behind her, went over to the patrol ships the Senate had loaned out for the trip. Sabé and Tonra were in the process of doing their final system checks and had their helmets on, which made conversation difficult as Padmé didn't have a comlink.

"Fly safely!" she shouted, wiggling her fingers in an approximation of wings.

Sabé replied with the sign they used to indicate a calm situation that could escalate at any moment, and Padmé grimaced. They would be on high alert. Tonra gave her a wave, and Padmé turned to walk back to the ramp.

"This makes me nervous, Senator," Typho admitted as they boarded.

"You have briefed us on a plan for if pirates attempt to steal the cargo and a separate plan for if they decide hostages would be more lucrative," Padmé told him. "I imagine you have a plan for what to do if they decide to do both at once, as well as multiple responses for scenarios I haven't imagined. We will be fine."

"I'm glad we'll have our own pilots," Typho said as he entered the bridge.

"Senator, we are just about ready to go," Varbarós said from the pilot's chair. "We'll rendezvous with the convoy in high orbit and stop to pick up the other ships at the agreed upon coordinates. Two jumps, and we'll be at Bromlarch."

"This is *Hazard One*, ready to depart," Sabé's voice sounded over the internal comm.

"*Hazard Two*, ready to depart," Tonra reported.

Padmé looked out the narrow viewports and saw the patrol ships lift up for their prelaunch thrust.

"*Hazard Three* standing by." This was Master Billaba, who had taken off from the temple separately and would rendezvous with them in orbit.

"Hazard Squadron, you are go for launch," Varbarós said. "We'll see you up there, *Hazard Three*."

The Jedi Master didn't answer.

Varbarós took them through the atmosphere as smoothly as usual, and the patrol ships took up their positions on the wings as soon as they were in space, with Master Billaba at the stern. They cruised over to where the convoy was assembling and took their place at the front of the formation. They put some distance between themselves and Coruscant.

"All ships, this is *Naboo One*," Varbarós said on a wide channel. "Prepare to receive navigation calculations and make the jump to hyperspace on my mark."

Padmé leaned back in her chair while the navicomputer did its work. She liked this part of travelling, the breath before the plunge into the full deepness of space. It reminded her how big the galaxy was and how lucky she was to live in it.

"Mark," said Varbarós, and they were off.

Although she knew she should go back and sit with the other senators, Padmé stayed on the bridge for the duration of the trip. She felt like it was the first time she had been in a room without politicians – herself excepted – in some time, and while that was a slight exaggeration, she still enjoyed the quiet.

The quiet came to an abrupt halt when the convoy dropped out of hyperspace at the second rendezvous point and found itself in the middle of a firefight with pirates.

"Activating the deflector shield!" Varbarós said. "Taking evasive action. Hazard Squadron, go wide for coverage."

Padmé watched as the two patrol ships peeled away, looping back to protect the whole convoy from a wider angle. It had been a while since Sabé had flown a single-person craft, but Padmé knew she'd been much better at maintaining her flight hours than Padmé had. Tonra wasn't a regular pilot, either, but Captain Panaka – both of them – had exacting standards, and Padmé felt only moderately alarmed to be in another battle. She couldn't see the Jedi ship at first but soon picked out Master Billaba's distinctive triangular Delta-7 starfighter closing in on the fight.

"Can we jump again?" Typho asked. He leaned forwards, and Padmé could tell he was itching to be more in control of the situation. She understood completely.

"The other half of the convoy is in the middle of shifting cargo between two of the haulers," a tech reported. "They can't go until everyone is back inside."

"Damn it," Typho said.

"Varbarós, move us closer," Padmé said. "We can draw their fire and give the haulers some time."

"Do not do that," Typho said, biting off each word like they were proton torpedoes.

"Sergeant, we have a far superior shield," Padmé reasoned. "We can take a few hits. Move us in, Varbarós."

"One pass!" Varbarós said, clearly considering this a

compromise. She couldn't make eye contact with either of them from the pilot's chair, which was probably for the best, all things considered. "Moving us in. Hold onto something."

The ship rolled into the action, and though the gravity generator kept them in place, Padmé felt her stomach flip as Varbarós completed the manoeuvre. It worked well enough. The royal ship took two shots across the underside of the bow, but the shield held firm.

"Their weapons aren't strong enough to break through without significant bombardment," the tech reported, their fingers flying as they cycled through system updates and relayed orders to the other ships.

"Sergeant," Padmé said, pouring a great deal of feeling into the word.

"Take us on another pass," Typho said, speaking through his teeth. He was definitely going to yell at her later, but this was worth it.

Varbarós rolled again, and three more shots rocked across the bow.

"*Naboo One*, *Hazard One*, we have targeted the cannons on the primary attacker," Sabé said through the comms. "Starting our attack run."

"*Hazard One*, you have a go," Varbarós replied. She pulled the royal ship out of their path, and for a moment, Padmé's view of the battle was replaced by a quiet and peaceful field of stars.

Not stars: the ballast that Master Billaba had dumped to deflect the cannon fire. Vacuum or no, the particles seethed in space as they absorbed the energy that was meant to have cut through hull metal. The Jedi Master returned to her position behind the silver ship, and Padmé could only track her movements on the scanner.

Watching space battles was deeply unsettling on account of the silence in which they were conducted, but once they were back in visual range, Padmé didn't take her eyes off the ship she knew Sabé piloted. She missed Tonra's successful assault on the first cannon but saw Sabé take out the second one.

"The haulers are ready to go," the tech reported.

"Firing up navicomputer," Varbarós said on the wide channel again. "All ships, all ships, prepare for coordinates and jump when you are ready."

"We're going last," Padmé said. "I want to be sure everyone is away."

"Senator," Typho said, and Padmé held up her hands in defeat.

"Almost last," she amended. "Hazard Squadron can follow us."

"Copy that," came three different voices over the comm.

Flashes of light indicated each time a convoy ship jumped. Sabé and Tonra continued to attack the pirate vessels, aiming for weaponry and drive systems to cover their retreat, while Billaba deployed another run of ballast between the attackers and the Naboo.

"We're going," Varbarós announced, and before Padmé could look out the viewport to confirm they were the last remaining, they jumped.

Varbarós blew out a breath in triumph, and Padmé reached out to touch her shoulder.

"Well done," she said. "You did an excellent job."

"Thank you, Senator," the pilot said.

Padmé leaned back in her chair and looked over at Typho, who didn't look as angry as she'd thought he would.

"Can you fly an N-1 fighter, Senator?" he asked after a moment.

"Yes," Padmé said. "Captain Panaka had us all learn how. I'm a little out of practise, but I think it would come back to me."

"Good," he said. "I don't imagine I'll be able to talk you out of risking your neck in the future, so the next best thing is to make sure you risk it in something with a laser cannon."

"Very well, Sergeant," she said. "As long as you are flying with me."

"My rank doesn't – " he started, and she laughed.

"I may call in a few favours. I have powerful friends," she said. "And you deserve it, Sergeant. I truly think so."

Padmé stood up and went below to tell the other senators what had transpired. They would have been kept apprised of the situation by the ship's computer, but it was always nice to hear a report from a living person. She met R2-D2 on the way. She knew the droid often ran scans when he hadn't been given any other tasks to do, and a thought occurred to her.

"Artoo, did you get a good look at those pirates?" she asked.

The little droid beeped enthusiastically and rolled over to a computer outlet. Padmé followed him, and after he hooked up, she watched as a series of scans of the ship whose cannons Sabé had destroyed played across the screen.

"Any significant markings or registration numbers?" she asked.

R2-D2 rotated his dome, indicating no.

"Please do a detailed analysis," Padmé said. "I'll read your report as soon as things calm down."

The astromech turned back to the screen, images flashing too quickly for Padmé to track them, and she left him to it.

The senators were waiting for her in the room that could serve as a throne room when the queen was aboard but was currently decorated with several white chairs and a table.

"We took no damage," Padmé said by way of greeting. She sat down next to Senator Gaans. "Two pirate vessels were attacking our secondary convoy. The haulers were transferring cargo, so they were vulnerable. Our patrol ships took out the enemy cannons and bought us enough time to jump away."

"It's troublesome that the pirates knew the location of the secondary convoy," Gaans said. "Though their timing was unfortunate for them."

"It was almost unfortunate for us," Padmé said. "We had no real scheduled time for leaving Coruscant. The haulers had been waiting for us for a few hours before we arrived. If we had been even ten minutes later, it would be an entirely different story."

Senator Yarua barked a question. A screen next to the Wookiee senator provided a quick translation, like Padmé's screen in the Senate did.

"I don't know," Padmé said. "I can think of half a dozen reasons someone in the Senate might have tipped them off, but I have no way of confirming my suspicions.

"I will ask Senator Mon Mothma if I can look into it when we get back to Coruscant," she continued. "If someone is trying to interfere with Senate-sanctioned missions, not to mention one of the most unified actions in recent memory, we should try to find out who and why."

"I agree," Gaans said.

Padmé didn't like that it always took danger and pain to provoke response. Mon Mothma had been perfectly content to continue passively treating with the pirates until her ship came through their contested space, and now she was willing to expend additional effort. Padmé hoped she would never need to confront something herself to believe it, even if it meant she would face an increase in personal moral discomfort.

"One of my droids took scans during the fight," Padmé said. "I'll let you know what, if anything, shows up in the analysis."

"Senators, we are coming up on Bromlarch," Varbarós's voice sounded from above them. "We'll go into synchronous orbit over the capital region and wait for further instructions."

"Senator Gaans," said Padmé. "Let's get you home."

CHAPTER 26

Once Mon Mothma completed her survey of the Bromlarch aqueduct and the flooding that had resulted from the damage, there was no need for them to stay on the planet. Indeed, Padmé suspected they were in the way, since none of them knew how to do the actual construction. Ninui was a gracious guide but was just as clearly overworked, and Padmé was happy to be able to lighten her load somewhat by returning to Coruscant as soon as possible. Senator Gaans stayed behind for a few more days, but the rest of them departed in good order. The trip back was done in a single jump, the Naboo ship just ahead of the Chandrilan vessel, and was therefore uneventful.

"I look forward to working with you again, Senator Amidala," Mon Mothma said when they were standing on the landing pad waiting for Mon Mothma's planetary shuttle to come and pick her up. "You have a unique perspective on the galaxy, but I think we are not so different as our squabbling would lead others to believe."

"We are far too dignified to squabble," Padmé said. "But I agree on your other points."

"It will not always be this easy to unite the Senate," Mon

Mothma said. "We respond to fear, of course, but anything drastic enough to cause that sort of unification will only lead to ruin."

"I know this was something of an outlier, in terms of procedure," Padmé said. She had confronted a few of her feelings on the return journey. The rush of working with Clovis had faded quickly, for several reasons, and Padmé realised that the process they had used was not sustainable in the long run. Eventually, there would be no more favours to trade, and the relationships they had built in constructing the bill weren't solid or reliable enough to be worth it. But Bromlarch would survive. "I hope someday the Senate can respond swiftly to problems without resorting to fast dealings. It made me uncomfortable, and I am not in a hurry to do it again, if there is another way."

"We will make that way together," Mon Mothma said as her shuttle landed across the pad.

"I look forward to it," Padmé said.

"You might consider adding an official representative to your delegation in the Senate," Mon Mothma added. "Not everyone does it, but it allows me to cover more ground with a fresh perspective."

"I'll think about it." Padmé smiled. "Actually, I have just the being in mind."

The Chandrilan senator and the aide who had accompanied her boarded their speeder and departed. Sabé extricated herself from her patrol ship.

"Well, Senator," she said, "will you stay?"

The question was easier to answer now. Padmé knew it with every fiber of her being. Yet it cost her something to say the words out loud. She knew politics was a difficult arena that required constant compromise. She *thrived* on it. She could lose herself in it, and maybe that was the problem. But there was no one better, and so her answer remained the same.

"I will," Padmé said. "I'm not always comfortable with who I am here, but I'll stay."

"You'll be Amidala," Sabé said. "And you'll be Padmé, too."

"And you'll be Tsabin and Sabé?" Padmé asked, even though she already knew the answer.

"For as long as you need me," Sabé said.

She and Tonra took the lift down to the public pedestrian level, where they would catch a transport back to their apartment. They were wearing Republic uniforms, but that was hardly a strange sight on Coruscant. They would fit right in.

Padmé, R2-D2, and Typho took the private speeder to the Senate building, because Padmé wanted to write up her report before she went home. She was tired, and she knew that once she stopped moving, it would be a long time before she wanted to start again.

The Senate building was emptying as she arrived, the session over and the committee meetings concluded for the day. Typho had no trouble finding a landing pad, and they walked up to Padmé's office through quiet corridors. She downloaded the files from R2-D2's memory and spent a few minutes looking at the pirate ships before passing the specs over to Typho.

"Do you recognise any of it?" she asked.

"No," he said. "But I'm not an expert on this sort of thing. You might ask Captain Panaka, though. He knows ship design better than I do, and he has more contacts."

"I'll have Mariek add it to one of her communiqués to him," Padmé said. She intended to ask around, as well. "Do you mind if I go down and see if Senator Bonteri is still here? I know she hasn't been involved lately, but she did help us get started with the Bromlarch situation, and I would like to update her in person, if she wants to know."

"Artoo and I will be fine," Typho said. "Just don't take too long. We both need to get home."

Padmé agreed, so she wasted no time getting to Bonteri's office. It wasn't far, given the size of the building, and Padmé was familiar with the route. The lack of other senators and aides sped her journey along. She didn't even see any cleaning or maintenance droids. It was almost too quiet. Padmé came around the final corner to find Senator Bonteri standing at a communications console in the corridor, speaking with someone Padmé couldn't see. The image was concealed by the screen around the holoemitter, which, combined with the anonymity of the console, made the conversation totally private. Padmé stopped walking as Bonteri looked up and saw her. She thought a flash of fear might have gone through the other senator's eyes but couldn't imagine what her friend would be afraid of.

"I will let you know," Senator Bonteri said. Her words were rushed, as though she had said the first thing that crossed her mind.

"See that you do, Senator," the figure said.

The voice was unmistakable. This was the man that Bonteri had been conversing with the day Padmé had accidentally overheard them, and now here he was again. He made her feel cold, though not in the usual way. She couldn't explain it. It was not in her nature to dislike people with no context, but Padmé found she didn't care for him one bit. The blue glow disappeared from the console, and Padmé was glad of it.

"You have been successful, then," Bonteri said. For the first time, she didn't invite Padmé into her office, leaving them standing in the hall.

"Yes," Padmé said. "Bromlarch is saved."

"Congratulations, Senator Amidala," Bonteri said. "You have done what few other senators before you have accomplished."

"I couldn't have done it without you," Padmé said.

"No," said Bonteri. "I don't suppose you could have. But your patience with the Republic is commendable, and I applaud you for it."

"Thank you," Padmé said. "I can give you more details if you like."

"I'm sorry, Senator," Bonteri said. "I have a call scheduled with my son. I will have to hear about it in the session report."

"Of course," Padmé said. "Please feel free to ask me any questions."

"I will," Bonteri said. She turned, went into her office, and closed the door.

Padmé drifted back up to her office, lost in thought. She had gained the full confidence of Mon Mothma only to lose Mina Bonteri. The two women were not dissimilar, and Padmé had been hoping to work with both of them, because she admired them for similar reasons. But it seemed that it was not to be. Bonteri's primary alliance was a mystery, and it was a puzzle Padmé was strangely afraid to solve.

She arrived back at her office just as Chancellor Palpatine did, accompanied by two guards instead of his advisors.

"Senator Amidala," he said, "I'm pleased to see you have returned safely."

"Thank you, Chancellor," she said. He had come to her office, but his tone indicated he was not merely a friend checking on her welfare. "We did come under attack, but with the help of the Republic ships and Jedi Master Billaba, we suffered no losses."

"Good, good," Palpatine said. It was clear he was light-years away, his relief at her safety the same as he might feel if he had made a particularly risky holochess gambit only to have the pawn survive it.

"I will have a full report for the Senate soon," she said, nearly lapsing into the queen's voice.

"I'm glad you have found a more suitable arena to utilise your talents," Palpatine said. He gestured sharply to his guards, and they moved off down the corridor.

Padmé stood alone in the hallway for several moments, parsing what he'd said. *More suitable.* He was glad she had moved away from the antislavery – "jurisdictional" – politics. She set her teeth. She hadn't come all this way to be a line in the programming. She could do more than one thing, even if it meant going against the Chancellor's implied wishes. She had, after all, only just begun.

"I'm ready to go home, Sergeant," she called to Typho from the hallway. If she went back into her office, she would find a hundred more things to do.

Typho came out, R2-D2 at his heels, and they went back down to their airspeeder.

"It's so good to be home," Padmé said, sinking into the sofa in her sitting room. Dormé, Cordé, and Versé were all with her, and the guards were pretending not to be there, which was always appreciated. Everything seemed soft and warm and solid, a welcome respite after the past few weeks of hard desks, desperate plans, and interplanetary cooperation.

"Home?" said Mariek, who was always worse at pretending she wasn't in the room.

"Well," Padmé said, "not home, I suppose. But I am glad for this cushion in particular."

She told them all the details of the excursion, including the firefight, though she left out her conversations with her fellow senators. She didn't like shutting the handmaidens out, but the boundaries were different now, and they would all have to adjust to them. There would still be times like this, when it was all of them together, but they wouldn't inhabit each other's skin any more, and that was probably for the best. She wouldn't even have to tell them. They were all professional enough to spot the shift and accept it.

Movement caught her eye, and Padmé saw an airspeeder rise from the dedicated traffic lanes to level off outside her balcony. It was Sabé, and she was waving for them to let down the screen that kept out intruders and high winds. Typho came running into the room as the proximity alarm sounded.

"It's all right," Padmé said. "It's just Sabé."

"If she's doing this," Typho said. "It's not all right."

He deactivated the shield, and Sabé jumped onto the balcony. Padmé tried not to think about the distance between the balcony and the ground. The airspeeder drove off, and the alarm ceased once the screen was back in place. Sabé came in at a run.

"There's news," she said. "It's not public yet, but my source is a holojournalist, and she was in the courtroom when it happened."

A courtroom could mean only one thing. The Occupation of Naboo had ended, but it was going to follow her forever. She couldn't regret it. She had done what she needed to do. But she was just so tired.

Sabé knelt in front of her and took her hands. Padmé knew that her dearest friend would see her weariness no matter how she tried to hide it, so she didn't. Sabé looked her straight in the face, as she had always done, and the message in her eyes was clear as crystal.

We are brave, Your Highness.

"Nute Gunray was found not guilty," Sabé said. "He retains his assets and titles until we file another appeal."

We are brave, Your Highness.

"Padmé, the rumour is that he has put a price on your head," she said. "Big enough to attract the attention of some unpleasant people."

We are brave, Your Highness.

"All right," Padmé said.

Naboo. Tatooine. Bromlarch. Trade. Slavery. Piracy. There would always be another planet that needed help, and she'd be damned if she would let anyone stop her. A light flashed on her personal console, the alert she'd set for any development on Chancellor Palpatine's jurisdictional bill. She'd make time for all of it. She looked up, and her people were ready for her.

"What do we do next?"

EPILOGUE

Padmé Amidala was completely still. The brown halo of her hair spread out around her, softened here and there by white blossoms that had blown through the air to find their rest among her curls. Her skin was pale and perfect. Her face was peaceful. Her eyes were closed and her hands were clasped across her stomach as she floated. Naboo carried on without her.

Even now, at the end, she was watched.

Theed was subdued as its citizens remembered. Even the Gungans in the procession walked slowly, no trace of the usual bounce in their steps. Throughout Naboo, the people mourned a queen, a senator. She had served well. She had grown in wisdom and experience, and had done both rapidly. She had faced the trials of her position unflinching and unafraid. And now, her time was ended.

After the funeral, Sabé went home. She had nowhere else to go.

It was a cramped little place on one of Theed's smallest streets. There weren't slums on Naboo, but if there were, that's where Sabé would be living. She didn't stay there very often, only when she was onworld and her parents started asking too many questions. It was the only place she could go now where no one would ask her if she was all right.

A knock made her jump. She was halfway through the list of disreputable types who might have tracked her down before she realised that it was Tonra, one of the few who knew where this place was. She let him in without saying anything and went back to where she had been sitting.

As usual, Tonra was content to wait her out, and her patience frayed long before his did.

"It doesn't make any sense!" Sabé's rage and bewilderment – held at bay by sheer force of will through-out the public response to tragedy – finally crept into her tone. "She wouldn't just *die*. And an empire? Headed by Sheev Palpatine? Nothing about this makes sense!"

Sio Bibble had finally retired, and instead of holding an election – in which Saché was heavily favoured – the role of governor had been replaced with a new position. By Imperial appointment Quarsh Panaka, of all people, now oversaw the daily operations of Naboo. Neither Mariek nor Typho had appeared with him when he made his first for-mal address to the planet. The changes were coming almost too fast for her to cope with in her grief. At least they still had a queen, though Sabé didn't know how she could help the girl, even if she were in a position to do so. She needed a moment to *think*, and Tonra was giving it to her.

"What will you do?" Tonra asked.

From her parents, that question would mean, "What will you do without her?" It was a question they had been asking Sabé for years, and she never had an answer for them, because she never considered life without Padmé's direction. From Tonra, there was more nuance. He knew what she had done in Padmé's service, after all. He wasn't asking what she would do without. He was asking what she would do *because*. He knew her too well to imagine she would do nothing.

She had walked with the surviving handmaidens in the funeral procession. They had barely spoken. Their grief was deep and profound but difficult to explain to those outside their select circle. Naboo had lost a senator, a hero, a queen. They had lost the friend they had all – every one of them over the years – risked their lives for. They hadn't taken those risks for politics or for Naboo or for the now-defunct Republic. They had taken them for Padmé, because they loved her. And now she was gone.

"I'm going to find out what happened to my friend," Sabé said. She got up and began to pace the small room. She couldn't sit still any more. She couldn't stay on this paradise of a world while there were dreadful secrets for her to uncover. Cordé was dead. Versé was dead. Obi-Wan was dead. Master Billaba was dead. Anakin Skywalker was dead.

Padmé Amidala Naberrie was dead, her dreams with her.

"I'll go back to Coruscant," she said. "I'll be Tsabin a little bit longer. One or two of our old contacts might still be there. They might know something, and that would be a place to start."

"I'll come with you, if you'll have me," Tonra offered.

She knew the offer was genuine. They had spent more time apart than together since Bromlarch, and Sabé knew Tonra hadn't spent all that time alone. She hadn't, either. But they had always been on good terms, even if they had rarely been on the same planet. She knew they worked well together. And she didn't really have anyone left. She stopped pacing and stood in front of him.

"I would like that," she said.

He heard the small crack in her voice and ignored it, placing a kiss on her forehead instead.

"We'll need entirely new identities," she said. "Even if we go back to Coruscant. Sabé, Tsabin, Tonra – they'll all have to go. We have to be people we've never been before. And we have to scrub off anything that indicates we're from Naboo."

Her hand went to her necklace. She could leave that behind, if she had to. For Naboo, and for her friend. There were plenty of places to hide something that small, and keep it safe until she could return for it.

"Tell me what you need me to do," Tonra said. "I can

get us a ship, I think. Or at least I can get us offworld, and then we can get a ship somewhere else."

"We'll have to make the credits we have left last for a long time," Sabé pointed out. "So any favours you can call in would be a good idea, as long as they can't be traced."

"Go and plot out the IDs," he said. "I can pack for you."

It was true. She didn't have that much any more, and her essentials were almost the same as his, when it came right down to it, except her boots were smaller.

She went to her workstation and closed the files she'd been looking at. They were Padmé's writings, the work she had hoped would be her senatorial legacy. A call to reinstate term limits on the chancellorship. Multiple bills advocating Clone personhood, both during the war and hypothetically for when the war was done. A motion to bring all hyperspace lanes under the purview of the Republic, to avoid territorial taxation and squabbling. Years and years' worth of drafts of antislavery bills. A legacy that would go largely unrealised, and Sabé burned with the need to know *why*.

She called up two blank idents. They would use basic ones to get off Naboo and then switch to a higher-quality cover when they were someplace else. It was safer that way, even though it meant a lot of work.

She heard her comm chime and ignored it. She really didn't want to talk to her mother right now, and the handmaidens would know to leave her alone. They didn't have to speak to communicate. They knew she'd tell them when they needed to know. They knew it might be dangerous to know before that. The comm chimed again.

She heard a soft murmur from the main room as Tonra answered it and spoke to whoever dared interrupt her peace. A moment later, he appeared in the doorway.

"Have them leave a message," Sabé said. "I don't want to take the call right now."

"I think you should, love," he said. He passed her a holoemitter. Whoever had called wanted to talk face to face.

Sabé held the device in her palm and activated it, calling up a familiar figure. When she spoke, it was in Amidala's voice. She had no intention of giving anything away.

"Senator Organa, now is not a good time," she said. "What do you want?"

ACKNOWLEDGEMENTS

I have been waiting for this book for twenty years, and I am endlessly thrilled I got to write it. It would not have happened without the generous help of several people:

Josh Adams, who phoned me in Iceland to see if I was interested, and who always takes me seriously when I say I'm good to go on a project.

Jen Heddle, who guided me from idea to book. Emily Meehan, who always has my back. Patrice Caldwell, who helped me make the world bigger.

The Lucasfilm Story Group and design team, who made sure everything worked out.

Everyone who did art or story for Naboo in Shattered Empire, Forces of Destiny, and *Battlefront II*.

Natalie Portman, Keira Knightley, and Trisha Biggar, who gave me the best fifteenth birthday present ever, and Cat Taber, who kept it going.

Several people who answered questions without knowing what we were talking about, including Emma Higinbotham, Rachel Williams, Bria LaVorgna, and Angel Cruz. Keeping secrets is rough.

MaryAnn Zissimos, who is somehow the most simultaneously excited AND levelheaded person I know.

And every girl who ever asked for more from *Star Wars*. You're my spark.